He presses his lips to mine, stopping not only my sentence but my breath in my throat. He takes my face in his hands and moves his mouth slowly across mine. Every nerve ending in my body is electrified.

He pulls away and searches my eyes. "You haven't lost me," he says, before bringing me back to him. Just when I decide that I could kiss him all day long, he says, "What if this is a Search?"

I stiffen. "What?"

"What if now, this very moment, isn't set in stone. What if you're just seeing a vision of what could be?"

Books by Kasie West

Pivot Point
Split Second

The Distance Between Us

KASIE WEST

PIVOT POINT

An Imprint of HarperCollinsPublishers

HarperTeen is an imprint of HarperCollins Publishers.

Pivot Point
Copyright © 2013 by Kasie West
All rights reserved. Printed in the United States of America.
No part of this book may be used or reproduced in any manner whatsoever without written permission except in the case of brief quotations embodied in critical
articles and reviews. For information address HarperCollins Children's Books, a
division of HarperCollins Publishers, 195 Broadway, New York, NY 10007.
www.epicreads.com

Library of Congress Cataloging-in-Publication Data
West, Kasie.
   Pivot point / Kasie West.
      p. cm.
   Summary: "A girl with the power to search alternate futures lives out six
weeks of two different lives in alternating chapters. Both futures hold the
potential for love and loss, and ultimately she is forced to choose which fate she
is willing to live through"— Provided by publisher.
   ISBN 978-0-06-211736-6
   [1. Divorce—Fiction. 2. Choice (Psychology)—Fiction. 3. Love—Fiction.
4. High schools—Fiction. 5. Schools—Fiction.] I. Title.
PZ7.W51837Piv 2013   2012019089
[Fic]—dc23   CIP
                                                                            AC

Typography by Andrea Vandergrift
19 20 21   PC/LSC   13 12 11 10 9
❖
First paperback edition, 2014

To Jared, I'm glad I chose the path that led to you.

PIVOT POINT

CHAPTER 1

am•bush: *n.* to pick a subject (me)
and lie in wait to attack

"Heads up," a loud voice called from my right. I looked up just in time to see a football smack me right between the eyes.

I never really understood the saying *heads up*. At least not as a warning. *Duck* or *watch out* or *flying object*, even *heads down* would've worked. I lie on my back, book clutched to my chest, staring at the purple-and-gold streaked sky—the Perceptives must've been gearing up for the football game that night. As if the school colors splashed across the sky would send us running to the ticket booth.

I mentally inventoried my situation. I'd landed on cement, so no mud was involved, thankfully. I'd only lost thirty seconds, at the most, so I'd still make it to class on time. I was fine. A little anxiety melted away with the thought.

A familiar face with a mess of blond hair and a wide smile appeared above me. "Sorry. I said heads up." His smile proved he wasn't very sorry at all, but more likely amused.

And I looked up, was what I wanted to say, but instead I ignored his offered hand and pushed myself off the ground. "Yeah, I heard you, Duke." I brushed myself off and continued walking. The spot the football had hit throbbed, so I pressed my fingertips against it, sure there was a nasty red welt.

Guess I should've Searched the morning after all, and I might've seen that coming. But I didn't Search all my choices— only major ones. There were already enough alternate realities floating around in my mind that sometimes it was hard to keep track of which one I had actually lived and which was the opposing choice never made.

And yet, earlier that morning when I climbed out of bed and saw the fog outside my window, I was tempted to see what would happen if I stayed home versus what would happen if I went to school. My mom made the decision for me when she opened my door and said, "Addie, I'm driving you this morning. I don't like you to drive in the fog."

"Okay, thanks." I knew better than to disagree. My mom was Persuasive. It was her mental ability. As far as mental abilities went, I thought my parents had the worst ones any teenager's parents could have. Who wanted her mom to be able to Persuade

2

her to do anything she wanted? My mother claimed she only used it when it was important, but I wondered.

My father was a human lie detector—although my mom didn't like it when I called him that; the technical term was Discerner—and he could immediately tell if I lied. He said he could even tell when I *planned* to lie. Irritating.

I slid into my seat, barely making it before the tardy bell. My best friend, Laila, wasn't so lucky. As usual, she came walking through the door a good five minutes later. Her bright red lipstick against her pale skin immediately drew my eyes to her defiant smile. We were an odd pair, constantly tugging each other back and forth over the line that represented normal teenage behavior. Everything she did made her stand out, made people notice, but I just wanted to blend in.

"Laila, what do I have to do to get you here on time?" Mr. Caston asked.

"Move the buildings closer together?"

"Funny, Ms. Stader. Warning today. Lunch detention tomorrow. Walk faster."

She plopped into the seat next to me and rolled her eyes. I smiled.

"Okay," Mr. Caston said. The lights dimmed, and our desk monitors lit up. Instructions appeared on the screen, and I meticulously copied them into my notebook.

"Seriously, Addie?" Laila asked, nodding her head toward my paper.

I made an exploding sound and kept writing. The school

computers hadn't crashed in more than twenty years, but preparing for the worst never hurt anyone.

"We're finishing up our partner work today," Mr. Caston said. "Remember, no abilities, please; just use your brain."

"We *were* using our brains," Bobby said from up front.

"The part of your brain that doesn't house your ability."

Everyone groaned. But, considering biology was a Norm-training class, we all knew the rule: Classes that taught us skills to exist on the Outside needed to be learned traditionally.

"Don't make me turn on the room's ability blockers. I'm not teaching middle school here. And turn off your phones, people."

Another collective moan sounded.

Laila flashed her phone at me with a conspiratorial smile. A barcoded football filled the screen. "Come to the game with me this time."

"You bought a pass? The sky thing worked on you?"

"What? No," she said as though the implication that she could be influenced by manipulation techniques deeply offended her. "I was going anyway. This had nothing to do with the— Whoa, what happened to your head?"

I rubbed the welt again. "Duke's football."

"You talked to Duke?"

"Not really, but his football and I seemed to hit it off."

Out of the corner of my eye, I saw Bobby walk up. His leg pressed against the edge of my desk, and my stomach twisted into a knot. I tried to ignore it and pretend I didn't see him.

"What do you want?" Laila asked. No matter how often I tried to convince her otherwise, she thought of herself as my bodyguard.

"I want to talk to Addie."

I bent over and rummaged through my backpack, hoping he'd get the hint. He didn't. I pulled out a yellow highlighter and set it on my desk. Still, he stayed. Finally, with a sigh, I looked up. "Bobby, please, just leave me alone."

"I thought now that the dance was over, you'd talk to me, tell me why you went from friendly to cold the minute I asked you."

"Nope."

"Yeah, so leave," Laila added.

He walked away, glancing back once. The look he gave me said he wasn't ready to give up yet. I hoped my look said, *You're going to have to*. I also kind of hoped it said, *I hate your guts*, but as long as it said one of the two, I was satisfied.

"Addie, you can't punish someone based on a Search. He has no idea what he did wrong."

"It's not my fault that if I went to the dance with him, he was going to shove his tongue down my throat and his hand up my dress," I whispered.

"I know, and I'm so glad you didn't go with him. But he didn't *actually* do that."

"But he would've." I nudged the highlighter. It rolled over the glass surface of my glowing keyboard and inched toward the edge of my desk before rolling back to safety. "That's who he is, and I can't look at him without seeing that Search."

5

"Do you want me to Erase it?"

"Have I asked you to Erase something before?" Every time she offered to Erase a memory, I asked her that question.

And every time she always answered, "If you did, I wouldn't tell you."

I made a face at her. "You're a brat."

She began painting her nails with a black Sharpie. "So, do you?"

"No. Because then I'll forget what he's capable of and his puppy-dog eyes might convince me to go out with him." I shuddered. I couldn't imagine ever thinking that his greasy brown hair and holey jeans meant he was misunderstood. But without the memories, I was sure, once again, I'd believe a good shampoo would wash the appearance of creep out of him.

"That's true."

"Hey, can you give me a ride home today?" I asked, ready to move past the Bobby subject.

"Sure, your car didn't start again this morning?"

I scrolled through the diagrams on my monitor until I found our current assignment. "No, fog."

"Ah, of course." She didn't need further explanation. My mom's overprotectiveness had affected a lot of our outings. She turned toward her monitor because Mr. Caston started pacing the rows. Up on the screen was a diagram of frog innards. "Where is the kidney?" she asked.

I pointed, and the bean-shaped organ blackened as the heat from my finger touched the screen. Mr. Caston passed our desk.

"So, back to Duke," she whispered when he was out of hearing range. "Tell me all the details."

"There's nothing to tell. His football knocked me down. He apologized."

"And you said?"

I thought back. "I said, 'Yeah, I heard you, Duke.'" A look of horror came onto her face, and I cringed.

"Addison Marie Coleman. You get handed an opportunity to flirt with Duke Rivers and you blow him off? All these years of being my friend and you have learned nothing. That was your chance. You could've acted like he hurt you and made him walk you to the nurse's office."

"He did hurt me. But he annoyed me more. He let a football hit my head."

"How do you know he let it?"

"Hello? Because he's Telekinetic. He could've easily knocked it out of the way."

"Come on, Addie. He can't use his powers all the time. Give him a break."

"He *let* a football hit my head," I repeated slowly.

"All right, all right, perhaps he's not the most gentlemanly guy in the world, but he's Duke. He doesn't have to be."

A loud sigh escaped my lips. "Laila, don't make me hurt you. It's girls like you who let guys like Duke get away with their behavior."

She laughed. "First of all, I'd like to see you try to hurt me, Miss Skin-and-Bones. Second of all, if I were with Duke, he'd be cut down to size in seconds." She leaned back and let out a dreamy sigh, as if a mental image of her with Duke played through her mind. "Hotlicious."

"What?"

"It's *hot* and *delicious* combined. In the dictionary it would be listed as a noun and wouldn't even have a definition attached, just a picture of Duke Rivers."

"Please. There are plenty of real words Duke's face is probably already attached to in the dictionary . . . *conceited*, *egocentric*, *arrogant*. And besides"—I smiled—"*hotlicious* would be an adjective."

"Girls," Mr. Caston said, "I don't think much studying is going on in your corner."

Laila pointed to the monitor. "We've located the kidney, Mr. Caston."

When I got home, my parents were both in the living room. They sat on opposite couches, hands folded in their laps, looking grim. My cheeks numbed as all the blood in them suddenly left.

My house was what Laila always described as old-fashioned cozy—overstuffed, mismatched furniture; plush carpet; honey-colored walls. The kind of house that was easy to curl up and relax in. I had the opposite feeling at the moment as tension spread across my shoulders.

"Is Grandma okay?" I asked. It was the only reason I could

come up with for them both being home in the middle of the day, looking so somber.

The smile that appeared on my mom's face seemed patronizing and immediately put me on guard. "Yes, honey, Grandma's fine. Everyone is fine. Why don't you take care of your backpack and then come sit down? We need to talk."

I went to my room and wondered what would happen if I barricaded myself inside. I even glanced at the tall bookcase next to the door as if the idea were actually a valid one. If I never came out, they wouldn't be able to deliver whatever news had etched worry onto their faces. I paced for a few minutes, reviewing my options, talked myself out of Searching, then walked back out. My mom pointed to the *lair* (so dubbed because it was smaller than a love seat but bigger than a chair). It sat against the wall between the couches, and I lowered myself into it.

I wedged my hands beneath my thighs to keep myself from biting my nails. "Is someone going to tell me what's going on?" I looked straight at my dad, hoping he would tell me. Whatever the news, my dad was better at a gentle delivery. He actually acknowledged the existence of feelings. Unlike my mom, who seemed to think people were like one of the programs she developed: easy to reconfigure when they didn't react as expected.

His face gave away nothing at first, then softened to what looked like pity. That wasn't a good sign.

But my mother spoke. "Addie, after trying for several years

now to work out our differences, your father and I have decided to go our separate ways."

It felt like a hundred footballs whacked me in the forehead. The throbbing returned, and I rubbed at the welt. I tried to process what she had said, but the only answer made no sense. My parents got along just fine. Why would either one of them leave? "You don't mean you're getting a divorce?"

"Yes, sweetie." Apparently the straightforward approach didn't trigger the right response, so she changed to the look-how-sympathetic-I-can-sound voice. "It has nothing to do with you. It's about issues we can't work through. This was the last thing we wanted—to split up our family. But no matter what we tried, it didn't help." She tilted her head and squinted her eyes. Was that supposed to be her sorry face? It looked forced. "We thought maybe you would've seen this coming. Haven't you Searched anything lately?" The last sentence was accompanied by a hand on my arm.

I started to look down at her hand, but it was gone in an instant and had moved on to pick a piece of lint off the arm of the couch, before joining her other hand in her lap.

It took me a moment to realize she had asked a question. "No, I haven't." My last Search was the week before last and went as far as the homecoming dance, which happened Friday. If I had just looked a few more days ahead, I could've seen this coming. "I don't understand. Why would you get a divorce?" The word tasted bad in my mouth.

"Because we're like strangers living in the same house. We

don't even care enough about each other to fight anymore."

I waited for my dad to speak up, to say he didn't want this, but he nodded his agreement. "Sorry, baby. It's true."

"But I care about both of you. You can't do this."

"Our choice has already been made," my mom said. "You're the only one left to make a choice."

"I choose for you to stay together."

My mom had the nerve to laugh. Okay, it wasn't a laugh as much as it was a small chuckle, but still. "That's not your choice, Addie. Your choice is: Who do you want to live with?"

CHAPTER 2

Un•just•ville: *n*. the land ruled by my parents

I sat in stunned silence, convinced the house must've initiated security protocol when I came home, and these were the holographic versions of my parents, programmed to fool intruders. That's how little sense what they said made. But they weren't holograms. They were right in front of me, waiting for my reaction. Considering none of us had moved for what felt like five minutes, I was surprised we hadn't been plunged into darkness. I didn't know what my parents expected from me, but I was waiting for the world to realign on its axis and return my life to normal. Not used to surprises, I decided I didn't like them very much.

My mom broke the silence with: "I know it's a hard choice,

Addie. And we fully expect you to use your ability to see which future looks more appealing. You don't have to answer us now."

"Can't I be with both of you? Isn't there like a fifty-fifty deal we can work out?"

"That would be okay, but your father's decided to leave the Compound. He's going into the Normal world."

My stomach went from twisting uncomfortably to dropping straight to my feet. "You're leaving, Dad?" Not many people left the Compound. No one I knew personally. So this news was almost as shocking as the divorce announcement.

My mom continued, "I don't think you joining him there would be good for your develo—"

"Marissa, you promised you wouldn't try to influence her one way or the other."

"I'm sorry. It's true. Addie, this decision is yours. Stay here with others like you, or leave the Compound and live in a world surrounded by people who use only ten percent of their brains."

"Marissa."

"Sorry," she said again. This time they both laughed. I was glad they found this situation *so* amusing, considering my life had just ended. I stood abruptly, and they stopped laughing. My dad's face crumpled into the pity look again, and I could tell he was about to apologize, but I didn't want to hear it.

Without a word, I walked by them, straight to my room. I slapped my palm against the panel inside, causing the door to swish shut behind me. Angry music blasted from above, the computer obviously sensing my mood from the palm scan.

13

"Off," I said, and silence took over. I walked around the bookcase, placed my back against the side, planted my feet firmly on the ground, and pushed. When it didn't budge, I slid to the floor and lowered my forehead to my knees.

There was no way I could make this decision. It would've been better had they just told me what needed to happen, left me no choice in the matter. Sure, I would've complained about that as well, but at least then I wouldn't have been forced to pick between my parents.

I crawled to my backpack, grabbed my phone out of the front pocket, and called Laila.

"Hey," she said. "I'm almost home. Did you forget something in my car?"

"Did I?"

"I don't know. I just thought that's why you were calling."

"Oh. No, I didn't." I lay on my backpack, not moving when the pens and other lumpy items pressed into my cheek. The discomfort created a momentary distraction from more unpleasant feelings. Closing my eyes, I listened to the slight static of the phone line.

"What is it then?"

"My parents are getting a divorce." For the first time since the announcement, my eyes stung and my throat tightened.

"Oh no. I'm so sorry. I'm coming back, okay?"

I couldn't answer. I only nodded.

• • •

14

Ten minutes later there was a knock on my window. The window was how she snuck into my room in the middle of the night. She didn't need to use it in that moment, but I was glad she did. I felt betrayed by my parents and didn't think they deserved to know how much I needed my best friend.

I powered open the window and screen. Laila climbed like a pro over the struggling bush in the flower bed and into my room. She immediately threw her arms around me. "I'm so sorry," she said again. "This sucks."

"My dad's moving away." Against her shoulder, my voice came out muffled. "I have to pick."

"What?" She brought me out to arm's length. "He's leaving the Compound? Why? Is he helping with containment?"

"I . . ." I had been too shocked to ask him what he'd do on the Outside. Most people only left the Compound to help in the process of keeping the Para-community a secret—investigating leaks, assessing damage, Erasing memories. But some left for high-powered positions, to help gather intelligence to send back to the Compound, keeping us informed on the world outside the walls. Only a few left because they wanted to integrate into the Normal world—essentially disappear. I had no idea which category my father fell into. "I don't know."

"But you might leave with him?"

I nodded.

"No. You can't do that. You can't leave. You'll hate it out there. When's the last time you've even had to deal with Norms?" she asked, putting one hand on her forehead and the other flying to her hip.

"I don't really remember. Years." I remembered perfectly. I was eight. We had to fill out tons of paperwork and take secrecy oaths. All for a weekend trip to Disneyland. It was crowded. Everything seemed so *normal*. All the rides were outdated, and the fireworks were nothing compared to a Perceptives light show. My parents argued the entire time.

"This is so unfair." She led me over to the bed, and we both climbed on, leaning against the headboard. She kicked off her shoes and turned toward me. "So then you're staying here, right? Otherwise you would have to leave school and all your friends . . . and me."

I hadn't even begun to think about the details of one choice over the other, but she was right.

"Are you going to Search it?"

"I need to make a list. Pros and cons." I jumped off the bed and grabbed a notebook and pen out of my desk. I opened it to a blank page and drew a line down the center, then sat on the edge of my bed, pen ready. The silence stretched as I stared at the page, trying to think of the good things about leaving.

My shoulders tensed as I wrote the first word, because I knew there would be no other words to add beneath it. *Dad*. When put that way, the choice seemed easy: Lose one person, or lose everyone and everything. But the thought of losing my dad consumed me with such sadness that my stomach hurt. He was my rock. The calming force in my life. I gnawed on my thumbnail. It wasn't like I'd never see my dad again. Of course he'd come visit, and I could go visit him in whatever Norm town he moved to.

I traced each letter over and over again until the word was black and bold on the page. As I went to add another line of ink to the *D* Laila grabbed my hand. "Addie, you need to Search it. It will help."

She took the notebook from me and set it on the bed beside us. "How long?"

The longest amount of time I'd ever Searched was when Bobby asked me to the dance. He'd asked me a week in advance, and because I chose not to Erase it, I had to live and then relive that week of my life. That was rare though. When I Searched, it was usually just for a few days, sometimes only for a few hours, at a time.

I shrugged my shoulders. "A month maybe. Six weeks?"

"How long will that take?"

"Five minutes. I don't know." The energies I focused on just seamlessly blended into my mind. It was sort of like a stream joining a river—instant "memories" of the two paths I could take. When it was over, it felt like I had already taken both paths. That's why I didn't like to do it too often, because it felt so real that it was hard to separate the would-have from the would.

"Do you think six weeks is enough?" My parents' surprise announcement was making me second-guess everything. I usually knew exactly what needed to happen and exactly what I would do to make it happen. Not because I Searched everything—I didn't—but because I liked to have a plan. Plans were good. But now I didn't know. I was confused and frustrated. I pressed my palms to my eyes.

"It should be plenty."

I let my shoulders rise and fall with a deep sigh.

Laila, always ready and willing to do just about anything, said, "Well, what are you waiting for?"

"You want me to do it now?"

"I think it would make you feel better."

I grabbed a pillow, pulled it against my chest, and lay down. On the ceiling above me, in black scrolling print, was the Aristophanes quote I had painted there: "By words the mind is winged." For some reason it stood out among all the other quotes that loomed above me. "I don't know. Six weeks is a long time. I'd hate to have so many detailed memories floating around up there."

"Why? That week leading up to homecoming was pretty awesome. I liked knowing that the heel of my red shoes was going to break on Wednesday after third period and that there would be a pop quiz on Friday."

"Since I live to serve you, why don't I just Search every day from now to death?"

"Seriously, why don't you?" She smacked my leg. "Are you waiting for me to offer, or are you just being ridiculous? You know I can Erase whichever path you don't choose, so you don't have to fake it. Sometimes I wonder if you just picked me as your best friend because of my awesome ability."

"Whatever. Your ability didn't even Present until the seventh grade." I paused, then tilted my head. "So wait, are you saying I use your ability a lot?"

"I'm not telling," she sang. "And it's true. You didn't pick me for my ability. You picked me because I shoved Timothy after he stole your virtual pet."

I smiled, then took a deep breath. I was avoiding the choice, still not sure if I wanted to know, if I was ready to know what my new life would look like. My parents admitted that the only reason they had left the decision up to me was because of my ability. And why wouldn't I want to know for sure which choice would turn out better?

"Are you ready?" she asked.

I nodded. I had to know.

"So what do I do? Just sit here? Do you need something?"

I laughed. "No, I'm fine. It might take awhile. Are you sure you want to wait?"

"Please, that's like asking someone if they want to leave the room while Picasso paints a masterpiece."

"You're comparing me to Picasso?"

"You know what I'm saying. Now start."

I settled deeper into the pillow and tried to relax. It was hard when I knew I was about to be flooded with memories of a life I hadn't lived yet. Really, two lives I hadn't lived yet. It would only seem like five minutes to Laila, but to me it would feel like a month. I concentrated on the energies around me, and everything went hazy.

CHAPTER 3

PAR•A•digm: *n.* something that serves
as a pattern or model

"Aren't kids of divorced parents supposed to get whatever they want due to the extreme guilt of both parties?" I ask at breakfast a week after my dad left. The house feels different without him . . . empty.

"You're not getting a new car," my mom says from where she sits at the kitchen table behind her laptop. A pen holds her blond curls in a loose bun at the nape of her neck, and she grabs it to jot something on the notepad beside her. The action sends her hair down over her shoulders and reminds me of how similar it is to mine. Just when I think she's forgotten we were talking, like she

20

often does, she adds, "Your car runs just fine."

"I'm not asking for a new car. Just a different one. Mine barely runs. Have you heard the latest noise? It's kind of like a *knock-clank-knock* sound."

"Talk to your father about it."

I scoop a spoonful of milk-engorged bran flakes and then watch them slide slowly off my spoon. "Oh good, at least we're not going to skip the pass-the-problems-to-the-other-parent part of divorce. I knew you wouldn't let me miss out on at least some fun." I know I'm being a brat, but I can't help it. Like a bad cold, every negative feeling or complaint I've ever had about my mom has decided to accumulate in my chest.

For the first time since the conversation started, she looks at me. "Addie, knock it off. I just meant that your father is better at knowing what weird car noises mean."

I stand, stick my bowl in the sink, and swipe my backpack from off the floor. "Well, I would ask Dad, but I don't think my car would make it the five *hours* to his house."

"We're going to get through this," she calls as I walk out the front door.

"And one day you're going to understand why I did it," I finish for her as the door shuts behind me. I don't know how many times she's said that line over the last week. She probably hoped that each time it was said the "one day" would get a little closer. It only seemed to push that day further away.

Once in my car, I pull out my cell phone and dial.

"Coleman," my dad answers.

His voice alone makes me smile. "Don't they have caller ID out there in Normville?"

"Yes, of course they do."

"Then how come you answer that way when you know it's me?"

"Habit. How are you?"

"Okay. My car's being weird. Are you ready for it?" I hold the phone out the window and press my thumb against the start pad. The seats and mirrors adjust to my thumbprint specifications, and the radio starts playing my preset playlist that I have to voice command off. But the engine sputters to its halfhearted existence. "See?"

"Yeah, that doesn't sound good. Is it fully charged?"

"Yes." I tap on the dash. The green bar that used to indicate its charge level had blackened long ago. "It was powering all night."

"Hmm. I'll talk to your mother about it, okay?"

"Okay."

In the background I hear a muffled, deep voice and my dad say, "Thanks. Stay cool." Then he gives a little chuckle, and a door shuts.

"Did you really just tell someone to *stay cool*?"

"What's wrong with that? It's hot here."

I laugh. "Who was it?"

"The mail carrier. Just got a package. But, anyway, we'll figure out the car situation. Sound good?"

"Yes. I'd better get to school. See you lat . . . I mean . . ."

I couldn't finish the sentence. Somehow saying *I'll see you in a month* didn't sound right.

"Addie," my dad says in his soft voice, "it won't be long. We'll see each other before you know it."

I give a little hum and hang up the phone.

In the parking lot at Lincoln High, I glance at the clock on my dash. The talk with my dad put me a few minutes behind schedule. Just as I open the car door, a football hits my windshield. "Are you flippin' kidding me?" I mumble.

"Sorry about that," Duke says, running up to retrieve it from where it had bounced five feet away.

"Do you go anywhere without that thing?"

"If I didn't have a football, people might not recognize me."

As if. I look up at him. His perfectly messy blond hair and gorgeous smile greet me. Hotlicious. Was that Laila's word? It fits, but I will never tell her or she might die of smugness. I grab my backpack off the passenger-side floor and stand. "And that would be a tragedy."

He laughs. "I've just been practicing. Big game coming up."

"Well, maybe you should practice on the field, away from people, because your aim seems a little off." I shoulder my backpack and walk away.

"My aim is always perfect, Addie," he calls after me.

What was that supposed to mean? That before he'd been trying to whack me in the forehead. And now he was trying to crack my windshield. What had I ever done to him?

Halfway to class Laila catches up with me, out of breath. I raise one eyebrow at her, surprised she ran in order to make it on time.

She provides the explanation: "I can't get lunch detention today."

"Nobody left to flirt with?"

"As a matter of fact, yes. Gregory had his last day yesterday."

I roll my eyes. "It's so nice to have a best friend who bases her choice on whether or not to be responsible solely on guys."

"I'm glad to see you're channeling the my-parents-were-just-divorced-so-I'm-allowed-to-be-pissy-anytime-I-want-and-everyone-should-understand attitude so well."

I smile. "I'm sorry I've been so pissy."

"Yeah, me too. Could you work on that, please? It's ruining my social life." She slips her arm in mine and lays her head on my shoulder as we walk. "I'm sorry your life sucks."

"It doesn't suck. I've just been spoiled by the ideal all these years."

"I know, your parents did you a major disservice by giving you such a great childhood."

"I'm sorry." I say it because I realize how selfish I've been. Laila has a horrible home life, and she never complains about it. Nobody would know that her father lost his job because he has a drug problem. He spends all the family's money to support his habit while her mom works all the time in order to support them.

As if reading my mind, Laila says, "Don't start feeling sorry for me. You know how much I hate that." She squeezes my arm and then straightens up. "You want to go to that party Friday? I promise not to leave your side the entire time."

My brain tries to come up with an excuse, any excuse, but I already know my Friday evening is wide open and I'm a horrible liar. "Sure. Sounds exciting."

"You are the queen of sarcasm, my friend, but I'll pick you up at nine so you don't stand me up."

I open the door to the morning meditation room. "What would I do without you?"

"Probably curl up and die of boredom." She pauses. "No, actually, you most likely already have your death penciled in sixty years from now, somewhere after homework and yoga."

"I'd better not have homework in sixty years." I step into my cubicle. The small, wall-mounted screen lights up at my entry and the acronym DAA—Department of Ability Advancement—pops up in bold letters. And if that isn't enough to wipe the smile off my face, the talking head that appears next finishes the job.

My mother.

She's a program developer for the DAA. It's rare to see her in my cubicle in the morning, but according to her smiling, obviously prerecorded face, a new mind pattern has been introduced, specialized for each of our "claimed" abilities. She doesn't actually use air quotes, but I can hear them in her voice. Adults like to make a point of adding the word *claimed* before *abilities* until we graduate and are able to officially prove ourselves by passing all the tests. It's like they want to remind us that we're not fully capable yet and still have to rely

25

on them to help us reach our potential.

"So sit back, relax, and let your mind expand," my mom's face says.

Tones sound in my ears as images flash rapidly on the screen. I sit back. The relaxing part is out of the question.

CHAPTER 4

NOR•Mal: *n.* conforming to the standard

I lie on the couch in our new house staring at the slowly circling ceiling fan. I decide it must be the least efficient way, ever, to cool a room. I long for the crosscurrents of my Compound house. My dad moved us into an already furnished rental in Dallas, Texas. Considering the state and style of the decor, I assume it was furnished forty years ago. Other than the ancient furniture, the house is bare—its walls white and empty.

On the floor around me I have spread out the required reading I received upon leaving the Compound. Considering I spent half the day in the Tower before I left—where I had to take a mandatory Norm-training class, be briefed on my new backstory, and receive Norm credentials like a driver's license and birth certificate—I didn't think there was anything else to cram into my head. I was wrong. They sent me off with reading materials—a very thick packet refreshing my Norm history knowledge.

I had done a lot to avoid this novel-size assignment written by someone who didn't care about making it entertaining in the least. I had unpacked and meticulously organized my room, down to color-coordinating my clothes. I had even searched through the unpacked boxes but couldn't find the one titled "Addie's books," which I clearly wrote in black Sharpie so as to avoid this very situation. I have no idea where that box is now. Probably somewhere in the garage, buried beneath the hundreds of boxes that should say: "Dad's crap."

I pick up one of the sections of the packet, World War I, and read. Norms believe Archduke Franz Ferdinand was not Paranormal. He was assassinated due to a power play, not because people feared he could control them with his mind. I say that to myself several times. "World War One was not started because of a Paranormal." I flip through a few more pages of Norm war history. I toss the packet aside, then grab the Space section, remembering some sort of weird beliefs they have about the moon landing.

"Bored," I moan. My hand starts to sweat from the tight hold I have on my cell. I know Laila won't call for at least another hour, since she's still in school, but I hold out hope that she decided to ditch. We haven't talked since yesterday.

The doorbell rings, and I practically trip over the study papers in my excitement to answer it. The sun assaults my eyes, and a burst of sticky, hot air hits me across the face when I open the door.

It's the mailman, holding out a clipboard. "Can you sign for a package?"

I pocket my cell and grab the clipboard. "Yeah." I scribble my name in the box he points to. He hands me a large, padded envelope and starts to walk away.

"How is your day going?" I blurt out. "Staying cool?"

He stops. "It's October. This is the start of our *cool* season." He winks.

"Really?"

"You'll get used to it. Welcome to Dallas," he says, and walks away.

"Thanks." The phone in my pocket vibrates. "Hello?"

"You miss me yet?" Laila asks.

I shut the door. "Let's just say I'm so desperate for conversation that I was just chatting it up with the mailman."

"Was he cute?"

"He was probably fifty."

"*Ew.*"

I glance at the padded envelope in my hand. It's addressed to my dad with no return information. I walk into the kitchen, and when the lights don't immediately turn on wave my hands in impatience. It takes me a second to realize they aren't going to. I toss the envelope onto the counter and leave without searching for the switch. "Not that I'm complaining, but shouldn't you be in class?"

"Yeah, probably, but I'd rather be talking to you. It's just Thought Placement. I have that down."

"You do?" I ask.

"Don't you?"

"Just short distances."

Laila hums and then says, "You know who's having a hard time with Thought Placement?"

"Who?"

"Bobby."

I curl my lip. "That's because he's not used to manipulating people's minds. Only mass." He can walk through walls, harden liquid, stretch objects. I will never admit it out loud, but he is really good at what he does. Probably the best Mass Manipulator I know who's his age.

"That's exactly what the teacher said. He said it's nearly impossible for people to master Thought Placement if their abilities aren't ones that work on others' minds."

"My mom told me that. She's an expert at it. Probably because she's the master mind manipulator."

Laila laughs. "True. So how are the Norms? Are they hard to talk to?"

"Not really, but I haven't really talked to many, just a few on the way here and now the mailman." I suspect my dad is trying to introduce me into the Norm world slowly, because he hardly stopped at all on the way here.

"You've inspired me. I think I'm going to a few away games this year with the football team. If you have to suffer through talking to Norms, the least I can do is experience a little bit of your pain."

I laugh. "You don't sound prejudiced at all."

"And you're not?"

"I'm not."

"No, you just think you're better than they are."

"Not better, just different because I can do more things."

She laughs like she won the argument.

I plop, back first, onto the couch and throw my legs over the armrest. It's warm from my earlier occupation, and after I remember how many other people have probably already occupied this couch, I'm grossed out. I sit up. "It's not so much the people who are different. It's the place. I swear it's hotter here and brighter. Do you think the sun is going to give me brain damage?"

She laughs.

"I'm serious. Why else would they filter sunlight in the Compound?"

"I'm sure they've found the optimum lighting for brain development. Just like everything else that's altered here to maximize our brains' potential."

"Exactly."

"Another reason you should come home immediately. Either

way, I have no doubt you'll come home eventually. Wouldn't want to risk your children being born without advanced minds."

I sigh.

"Oh, speaking of perfect marrying genes, guess who asked about you today?"

"No idea."

"Duke Rivers."

"Uh . . . why?"

"I don't know. I thought you'd tell me."

The door that leads from the garage into the kitchen opens, and the sound of keys landing on the counter rings out. "Hey, I'll call you later, my dad just got home."

"Okay, bye."

Duke Rivers asked about me? Weird. "Hi, Dad." I gather my scattered papers and stand up. "You're home early."

"Considering I wasn't supposed to go in at all today, I'm home very late." He picks up the padded envelope on the counter and looks at both sides.

I place my cure-for-insomnia reading on the table. "Oh, that came for you a little while ago."

He lowers his brow.

"What is it?" I ask.

"Just something I'm consulting on for the Para-bureau."

"I thought you weren't working for them anymore. I thought we were trying out this whole Normal thing." *We're going to live like the rest of the world, Addie,* he had said. *It will be refreshing.* The words sound cheesy now, but at the time they made me feel like we were marching into battle or something.

"Well, when I left I said I'd do some side jobs if they needed me."

I grab an apple from a bowl on the counter. "You're gone less than a week, and they're already calling on you? They must be hurting without their best lie detector."

He rolls his eyes.

I take a bite of my apple. "Sorry, I mean Discerner. I bet the bureau here is happy to have you, though. Where do you work again?" I try to remember the acronym. "The EBI . . . SBI . . ."

"FBI. Federal Bureau of Investigation."

"Right. FBI. I guess I should remember that. So are you stickin' it to all the bad guys? No lies will be told in Dallas ever again."

"Funny. My daughter is a comedian. Not to mention surprisingly good at talking with her mouth full."

"It's a gift."

He bonks me on the head with the envelope, then opens it. First he pulls out some sort of ID card.

"What's that?"

He turns it toward me. "I left my Compound Clearance card at the office."

The holographic logo seems to jump off the surface. It looks exactly like mine except where his says Discerner, mine says Underage. Oh, and of course our pictures are different. I stare at his. If my dad didn't wear his hair with such a harsh part, slightly off center, he could pull off cool. With a full head of dark hair and a strong jaw, he's handsome enough. "Dad. Not smart. Are you subconsciously trying to never go back?"

His jaw tightens then loosens again, which surprises me. It was a joke, but his reaction makes me wonder if there is some truth to the statement. He takes out his wallet from his pocket and tucks the card behind his Norm license, then offers me a smile. "I have it now, so no need to analyze me." He dumps the envelope upside down and a circular disc inside a clear plastic case slides onto the counter.

"What's that?"

"It's a DVD."

I pick it up. "Oh, I've seen these on TV before. It's so big." I turn it over in my hand, then set it back on the counter. "I don't get it; someone sent you an old movie?"

"No, the Para-bureau transferred the interview onto a DVD because that's the technology used here, and we're not allowed Compound technology Outside. I'll have to pick up a player for it." He lets out a sigh, then turns his attention to me. "How are you today?"

"Bored."

He smiles. "I'll go change and then we can go get something to eat."

Before he even finishes the sentence, I put my hand behind my back and he does the same. "One, two, three," I say, and I reveal my hand shaped like scissors at the same time he reveals his flat like a paper. "Ha! I won. I choose Mexican food."

He groans through a smile, then leaves to change.

I pick up the DVD again. Across the silver surface, written in black letters, is the name Steve "Poison" Paxton. *Poison? Really?* I wonder if it's a self-appointed nickname. There was a kid in seventh grade, who, after he Presented, insisted everyone call him Flash. He had developed the ability to speed up the connections in his brain, allowing him to run the mile a whopping one minute faster than the rest of us. One lousy minute. I wasn't calling anyone Flash unless he could create a tornado around me with his speed. Had that been my ability, I would've kept it to myself as long as I could, until I had no other choice and it was permanently embedded onto my Compound Clearance card.

I'd love to see what a guy who calls himself Poison looks like, but I can't. The stuff my dad gets from the Bureau is classified. I drop it back on the counter and get my shoes.

CHAPTER 5

PAR•A•dox: *n.* a statement that seems contradictory
but speaks a truth

The party is like every other one I've been to—loud and crowded. It's outside but still packed because people parked too close, creating a barrier around one side of the clearing. The other borders are the lake and then the Compound wall—which no illusion can keep from being an actual blockade.

I've sneaked to Laila's truck, climbed in the back where she had a couple lawn chairs set up, and retrieved the book she didn't know I brought out of my bag. Just when I start to settle into a reading rhythm, the book is ripped from my hands. In vain, I try to grab for it and end up swiping at the air a few times.

"I don't think so," Laila says. "This was not part of the deal."

"Come on. I came. I'm still involved."

"How is this"—she points at the floor of the truck bed where she stands—"involved?"

"I could've sat in the cab." I look at Laila. She's beautiful with her dark hair piled on her head and her big, dark eyes staring down at me in mock anger. She belongs here, with these people—the popular kids. Sometimes I wonder if Laila would be my friend if we had met now versus in kindergarten.

She laughs and sits in the chair next to me. "Are you really that bored?"

I lean back, resting my head on the chair. The night sky shines bright with an oversize moon and two smaller ones. Someone at the party obviously wanted extra light. I look around to see if I can pick out the Perceptive responsible for the altered sky.

"You're the only one I know who still lugs around actual books," she says, flipping through it.

I take it from her and put it back in my bag. "I like books. They're pretty."

A drink floats through the air, and Duke, who is leaning against a tree, catches it. He smirks at me as though I should be impressed. I raise my eyebrows and nod at all the other drinks in the air. Telekinetics are such show-offs.

"Okay, what's up with you and Duke?" Laila asks. "That seemed like the kind of look only exchanged by good friends.

Like you have some sort of inside joke or something."

"We don't."

"Yeah, well, it's obvious you know him well enough to introduce me."

"You know him too," I say.

"The whole school knows him. The whole Compound. He's the quarterback. But he has no idea who I am. Come on, you're going to remedy that."

She drags me out of the truck and through the crowd. I have to apologize to several people she plows me into as we go.

"He has no idea who I am either . . . ," I start to say, but then remember he had called me by name the other day when his football hit my car. How does he know my name?

Halfway to Duke, a guy steps in front of us. "Hey, Laila. Interested in a block enhancer?" He holds up a clear plastic bag full of electronic chips. "Twenty bucks."

"Who does it help block?"

"Telepaths."

Laila reaches into her pocket as though she's going to pull out her card and clip one of his chips to it. "What's the—"

"No." I push the guy's hand away. "She's not interested." When he walks away, I turn toward her. "What's wrong with you? You're going to waste your money on some unproven, untested mind-expanding pattern?"

"I wasn't going to buy it. I was just curious. If your father were Telepathic, you might be a little more open-minded about

38

alternative methods of blocking too."

"Just stick with the programs on our meditation track. They're the only ones proven to help."

"They're just so slow. . . ."

I sigh, but before I can say anything, she says, "Yeah, yeah, I know, slow and steady is the best way to come into our full abilities. Blah, blah, blah. You sound like your mom."

"Ugh. Don't say that." My mom is the last person I want to be compared to.

"Come on, you still have to introduce me." We stop in front of Duke, and she looks at me expectantly.

"Um, hi," I say. Have I ever introduced two people to each other before? Laila had always been in charge of introductions. Considering I have no idea what to say next, my guess is that I haven't.

"Hey, Addie."

Laila clears her throat.

"Duke, this is Laila. Laila, this is Duke." That sounded right. But maybe I'm supposed to include a little something about each of them. Like, *Duke, this is Laila; she thinks you're hot. Laila, this is Duke; he and his mirror share a close relationship.*

Obviously they don't need my help with conversation starters, because they begin a perfectly comfortable exchange all on their own. "Yeah, I've seen you around. Nice to meet you," Duke says.

"Great game tonight. That last touchdown pass was amazing."

He smiles. "Thanks."

"What's your secret for throwing so far?" She pats his arm. "Killer biceps?"

"He's been practicing," I add unhelpfully. I hadn't gone to the game, so it's the best contribution I have.

He laughs. "Yes, I have."

Even though Laila is an expert at flirting, I feel so uncomfortable. "Anyway, good to see you. We're going to talk to our friend now." I point blindly to the side and then let my gaze follow. I'm now staring at the lake and a group of people standing on the sandy bank. I realize I'm pointing right at Bobby, who's showing everyone he can manipulate mass by walking across the water. *Speaking of show-offs.* Ugh. I roll my eyes.

"Bobby? He's one of my best friends."

It makes sense that the two of them would be friends. It confirms my feelings about Duke's true nature. This also solves the mystery of how Duke knows my name. Bobby probably told him who he was going to ask to homecoming. "Really? You're best friends?" Laila asks. "But I've never seen you hang out. I thought you and Ray were best friends." She looks around as if she just realized Ray wasn't there to prove her point and she now must find him.

"Yeah, we are. All three of us. We live on the same block, grew up together. We've known each other since we could walk."

"Oh." Laila hums as if the relationship now makes complete sense.

"Good to know." I grab Laila's arm. "We'll see you at the

next football game." I start to pull her away.

"Well, *you* probably won't see me at the next football game," he says, and Laila jerks to a halt.

"Why not? Did you get hurt or something?" she asks.

"No, I meant Addie." His eyes lock on mine. "What is it? You don't like football, or you just don't believe in supporting your school?"

"Ever since a football hit me in the head, I can't seem to look at them the same."

He scoffs. "So you're telling me before two weeks ago you went to every football game?"

"How do you know I didn't?" Did this guy do a background check on me or something?

"I don't. It was a question."

"It sounds like one you think you already know the answer to."

"I believe I do. But you can still tell me I'm wrong."

He wasn't wrong. I'd only been to one football game. It was my freshman year. I learned rather quickly that Para-football wasn't really my thing. Aside from the fact that it was a complete waste of my time, it wasn't like the Norm football I sometimes watched with my dad. They rarely tackled one another, the Telekinetics on the team kept the ball airborne, tugging it back and forth. Occasionally a player would trip with no one around. In the end, the team with the best abilities won. But because I can't stand the smug look on his face I say, "You're wrong."

He takes a drink. "Well then, I'm sorry I've ruined your

41

football enjoyment for life with my stray ball."

"I thought you had perfect aim," I remind him.

He raises his glass slightly in a mocking toast. "I do."

Confused, I start to question him, but instead shake my head and successfully pull Laila away.

"Holy crap. What was that all about?" she asks, when we're out of earshot. "He likes you. In a big way."

"He does not. It's Duke. He flirts with everyone. Besides, you heard him, he's Bobby's good friend. I'm sure man code applies."

"But you hate Bobby. It's obvious he knows that and now wants to swoop in."

I stop by a speaker. The music is loud, and I yell, "Swoop in?"

"Don't you dare get sidetracked by my word choice. The boy likes you. You have to Search it. Find out if . . . I don't know, find out if he asks you out or something."

"First of all, I can't just ask the universe if Duke likes me. It doesn't work that way. I have to be faced with a choice. There is no choice here. Second, even if I did get the opportunity to find out my future with Duke, I wouldn't, because if it tells me I end up liking that guy then I'll just kill myself now."

"That guy? That *guy* is Duke Rivers, Addie. What is wrong with you?"

"He's a player." The song has ended and my words seem to echo in the new silence. My head whips around to Duke, and he holds my eyes for a single count, then looks away.

Laila lowers her voice and leans toward me. "And maybe you can be the girl to help him change his ways."

I shake my head. I don't want to argue about this. And I definitely don't want to be *that* girl. Every other girl may go weak in the knees anytime Duke is around, but I don't.

The next song starts, and a group of people behind us cheer and start dancing.

This is ridiculous. Even if I was interested, I didn't get "fought over" or "handed off" or whatever this was. Laila is reading way too much into this.

"I must be their charity case. The popular crowd is having 'do a good deed' month. Or maybe they're having a bet or something. I see it in the movies all the time—two popular guys see who can get the average girl first."

Laila throws back her head and groans. "Seriously, who taught you to be so cynical? You're gorgeous and smart. Who wouldn't like you? Just relax a little and give the guy the benefit of the doubt."

"Hey, I'm still in my-parents-just-got-a-divorce mode. Remember? This is the time when I'm allowed to question all relationships, wonder if true love exists at all anymore, and swear to a life of celibacy."

"Are you trying to live out every cliché?"

"Yes. If I'm forced to live through a divorce, it better be exactly like I've seen it play out in books and movies." I start listing the characteristics on my fingers. "Teen's parents fight over her through bribes, teen gets to be full of angst, teen's friends feel sorry for her, teen trusts no one. . . ."

"Except her best friend."

"Of course. And then teen's parents realize they made a huge mistake and teen helps them get back together after she matures or has an 'aha' moment or something." All five of my fingers are extended with my list, and I hold up my hand as if that reiterates my point.

Laila laughs. "Have you seriously planned out how you're going to deal with this divorce? What movies have you been watching, anyway, *The Parent Trap*?"

My chest tightens, and I try to ignore it. I glance over her shoulder to where some people are throwing rocks at the Compound wall, creating a ripple in the mountain illusion. "No. Lots of movies and books end that way. The plot point is obviously based on some sort of reality."

"Your parents aren't getting back together. And you read entirely too much. It's not good for your brain. I hereby ban you from all books."

I look down to hide my stinging eyes.

"Oh no," Laila says, her voice now serious. "You really thought your parents might get back together?"

"No, of course not." I'd been holding out hope, but she was right, there's no chance. A guy dancing slams into Laila's back and she growls at him, then takes my hand and pulls me away from the crowd and behind some trees.

She wraps her arms around me. "I'm so sorry, Addie."

The words make me realize just how final the situation is. My heart aches, and my throat is sore. "It's good for you," she says, rubbing my back. "Just let it out."

I can't. My emotions feel lodged in my chest and push against my lungs, making it hard to breathe. "I'm fine, really."

"You'll get through this," she says. "I'm so glad you stayed with your mom. I don't know what I'd do without you."

A deep voice behind me says, "Am I interrupting something?"

I look over to see Bobby standing by a group of trees, staring between the two of us. He has a satisfied look on his face as though he just solved some mystery. "Had I known, I would've never asked you to the dance. You should've just told me you were already taken." He nods his head toward Laila. "Mind if I watch?"

Laila's face hardens, and she whips around to face him. "Listen, we already know you're a perv, no need to prove it again. Get out of here."

He raises his hands in surrender. "Fine. Fine. I'm leaving." He walks backward through a tree trunk.

Laila walks over and hits the tree as if that will somehow hurt him. "Idiot."

"You don't think he really thinks . . ." I trail off, and let my finger float back and forth between Laila and me.

"Please. He's just trying to soften the blow of your rejection. Come on. Let's go back to the party."

CHAPTER 6

NOR•Mal•i•za•tion: *v. reduced to a normal state*

My dad walks in the house after five on Friday afternoon. "I'm so sorry, Addie."

I melt off my chair and land in a pile on the floor.

"That bad?"

I roll onto my back. "I know no one, I have no car, and you've abandoned me."

"You didn't want to watch the movie I rented?" He points to the TV and this huge, boxy player he set up the night before.

"I couldn't figure out how to work that stupid thing. There's just a bunch of buttons with triangles and squares."

He laughs. "No voice activation here. I'll teach you how to use it later. It's not that hard. But right now I have a peace offering." Out of his back pocket he pulls two strips of paper.

I sit up. "What are those?"

"Tickets. Your new high school has a football game tonight."

At this point even football sounds decent. "What time?"

"Kickoff's at seven." He sits on the couch.

I plop down next to him, sideways, one of my feet nudging my dad's leg as it settles on the cushion.

He pulls on the toe of my sock, causing it to form a loose pucker above my big toe. Then he stares at me, waiting to see how long I'll leave it like that. I count to twenty to prove that it doesn't bother me at all.

"You're a nuisance," I say, fixing my sock.

He laughs, then pats my ankle. "So, how is your cover story going? Are you going to be okay for school on Monday?"

"I think I'm good."

"Need me to quiz you?"

"Sure."

He squares his shoulders and raises his chin, assuming what I guess he thinks is a teacher's pose. "Welcome to class, Addie Coleman. Where did you move from?"

"Jackson, Texas. It's about five hours southeast of here. Half an hour from San Antonio. If you went there you'd find a tiny town surrounded by a mountain range. That mountain range is actually just an illusion though. It's really a sprawling city full of people with mind powers." I laugh. "How's that?"

He doesn't crack a smile.

"Oh, come on. It was a joke."

"Addie. That's not something to joke about. You can't tell anyone about the Compound or your powers. Not anyone. The Compound Containment Committee works very hard to keep the psychologically advanced a secret. And if they ever found out you told someone . . ."

"Yeah. I know." Of course I did. We had a major debriefing in the Tower before we were allowed to leave. But in a way I thought it was more talk than action. I didn't think my dad would be so strict. Of course I'm not going to announce my ability at school, but realizing I can never tell anyone . . . ever . . . is hard. I've never had to lie about who I am before.

My dad still has his stern look on. I nudge his leg with my foot. "Loosen up. I'm not going to tell anyone. Finish the quiz. Ask me another question."

"Okay. Why did you move here?"

"My dad's work." I start to say *as a human lie detector* but stop myself. He is obviously not in the mood to joke about it. The jokes were helping me feel better and without them the seriousness of the situation settles onto my shoulders.

"What do you like to do for fun?" he asks, still in teacher mode.

"Read . . . mostly."

"Good. You'll do just fine."

"You think that's all they'll ask?"

"I'm sure you'll get more questions, but it sounds like you have your story down." His lips pucker into his concerned face. "Are you okay?"

No. "Yes, I'm fine. This is just so new to me. That's all."

I know he doesn't believe me. He is the lie detector after all, but still he says, "You'll feel better once you start school and realize the cover story isn't a big deal."

"Yeah, probably. I'll go get ready for the football game."

I shut myself in the bathroom and lean against the counter. My ability had been my entire life. It Presented earlier than most—at the beginning of the sixth grade. But even before that, from the time I was little, my mom was constantly assessing my strengths, testing my mind patterns, seeing what I was drawn toward. Without my ability, I'm not sure who I am.

I dig out my phone from my pocket and dial Laila. On the second ring she picks up.

"Hey, what's up?" she says.

"I have to pretend like I'm average."

"The horror!" she says in faux offense.

"It *is* horrible. You know what this means, right? Everybody is going to think I'm . . . Normal. My ability is what makes me halfway cool. I'm nobody without it."

"Oh, please. You aren't average—with or without your ability."

I lower the toilet lid and sit down. "What am I supposed to talk to people about? The weather? I already tried that and it went horribly. I'm doomed."

"Did you hear what I just said?"

"Yes, but I don't believe you because you only know the me with my ability. You haven't seen the me without my ability in a long time. The me without my ability is boring, whiny, and plain."

"The you *with* your ability is pretty whiny as well."

"Not helping." I pull on the string hanging from the blinds beside me and they raise with a clatter, making me jump. After tugging on the bottom a few times, I give up, not remembering how to put them back down again.

"So let me get this straight. If I didn't have an ability, you wouldn't like me?"

I sigh. "Of course I'd like you. But that's because you're outspoken, bossy, and don't care what anyone else thinks."

"You just made me sound like a total witch."

"I know, but let's not get sidetracked. This is my meltdown."

"Addie, come on, you usually don't care what anyone else thinks either. What's going on?"

"I don't care when people think I'm an antisocial, controlling bookworm because that's what I am. It's when they interpret me wrong that I have a problem."

She gives a short burst of laughter. "Well, I'm sure you'll prove yourself to be just what you are soon enough. I gotta run. I'm getting ready to go out."

I pull the cell phone away from my ear to check the time. "Yeah, me too. Football game. Actually I'd better go take a shower."

"Wait. You're going to a football game?"

"My dad's taking me."

"Wow. Well, that's not going to help your image."

"Ha-ha."

"I'm proud of you. Find the student section and make some friends."

I wish she were going with me, and I think about blubbering this to her in an ever-so-dignified manner but settle with, "I'll try."

My dad and I sit on the cold cement benches of the stadium as we watch the game. It's a lot louder than I remember. The crunching of helmets and the cheering of the crowd echo through the air. The moon hangs over the stadium, a sliver in the sky. I try to remember the last time I've seen the moon anything but full.

"Is it disappointing?" my dad asks.

"Not at all," I answer quickly, and then realize I'm not sure if he's talking about the moon or the game. I decide the answer applies to both.

"Addie, why don't you go sit in the student section? It looks like they're having a lot more fun."

I look over to where a whole section of high school students are cheering and waving signs. Some have even painted their bodies in the school colors. I wonder how they can be so excited without Mood Controllers rallying their emotions. My dad nudges my shoulder with his.

"I don't know anybody."

"And that's never going to change unless you try."

"I don't want to leave you here alone."

He chuckles. "I'm a big boy."

The night, which has turned quite cold considering how hot the day was, sends a shiver down my spine. After another nudge, I stand and walk over. My dad always knows when to push and when to back off. I needed that push.

The student section is pretty full, so I squeeze my way down several rows. Faces that hold no history for me flash by, their most prominent features lingering in my mind for a moment or two—bright red hair, a large nose, green eyes, a gap-toothed smile. Finally, I find an empty seat next to a guy wearing cowboy boots and a wool-lined jean jacket. His hands are shoved in his pockets, and he watches the game intently.

"Excuse me, are you saving this?"

He looks up. Long lashes surround chocolate brown eyes. "No, have a seat," he says in the Southern accent that prevails here.

I sit down. "Thanks. And can we just get this out of the way? Your eyelashes make mine want to commit suicide from shame." Yeah. I'm not very good at small talk.

He laughs.

"I'm sure you've heard that before."

"Never put like that . . ." He looks around. "You here alone?"

"Well, sort of. My dad's over there." I nod my head toward my dad. "You?"

"No. See those idiots right there?" He points to the front

railing, where several guys stand shirtless with painted chests and wigs on. "Those are my friends."

All his friends are making fools of themselves, and he's not. Right away that says almost everything I need to know about him: He's not a follower, he can make up his own mind, and he's perfectly okay with sitting alone. "Why aren't you participating?"

"Because a coat of paint doesn't conceal my layer of fat very well."

I give him a quick once-over. He looks like he's in good shape, but it's hard to tell with his jacket on. I glance back at his friends. "It's not doing them any favors either," I note.

He smiles. "Plus, it's cold tonight."

"Your layer of fat is supposed to help with that."

"True." A whistle sounds, and he turns his attention back to the field. The quarterback snaps the ball and is almost immediately tackled in a hard hit near the thirty-yard line. I suck air between my teeth.

"I'm Trevor, by the way," he says, now that the play is over.

"Addie."

"Addie?"

"Yes, short for Addison."

"Do you go to this school, Addison?"

The fact that he has to ask makes me realize it must be a very big high school. I may not have known everyone's name at my old school, but I would easily recognize a new face. "My father and I just moved here. I start school on Monday."

"Ah, very good. Welcome to Dallas."

"Thanks."

"You're a senior?"

"Junior. You?"

"Senior." His gaze goes back to the game. My attention is drawn to the sidelines, where a person dressed up in a large cougar costume runs circles around the cheerleaders. We have a mascot at Lincoln High too—a lightning bolt. And thanks to the Perceptives, I've heard most home games include an actual lightning show (probably to divert the attention from the boringness happening on the field).

I cringe when the play ends in a bone-crushing pileup.

"You don't like football?" Trevor asks.

"Actually, I like this kind better. It's more exciting."

"More exciting than . . ."

"Um, than flag football," I say, proud I remembered another version so quickly. This whole business of not letting things about the Compound slip is going to be harder than I thought. It had been my entire life, after all.

"You've watched a game of flag football before?"

"Well, no, but this is more exciting than that, you have to admit."

"A lot of things are more exciting than flag football."

"True."

The rest of the game passes in comfortable silence interspersed with a few comments. By the end I've adopted his closed-off position of hands in my pockets, shoulders hunched against the wind. The final whistle sounds, and his friends rush toward him, a rowdy mass of painted bodies. I try to slip away, but one of them stops me with a loud, "Hi, who are you?"

I start to answer, but Trevor is faster. "Guys, this is Addison. She's new here."

"Just Addie is fine," I say, but my voice is swallowed by their boisterous hellos.

He goes on to list several names. To remember names, I usually advance my memory by relating the person's name to one of their physical features, but since theirs are covered in paint, I won't remember who is who after tonight. "Nice to meet you. I'm sure I'll see you on Monday." Again, I attempt to leave. The same guy who stopped me before—Rowan, with red stripes of paint down his face—stops me again by saying, "We all party at Trevor's after the game. You should come."

I really don't want to hang out with a bunch of Norm guys I don't know. I check the time on my cell phone. Nine thirty. Still too early to claim tiredness or curfew restrictions.

"Didn't you say your dad wanted you home early tonight to help unpack?" Trevor says, surprising me. Was my body language that obvious?

"Yes, he did. I'm supposed to meet him now, in fact. Next time?" I say to Rowan.

"For sure."

I back away slowly. *Thanks*, I mouth to Trevor when the others get distracted by a shoving match.

He nods. "See you Monday."

CHAPTER 7

PA•RAl•o•gize: v. to draw illogical conclusions
based on assumptions

I stare at the two doors. They both look so real. But I know one of them is an illusion that a Perceptive has made me imagine. When I figure out which one is real, I'm supposed to walk through it to Mrs. Stockbridge, who is on the other side, probably with her tablet already scrolled to her grade book. Imagining the big F she's about to type there is not helping my concentration. I need a good grade in this class since I've been bombing Thought Placement. I wonder if she'll highlight it red to emphasize my failure. I would.

Stop. Concentrate.

In my mind, I scan through the lessons we've had on detecting illusions. Inconsistencies in the image. My eyes go back and forth between both doors. They're identical. Ripples, movement, or haziness on an otherwise solid surface. None. A thinness or transparency to the object. They both seem like perfectly solid pieces of wood to me. My time is running out. Then I see it, a small smudge of black in the center of one door. I smile and step toward the smudge-free door. I reach for the palm scanner, and my hand goes right through it. "Crap."

After I walk through the right door, Mrs. Stockbridge clucks her tongue and types something into her tablet. The clip attempting to tame her frizzy red hair has been unsuccessful in its efforts, leaving several strands sticking out at odd angles. If I were a Perceptive, like she is, I wonder if I would try to make others see me at my best all the time.

"Reasoning?" she asks.

I almost answer my own hypothetical question but stop when I remember she can't read my mind. "What?"

"Why did you pick the door on the left?"

"Oh. There was a black smudge on the real door. I thought that meant it was fake," I admit.

"Sometimes perfection reveals the lie, Addie, not the truth," she says. I nod and wait with the others who have already completed the task.

A memory involuntarily works its way into my mind, filling the corners and taking me back to that moment. I am a little girl of five. My father has taken me on a picnic to a beautiful park near the lake. After picking at my sandwich for a few minutes,

I lie back on the blanket. Suddenly thousands of colorful but-terflies appear overhead. They gently float downward, twisting and turning, like fluttering leaves. At any moment they will land on and around me. I can almost feel the soft touch of their wings on my skin. With a smile I reach up.

"Addie," my dad says, "they're just an illusion."

I sit up, my brow drawn low. "They're not. I see them." They swirl between my dad and me, warping his image.

An old man walks by and smiles. "A gift for the little lady," he says. My dad waves politely. When he's gone, along with his butterflies, my dad takes me by the shoulders and points. A sin-gle butterfly rests on a flower five feet from us, its plain white wings moving slowly up and down. "That is real, baby. Isn't it pretty?"

I curl my lip in disappointment. "It's boring."

A barking laugh pulls me out of the memory. I glance over my shoulder to where a few girls quickly stop whispering. I shoot them narrow eyes. Am I the only one who failed the stu-pid door test?

At lunch, Laila gives me one look and says, "What's wrong?"

We walk toward the outdoor stage—our normal lunchtime hangout—and I give a frustrated grunt. "I failed an Illusion Detection test today."

"Failure is so relative," Laila says.

"No. It's not. You either pass the test or you don't. There's nothing relative about it."

She shrugs. "But you've aced all your other ones, so it averages out." She sits on the cement stage, letting her feet dangle over the side. "So, therefore, it's relative." She jerks her head to the side. "Sit down."

Seeing her so calm makes me think I've completely overreacted. I'm prone to do that. I take a deep breath, dig out my lunch from my backpack, and hop up beside her. A semicircle of grass fans out to surround the stage and soon it's full of people.

As I open my bag of chips, Laila leans forward. "This stage isn't very high, right?"

What is she talking about? I follow her gaze to the ground. "I guess not."

"So it wouldn't hurt too bad if someone got pushed off?"

I look to the left, where several other regulars are lined up along the stage, lunches on their laps, feet dangling. "Who's getting—" Before I can finish my sentence, she grabs my arm and flings me off the stage. I gasp in shock, wondering what evil plan this act has accomplished. I don't have to wonder too long when Duke practically trips over me.

"Are you okay?" he asks as I collect my scattered lunch.

"Fine." I shove my sandwich and chips into my ripped lunch bag and straighten up.

"Addie," Laila says, feigning concern and jumping down next to me. "Did you get hurt? What happened?" But her "concern" is instantly replaced with a smile for Duke. "Hey,

Duke, we didn't see you."

More like *I* didn't see him. Laila quite obviously saw him from a mile away.

Ray bends over and picks up my water bottle, which had rolled up against his massive foot. Seriously, he has to wear at least a size fifteen. The guy is huge. "Here," he says, handing it to me.

"Thanks."

"Where are you two headed?" Laila asks.

Duke points in the general direction of the parking lot. "Off-campus."

"Really?" Laila says as though this is the biggest coincidence ever. "We were just going to get something from my car. Mind if we walk with you?"

I could murder Laila right now. If only I could get my hands on a weapon—a size-fifteen shoe might work.

"Of course not."

And of course Laila squeezes herself between Duke and Ray, leaving me with no other option but to walk next to Duke. After only a few steps she has managed to become so engrossed in a quiet conversation with Ray that Duke and I are left in awkward silence.

"Sorry," I finally say, because unless he's an idiot, it's pretty obvious what Laila just did.

"I'm not. Now I don't have to make up some sorry excuse to talk to you."

I'm confused. "Don't you have man code?" I don't know why

60

I said it; it just flew out, but I can't take it back.

"What do you mean?"

Now I have to explain and I don't want to. I let myself get distracted for a moment by a backpack floating through the air in front of me. Eventually it lands in its owner's arms, and I look over at Duke, who is waiting for me to speak. "You and Bobby are good friends."

"Yes."

"Bobby asked me to homecoming."

"And you said no."

"So don't you have that thing where if your best friend likes a girl, she's off-limits?"

"If every girl Bobby liked was off-limits, I'd never get to go out with anyone. The only girls Bobby restricts me from are those he's kissed. You haven't kissed him, right?"

"No!" At least not in my real life. I had in my Search, but Bobby didn't know that. I feel my face go bright red.

Duke lowers his brow. "Are you sure?"

"Yes, I'm sure. I haven't kissed him."

"Well, then there you go. Man code does not apply."

I'm trying my best not to be flattered, but it's hard. This is Duke Rivers. He smiles, and I find myself smiling back.

"What do I have to do to get you to come to one of my games?"

"Play on a Norm team," I say before thinking.

He tilts his head. "Really? So that's what this is about? You don't like people using their abilities to win at sports? Are you a Naturalist? Do you want us to merge with Normal society?"

We round a brick building and walk down a wide hall toward the parking lot. "No, not at all. I fully support abilities. People can use them to advance in any areas of their lives. I know mine has helped me. I can't imagine life without abilities. I just personally find Para-football boring."

"Ouch. So you want to see more bodies slamming into each other? Is that it? Wait," he says, before I can answer. "Are you telling me you regularly watch Norm football?"

"Not *regularly*."

"This is getting worse. Tell me one thing: Have you ever seen *me* play?"

I rub my forehead. The welt has long since disappeared, but I wince for his sake.

He laughs and nudges my arm with his elbow. "That doesn't count. I mean, in a game."

"No. I haven't been since my freshman year."

The contagious smile is back on his face. "You're not very good for my ego."

"I think I'm perfect for your ego." I smile sweetly.

"Addie, you're a different girl, aren't you?"

Rude. I try to nudge my shoulder into his arm, like he had done to me. Only it doesn't work and the act of trying almost causes me to trip.

He reaches his hand out. "You okay?"

"Yeah." I look over my shoulder, pretending to search for what tripped me.

"How has your ability helped you advance?" he asks.

"What?"

"You said earlier that you're perfectly fine with people using their abilities to advance. You said yours has helped you. How?"

"Sometimes I'll see which classes I'm better at, which projects work out better. Things like that."

"So you're Clairvoyant?"

"Oh." I'm surprised because I assumed Bobby had told him my ability. "Yeah. Sort of." My ability is actually called Divergence, which means extending in different directions from a common point. It was one of the first words I looked up back when I Presented. But I don't feel like explaining that to Duke. I stopped correcting people a long time ago. Clairvoyance is a Time Manipulation ability as well, so close enough.

"With an ability like yours, you've probably never made a mistake in your life. You always know what you want." He meets my eyes.

That's mostly true. I generally know exactly what I want, and the steps I'm going to take to get it, but not necessarily because of my ability. "I don't Search everything. I've made plenty of mistakes. But you're right, I've avoided many." *Like Bobby*, I want to say.

"Have you ever Searched me?"

"No. I've never had to make a choice regarding you."

He stops abruptly, and I watch helplessly as Ray and Laila keep walking. He steps in front of me, putting his back to the ever-increasing distance between our friends and us. "What if I gave you a choice? How long would it take to Search it?"

"It depends on what it is," I say, instantly nervous.

"Maybe I want to ask you out."

"Don't." I grip tightly to the straps of my backpack and rock back on my heels a little.

"That was fast. What happened in the Search?"

"I didn't look. Like I said, I don't need to Search everything to know what I want."

He takes a step closer and leans down. "I didn't mean right now anyway. Just one day."

My eyes dart to his lips and tingles spread down my neck. "I have a personal rule."

"What's that?"

"I refuse to kiss a guy who's kissed more than five girls."

He raises his eyebrows, a playful gleam coming into his eyes, and I realize what I just said. My cheeks catch fire.

"Date! I meant date!"

He laughs a deep throaty laugh. "That's the most ridiculous rule I've ever heard. Did you make it up just now?"

I laugh. I had. But it was a good rule. If I had it before I met Bobby, it would've saved me a lot of trouble.

"That's what I thought. But that's okay. Keep the rule. It doesn't affect me."

I freeze in shock, trying to decide if I heard him right. *The*

Duke is implying he hasn't kissed more than five girls? Or maybe he's saying he hasn't dated more than five.

"That surprised, huh?"

I nod slowly.

"Duke!" Ray yells from where he and Laila have stopped by his truck.

Duke lifts his hand, acknowledging Ray, but doesn't take his eyes off me. "Stick around. I'm full of surprises." He turns and walks away. I watch Duke retreat, noticing the width of his shoulders and the confidence in his stride. It's then I know I'm in trouble.

CHAPTER 8

eNOR•Mous: *adj.* really big

I stir around the last few Cheerios in my bowl, the effort required to fish them out one by one too hard to find on a Monday morning. When my dad walks in the kitchen he says, "Ready for your first day of school?" like he's a contestant on a game show and the category is: Worst Things to Say to Your Teenager in the Morning.

"Tell me there's a way to get some mind-expansion sessions or something." I need at least that part of my morning ritual. It's what usually wakes me up.

"It's really hard to get Compound technology Outside. We'll have to apply."

"What? That rule extends to our programs as well? I might not get them?"

"You'll be fine, Addie. You don't need them. I never had that when I was a kid. I've always thought natural progression was the best for an ability anyway."

Only because when he was a kid that's all they had. But even way back then they did mind exercises to enhance their natural abilities. I stand and put my bowl in the sink.

"You'll be fine, right?"

"Dad. It's morning."

He smiles and gives me a hug. "Okay, I get it. We'll talk when you're awake."

"Thanks."

At school my head is still buzzing. I feel lost in a huge sea of people. I've never seen a school so big. In the hallway before class I get herded right past my door. I turn around and swim upstream. If I were better at Thought Placement I could've forced the word *move* into the minds of those around me.

I pull over to the side of the hall and wait for the crowd to thin before I make it back to my classroom door. The number on the door is C14 and, even though I memorized it, I check it against the paper schedule in my hand twice to make sure I'm not about to walk into the wrong class. The schedule confirms it, C14 Government.

I took one semester of US Government a few years back, part of Norm-training, so I hope I can remember some of it.

I walk inside and hand the slip of paper to the teacher.

"Welcome," he says. "Everyone, we have a new student: Addison Coleman."

"Just Addie," I say.

"Make her feel welcome."

I don't know if there is some ritual that's supposed to follow those words, but I look around expectantly. A few blank stares greet me. Almost everyone else is still talking to their neighbor or studying their phone. I'm glad that "making someone feel welcome" doesn't involve sharing three fun facts about myself or any other opportunity for embarrassment I had been dreading. Maybe I wouldn't have to test out my cover story on my first day after all.

"You may have a seat," the teacher says, pointing to a chair front-row center—the seat everyone else had quite obviously avoided.

"Oh, okay." I try to find a different open seat, but the only other one is beside a guy who is using half of it, along with all of his. In my scan for a chair, however, I notice Trevor in the back right corner. I smile, and he gives me a nod.

It seems my only choice is the dreaded seat, so I take the two steps required and sit down. Mr. Buford—according to my all-knowing class schedule—walks to his desk and hits Play on an iPod docked in a stereo. Music blares through the room, and nearly everyone throws their hands over their ears. I mentally muffle the sound. He fumbles with the controls until the music softens. It's only then I hear what's playing—the theme music to James Bond.

A satisfied smile steals across his pudgy face as though he just used the best teaching method ever. I have a feeling it's the only excitement I'll see in this class. He turns off the music and then faces us dramatically. "Our topic for the next several weeks is . . ." He pauses and looks around. Nobody volunteers the answer. "Any guesses? Justin?"

A guy several rows back says, "Old movies?" The other students laugh.

"Hot women?" someone else volunteers.

"No, guys, come on. Anybody?"

Just as I think about offering the answer he wants, to put him out of his misery, a voice from the back says, "Government-funded investigative agencies."

That was more specific than the "spies" answer I was ready to offer.

"Yes, thank you, Trevor."

I turn around and raise my eyebrows at him. He just shrugs.

Mr. Buford writes several acronyms on a big whiteboard using a pen I can smell from where I sit. How is he not high from that thing? I'm amazed at the lack of computers at this school. "Study them and know them by their full names. This will be on the test." Those words cause an eruption of notebooks to fly open so fast that, had I been in my old school, I would've thought Mr. Buford had used Telekinesis. He laughs. "Ah, the magic word gave you a little motivation to get in gear. Good. Today we're going to discuss the FBI."

When class is over, I slowly put away my notebook, giving Trevor plenty of time to come up and say hi. After zipping my backpack, I casually look over my shoulder—he's gone.

There went my only friend in Dallas. And that's using the term *friend* a little loosely. Okay, a lot loosely. I could barely call him an acquaintance. Whatever he is, I had been hoping I would run into him at some point today so I wouldn't feel like too much of a loner loser.

Out in the hall, I look both ways, hoping to catch a glimpse of his back, but all I see is a mass of people. Trevor is nowhere in sight.

I make it to lunch without having to come up with any fun facts except name, age, and where I moved from. Regardless of my practice session with my dad, California came flying out of my mouth without warning and I had to go with it. I had been so careful, trying not to slip up and call it the Compound, that a whole different state had resulted from my nervousness. Oh well, either story would've been a lie. At least this way, I won't have to tell half the truth and risk spilling the other half along with it. I'll go home and write my own backstory. It will be easier to remember.

The common area in this school is a big section of grass, interspersed with trees and surrounded by stone benches. For as long as I can remember, Laila and I have been friends—ever since she stood up for me on our first day of kindergarten. I've never been alone at school since. Now I'm very much alone, and it feels wrong. Rather than eat lunch by myself with an audience, I search out the library.

The smell of books, a mix of dust and leather, greets me as I walk through the door, and I smile. At Lincoln High, the library is three rows of computers where we can download information onto our cards. I get all my books from the one remaining bookstore in town, which without me there will probably go out of business. But that bookstore is nothing compared to this. This library is two stories high with a wide staircase leading up to the second level. Windows line the entire upper portion all the way around, blanketing the floor with light. If I were alone I would throw my arms out and spin in a circle. Instead I walk up the stairs, running my hand along books as I go.

I find the classics section, and after perusing for a while, pull out *A Tale of Two Cities*, which seems appropriate, and start to read. Just when I begin to realize Dickens's "worst of times" seem a lot worse than anything I've been through, I hear the sound of a crowd of people walking along the tile-floored entrance downstairs.

Crap. I must've missed the bell signaling lunch was over. A class is obviously meeting in the library today. I pull out my schedule from the front pocket of my backpack, hoping to find something different from what I know is printed there. PE.

The two little unassuming letters make me cringe. Tomorrow seems like a better day to start PE. Nobody should be forced to do physical exercise on Mondays. The decision to ditch on my first day produces a twinge of guilt in my gut. But knowing I can claim "new kid" status for at least a week, I push down the feeling.

I scoot farther back into the aisle, certain no one will find me. Why would they? It's the classics aisle. It has to be one of the least visited sections in a high school library. So when footsteps scuff the flooring, I'm genuinely surprised.

I look up to see Trevor intently focused on the row of books to his left. His finger trails along the bindings and then he stops and slides the book he holds in between two others.

"Hi," I say when he turns.

His shoulders jerk back in surprise before his face fully registers recognition. "Oh, hey, Addison. What are you doing?"

"Apparently I'm ditching PE."

"I was surprised to see you in Government this morning. I thought you said you were a junior."

"I . . . uh . . ." Panic wells in my chest. Had my dad put me in an advanced class? What am I supposed to say? *Well, yeah, my mind is at least ten times more efficient than a Normal person's, so my dad probably wanted to challenge me as much as possible.* Even if I were allowed to say that, it probably wouldn't go over well.

"Did you test into it?"

"Yes!" I say entirely too loudly. "I mean, yes, I did." I point to the book he just put back, trying to change the subject. "What are you returning?"

"Oh." He looks at the spine of the book. "*Nineteen Eighty-four*, Orwell."

I loved that book, but I don't like to influence people from giving their honest opinions about a book before I tell them how they should've felt. "Did you like it?"

He laughs and leans his shoulder against the bookcase. His whole presence, from his casual smile to his relaxed posture, oozes laid-backness. "I didn't read it. I don't know who would." He points to the books that surround him. "The only time the classics ever get checked out is when they're required for English."

"Uh." I hold up the book in my hands with raised eyebrows.

He tilts his head sideways to read the title. "*A Tale of Two Cities*. Oh, you like classics. Sorry."

I smile. "No. It's okay. I just like books in general. Today I felt like hurting my brain with archaic language and deep thoughts. What about you? If you didn't read it, why are you returning it?"

"I'm an aide in the library during sixth period."

"Nice." That would be my dream class. "How did you manage that?"

"I got hurt and couldn't do PE." He smiles. "If they had given me a more exciting class, everyone would start faking injuries."

By the time he gets to the last word of the sentence, my "fake-injury list" is already at five. "Wait, so you're telling me this is like a prison sentence for you?"

"More like a torture chamber."

I gasp. "I'm deeply offended."

"It's just this place is so quiet and these books all start to look the same after a while."

"Charles Dickens is turning over in his grave right now," I tell him.

He forces a serious expression, straightens up, and nods. "Noted. I will not criticize your personal friends when you are within hearing range." He shifts the books in his hands then looks at one of the spines. "Well, I'd better get back to work. The librarian"—he checks over his shoulder—"is a Nazi."

My eyes go wide. "She is?"

He lowers his brow. "Not literally."

"Oh. Right."

He gives me a half smile that only half hides the confused look in his eyes. "Okay, bye."

As soon as he's gone, I pull out my cell phone and text Laila: *It's hard to play Normal. Oh, and I've found your eventual replacement.*

Thanks a lot. Who is she?

It's a he. And for a Norm, he seems pretty cool. Definitely best friend material.

I'm irreplaceable. Gotta go, Mr. C is giving me the eye. I think he's reading my mind. Better concentrate on blocking it.

Trevor walks past the row, his stack of books half as tall, stops midstep, and backs up. "You really are ditching class."

I smile, feeling like the rebel I'm not. "Yep."

He shakes his head and keeps walking.

I pull out my notebook, turn to a blank page, and write, *The ghost of Charles Dickens told me that after he turned over in his grave, he couldn't go back to sleep. He's decided to leave eternal rest, reinhabit his decaying body, and exact revenge on you for disturbing his slumber. You've been warned.*

I rip out the page and fold it in half twice, making sure the corners are perfectly lined up. I haven't had to make a friend since kindergarten, and apparently my tactics haven't changed much. I write his name on the outside of the paper. Now, how to give it to him.

CHAPTER 9

ap•PA•RA•tus: *n.* any organization of activities
aimed toward a set goal

At lunch, I make it a point to sit more than an arm's length from Laila.

She laughs. "You're not still mad at me for yesterday, are you?"

"No, I love it when you throw me off the stage to make me talk to a guy I hate."

"You do not hate him."

"You're right. That would require too much energy. I have no feelings toward him whatsoever."

"You should tell that to your face, because it was looking at him pretty dreamily in the parking lot yesterday. Duke's charm is already working its magic."

She's right, but I'm trying to talk myself out of it. Duke and I have absolutely nothing in common. "No," I say defensively. "I'm immune."

"Nobody is."

Students talk in concentrated clumps on the grass surrounding the stage, and my eyes are drawn to a pair of guys fighting a hazy ninja. A teacher walks over, picks up the hologram simulator, and pockets it, the ninja disappearing. The guys moan their objection. I take a big breath and look back at Laila. "I'm not acting out enough."

Most of the time Laila can follow my erratic subject shifts, but this time she says, "Uh . . . what?"

"I've been thinking about books where the main character's parents are going through a divorce. A big theme is rebellion. I think I should give it a try."

She laughs. "Addie and rebellion. Those two words don't fit together."

At first I'm tempted to be offended by the comment, but she's right. I'm not rebellious. Not even a little bit. But considering the insane amount of tension still present between my mom and me, I'm pretty sure I can channel rebellion right now. "I can totally do it."

"You do know you're speaking of fiction, right? Your novels aren't supposed to be study guides for human behavior."

I shrug off her comment. "I have at least a six-month window where my parents will blame themselves instead of me for anything I do wrong. I was thinking of a blue streak in my hair."

Her eyes light up as though she's suddenly on board. "Really? Because that would be so awesome."

"Is that enough? I don't want to go over the top, but I don't want to undersell my suffering either."

"It's only enough because your parents have told you not to touch your beautiful blond curls before. My parents wouldn't even notice."

"Am I too late to join the conversation?" Duke asks, jumping up to sit on the stage beside me. It surprises me because I didn't see him coming. The other thing that surprises me is how I forget how gorgeous he is until he's next to me again. If he's going to start coming around more, I need to find some flaws to focus on. I study him for a moment but come up empty. He's flawless. Not even a single zit. New strategy. I will not look at him.

"Addie was just telling me how she was going to add a blue stripe to her hair today after school," Laila says, filling him in.

"That would bring out your eyes," he says.

"How would that bring out my eyes?"

"Because your eyes are . . ." He trails off as I meet his gaze. "Uh, brown. Your eyes are brown. I could've sworn they were blue."

"It's hard to keep track when you're looking into so many, isn't it?"

He narrows his eyes in confusion and I try not to laugh.

Laila hits my leg. "So you should come help us dye Addie's hair after school."

I keep myself from gasping my objection to her offer and add, "Yeah, sure. We're doing it at Laila's house."

She scrunches her nose and throws me the thanks-a-lot look. "We are?"

"Yes."

"But no one will be at your house. My dad and brothers will be at mine." That's her nice way of saying she doesn't want Duke at her house.

I don't want him at mine either, and since she's the one who brought it up, I don't back down. "I know, but my mom might come home early today and in order to achieve maximum impact, she can't walk in when my hair is wet."

"Maximum impact?" Duke says.

"Yeah, she's rebelling," Laila tells him.

"Against what?" he asks.

"I'm not sure exactly. Against what, Addie?" Laila asks with a smirk.

"Against unnormalcy. Antiaverageness."

"Let me get this straight. You're rebelling against being Paranormal?"

"No, this has nothing to do with abilities. I'm promoting the norm. The cliché. The typical."

"I'm lost."

"She thinks if she can check off every item on the list of

'how the average teen deals with divorce,' her parents will get back together."

I glare at Laila, irritated she would share that with Duke. "That's not true. I don't think they're getting back together." Anymore. "But since they're getting divorced, I don't want to miss out on any of the fun experiences that go along with it." I hold up a strip of hair.

"Ah, man. Your parents are getting a divorce? Sorry, that sucks."

"Mine and half the other kids' parents on campus at some point, right? Nothing new or exciting. Just average."

He raises his eyebrows. "And average is . . . good?"

"Exactly. See, you're learning. It's all about expectations. If you do the typical, you can expect the typical result, no surprises." In my attempt not to stare at him too much, I have gone from looking at the cloudless sky to a small rock by my hand and now to the vines growing up the building in front of us. They have covered nearly every inch of red brick as they climb their way up the wall, searching for open space.

Duke speaks, bringing my attention back to him. "So you're acting out against your parents, and what exactly is the typical result of that?"

I lean back on my palms. "Well, before the divorce, my mom would've flipped out. I would've been grounded and she would've taken me to the salon, made them dye it back at my expense."

"But now?"

"Now she'll flip out, but because she'll recognize it for what it is—me begging for love and attention—she'll tell me she's disappointed but then take me to a movie or something."

"Really?" He looks to Laila as if checking to see if I'm serious. When Laila shrugs, he turns back to me. "She'll reward you?"

"For sure."

Both he and Laila look doubtful. I assure them with, "You'll see."

He hops to the ground, then moves in front of me. Leaning against my legs that are still dangling off the stage, with one hand on either side of my knees, he says, "Sounds exciting. I'll see you after school then, Blue Eyes."

I hold back a curse.

"I knew they weren't brown. I didn't know you were studying Light Manipulation. I'm impressed. But it takes concentration." He leans forward slowly until his mouth is inches from my ear. My eyes flutter and I know he heard the gasp of air I took no matter how quiet it was. "You got distracted," he whispers, then grabs his backpack from behind me and leaves.

"Not by you," I call after him.

He turns and walks backward for a moment, a wide smile spread across his annoyingly handsome face. He knows I'm bluffing. He raises his eyebrows and shrugs his shoulders before he pivots and is gone.

"You know I want to kill you, right? Again," I say to Laila as we sit in her living room waiting for Duke to arrive. "Why would you invite him? You're making him think I like him or something."

"You do."

Her brothers dash by the couch, one chasing the other. They knock into one of the few remaining paintings on the wall, sending it swinging. Five years ago, Laila's house looked like a page out of a magazine. Now it's stripped bare. Only the essentials are left.

Laila yells after the boys, "I have company today, so stay caged somewhere until Mom gets home from work." She stands to straighten the picture. Even though she hides it well, I realize she must be embarrassed. Why did I insist on doing this at Laila's? I'm a horrible friend.

The doorbell rings, and my heart flips. She raises one eyebrow and skips to the door.

"Duke," she gushes. "How are you? Come in."

"I'm good. I brought some supplies." Out of his back pocket he pulls a pair of elbow-length, bright orange rubber gloves.

"We're dyeing hair, not scrubbing toilets," Laila says.

"I thought hair dye was like flesh-eating acid."

I laugh. "Because then everyone would want to dye their hair."

"So there isn't some flesh-burning caveat on the box?"

Laila draws down the corners of her mouth as though she's impressed. "I think Duke's been reading hair-dye boxes, Addie, what do you think?"

"Have you been doing your homework?" I ask, standing.

"I didn't want to look like an idiot, but apparently I didn't save myself from that fate."

Laila hits him on the chest. "It wasn't idiotic, it was cute. Come on, I can probably even find you some toilets to clean."

"Ha-ha."

In the kitchen Duke pulls on his rubber gloves and holds up his hands like he's about to perform surgery. He even makes orange gloves look adorable.

"What do I do?" he asks.

"Why don't you just sit over there so you don't hurt yourself?" I say, pointing at the table.

Laila says, "Oh, Addie, don't be a poor sport."

"Says the girl who isn't getting flesh-eating acid put in her hair."

Laila sits me on a barstool and separates a section of my hair out from the rest. "Duke, come hold this while I get the stuff ready."

He stands way too close and smells way too good. I avert my eyes, looking at the green numbers of the microwave clock. Laila walks across the kitchen and turns on the water to fill a bottle.

"You know what else the average girl who's acting out does?" Duke asks quietly.

I glance once at Laila, but it's obvious she can't hear us. "What?"

"She starts spending all her time with a boy who's no good for her."

"And that boy would be . . . ?"

"Me, of course."

"You're no good for me?"

"Horrible. I'll take your mind off schoolwork, force you to

83

constantly think about kissing, and make you want to spend all your free time away from home."

I can hardly breathe. "Sounds tempting . . . you know, just to go along with my acting-like-the-average-teen plan."

"Exactly."

I look up and meet his eyes. "You know we're nothing alike, right?"

"Isn't there a reason for the saying 'opposites attract'?"

"Yes—magnets."

A spray of water hits me on the side of the face. "Watch out, I'm armed and dangerous," Laila says, laughing. She turns the spray bottle on Duke.

"No, I'm defenseless." He drops my hair and scoops me up by the waist, facing away from him.

"You're using me as a shield?" I ask.

"You don't make a very good one," he says. "You're too small."

As if to prove his point, Laila lets off a series of squirts. Most hit me, but several hit him. The whole time I push against his forearm in an attempt to get free. He plops me back down on the stool and goes charging after Laila. She screams and runs. When they walk back into the room, he's holding the squirt bottle and water is dripping down her face.

"I defended your honor," he says to me.

"You used me as a shield."

"So what's this for?" he asks, holding up the bottle.

"We need to get Addie's hair damp."

"I'll be in charge of that," he says too readily.

"I don't trust you or your toilet gloves."

He squirts me once, right in the face. I blow air between my lips, spraying water everywhere, and try to suppress a laugh. "You're so dead."

A booming voice calls out from down the hall. "Laila, what's all this water?"

"It's nothing, Dad, I'll clean it up in a minute."

He pokes his head around the corner and sees Duke and me. "Oh. I didn't know you had company."

"Yeah, I do."

His hair sticks up at odd angles, like he just woke up from a nap. His cheeks seem bonier than the last time I saw him, and the circles under his eyes twice as dark. "Do you have a few bucks I can borrow?"

Laila pats her pockets. "Nope."

He rubs at his nose, and I'm tempted to rub mine as well. Not just because he did, but because the smell of smoke he brought with him finally reaches me. "Come on, Laila. I'll pay you back. Your mom didn't leave me any, and I have a friend coming over in a minute. I owe him money."

"Sorry. I really don't have any. I spent my last five bucks on lunch today."

He stares at her for a long time, probably trying to verify that her thoughts are saying the same thing as her mouth. Laila's thoughts have most likely shifted to words like *jerk-wad*. Okay, maybe not the *wad* part—she probably thought of a more color-ful expletive—but still. I can tell Laila feels uncomfortable and I search for a way to change the subject.

"Hi," Duke says. "You must be Laila's dad. Nice to meet you. I'm Duke—"

"Duke Rivers. Yeah, I know you. Best high school quarter-back in or out of the Compound in over a decade."

I roll my eyes. Like it's fair to compare guys outside the Compound to Duke. He has an ability; they don't.

"Thanks. So you go to the games, Mr. Stader?"

"Not usually, but I read the news feeds. Have you decided which college you're going to next year?"

Duke rests a hand on my shoulder, and even though it's wear-ing a rubber glove it still manages to set my heart racing. "Not yet. I'm working on it."

"How many offers have you gotten outside the Compound?"

"Several."

"Wait," I interrupt. "You're going to college on the Outside?" Not many people do that.

"There aren't exactly a lot of opportunities to play football after college in the Compound."

"You mean to tell me that Norm colleges come here to scout? I thought outsiders weren't allowed in the Compound. Do they bend that rule for sports?"

"No. They don't. But I've been to a few open tryouts. And we play several schools outside the Compound. You really don't follow football, do you?"

The doorbell rings, cutting off my attempt to answer—probably a good thing since the answer would've included the words *my lowest priority*.

"Laila, get the door," her dad says. "Tell him I'm not here."

"Dad, come on."

He slips away without another word. Laila follows.

"What's he on?" Duke whispers, nodding his head to where Laila's dad had been standing. "Suppressors or enhancers?"

"He's Telepathic" is all I have to say. Everyone knows that's an ability that can slowly drive a person insane. I wouldn't like other people's thoughts inside my head all the time either, but still, I don't think I would try to suppress my ability like that. Especially not at the expense of my family.

The doorbell rings again, followed by pounding. Laila comes back into the kitchen, looks out the window, and lets out a long sigh. She turns around and leans into the counter. "If he's not going to man up, I will."

"You're going to *man up*?" I say.

"You know what I mean. We're going to take care of that freak. Are you ready?"

"Ready for what?" I ask, but she's already heading for the door. I slide off the stool and follow after her.

"Just play along," she says over her shoulder.

"What's going on?" Duke asks, following close behind.

"I have no idea."

Laila palms the wall monitor, and as the door slides open she places a hand high on the frame. A wiry man with an eyebrow ring and an attitude nods his head at her. "I need to talk to your dad."

"He's not here."

He wipes his mouth, revealing a skull-and-crossbones tattoo on the back of his hand. "I know he's here."

"Look, loser." Laila moves her hand to her curvy hip. "I thought I asked you to stop coming around here."

"Just get him."

"He's not here. But you see my friend here?" She steps aside to reveal me in all my nonintimidating glory. He barely glances my way, but still I tense. "She's Clairvoyant, and she told me something interesting about your future. Right?"

I wait to hear his response to her question when I realize it's directed at me. She wants me to confirm her lie? Doesn't she remember I am not a convincing liar? "Yes. Your future. It wasn't good."

Laila gives me the is-that-really-the-best-you-can-do? look and then turns toward him again. "This is your warning. Do your business away from my house."

"Listen, little girl, get your dad and I'll pretend like you didn't just make a sad attempt at a threat."

Duke steps in front of me, and I'm surprised at how relieved that makes me feel. I shift to the side so I can still see. "Is there a problem?" Duke asks the man.

"Yeah, kid, someone owes me money. Are you going to settle the debt?"

Duke smiles. "Do you really want to take care of this business in front of the ladies? Can't this be done another time?"

The loser's eyes shift between Laila and me, his anger deflating. "When will he be back?" His voice is sarcastic, like he's decided to play our game for now.

"Probably not until tomorrow."

"Fine," he growls. "I expect my money tomorrow."

"We'll pass on the message."

The man gets into a low-riding car complete with red-and-orange flames. Duke shuts the front door.

"He's gone."

Laila leans against it. "That didn't solve the problem, Duke. It only postponed it. Poison will be back."

"His name is Poison? Seriously? Remember *Flash* Davis," I say, trying to lighten the mood, even though deep down I know Poison is no Flash. Poison looks like he actually earned his nickname.

Laila grabs two fistfuls of her hair by the roots, grunts, and then marches off to the kitchen.

Duke and I stare at each other, then I nod my head toward the front door. "Does it always work?"

"What?"

"Flashing your smile."

"It tends to. You'll have to let me know."

I shake my head with a smirk. He is good.

CHAPTER 10

NORM•date: *n.* an outing with a Normal guy

I shouldn't be here, I shouldn't be here, I shouldn't be here. . . .

My mind says these words over and over, and yet instead of turning around and walking back down the long, deserted hallway, my body seems to think pressing my ear against the door marked Athletic Trainer is a good idea.

In Government, I had left my stupid kindergarten-style note on Trevor's desk. I knew he got it because he picked it up and looked around when he came in. But after class, Mr. Buford had stopped me to tell me about a study group that meets on Thursdays. Sure, I had failed to answer one of his questions, more because I was distracted about my note than because I didn't know the answer. . . . Well, I didn't know the answer either, but still, Mr. Buford didn't have to act like I was an academic failure based on one unanswered question. More importantly, his keeping me after had made me miss my opportunity to talk to Trevor. So when I rushed out the door and saw him round the corner, I followed him. Here. To the kinesiology department. And pressed my ear against the door marked Athletic Trainer. Now my mind screams at me that I'm exhibiting stalkerlike behavior.

"Did you get approval from your physical therapist?" an unfamiliar voice asks.

"Not yet, sir." That's Trevor. "But I was hoping you could clear me."

"That's not how it works. How is it feeling?"

"It feels much better."

"Really? Because last time I saw you, it seemed you were in a lot of pain." There's a long pause. "I know you want to play, but you have pins in your shoulder. It takes awhile to get used to something like that. Your body needs time to recover."

"It's been almost a year."

"Why don't you do some windmills for me?"

I slowly raise my head to peer through the window. Trevor's back is to me as he sits on a table. His shirt is off, and two purple scars run down his right shoulder. I can't look away. I haven't seen many scars. There was this kid my freshman year who didn't want to see a Healer because he thought the cut across his knuckles would make him look tough, but a month later he changed his mind and got his skin regenerated.

My eyes wander from Trevor's scars to his back. Despite his claim otherwise, the boy doesn't appear to have an ounce of fat on him, let alone a layer. Considering Trevor is my future best friend, I let my gaze linger a little too long on his back.

He lifts his arm to do a rotation and lets out a grunt of pain.

"I thought you said it was feeling better."

"When I do that, it feels slightly less better."

"Trevor, I know how much you were hoping to avoid it, but I think another surgery might be in your future."

Trevor hangs his head, and his shoulders rise and fall.

"I'm sorry."

He straightens up. "Not your fault, sir." Then he stands and grabs his shirt. I duck back down and make a run for the exit. Back in the bustling hallway, I slow down and move with the flow of the crowd for a moment, my mind too preoccupied to remember the direction of my next class.

Lunch comes, and I haven't stopped thinking about Trevor and his injury. I wonder what happened to him. I stand by the commons again, looking around. I'm starting to recognize a few faces here and there, but nobody I feel close enough with to invade their group. I have no idea where Trevor and his friends hang out for lunch (maybe they go off-campus), and since he hadn't stuck around for even one minute after Government to say anything about my note, I'm beginning to wonder if he's trying to avoid me. He probably senses the you-are-being-stalked vibes I'm giving off. Maybe I should go to that study group Mr. Buford recommended after all and meet some people.

I suck at making friends.

The library is the only option that makes me feel halfway decent, so I head there. I pull *A Tale of Two Cities* from its place and sit down. When I turn back the cover, it automatically opens to where an index card is stuck between two pages. I furrow my brow and read, *Wanted: good zombie hunter. Call 555-3681. Be prepared to provide references and past experience.* On the back Trevor had drawn a stick-figure zombie wearing a powdered wig and chasing a man. A smile creeps onto my face. He has a sense of humor *and* creativity. I wonder when he put this in the book. I search the aisles for a while but can't find him anywhere. I program his number into my phone for later and slip the card into my bag. *And we're back on track to best-friend-land.*

After school I pull out my phone and call Trevor.

"Hello?" he answers.

I sit on the end of my bed. "I'm answering the ad for a zombie hunter."

"Would you be able to start immediately? Apparently my life is in danger."

"Can you describe the zombie that's after you?"

He hums a little. "He's a really old guy with an English accent, he might have a goatee, and he'll definitely be carrying around a really thick, boring book. You might be able to pry it from his decaying hands and beat him back to death with it. Or maybe just reading it to him would work."

He had to go there. "Boring? I could get a really thick book of my own and join his cause."

"Oh no, did I just lose my zombie hunter?"

"Are you offering me the job?"

"Well, there's one more step. Friday night a group of us are going to watch a movie at the Cineplex. Coincidentally enough, it's the newest zombie one. It will be your official study guide."

I notice he made a point of saying a group would be there; it wouldn't be just the two of us or anything. He's definitely not interested in me. So this confirms the fact that he is perfect best-friend material.

"Are you up for it?" he asks.

I have a very sensitive gag reflex and watching maggot-eaten skin for two hours probably isn't the smartest idea. "Yeah, sure. What time?"

"The movie starts at eight."

"Okay." It's silent for a few moments.

"Addison? Can you hold on a minute?"

"Sure."

"What's up, little man?" I hear him ask. I'm not trying to listen in on his conversation, but he's not attempting to hide it.

"Will you play catch with me?" the voice of a young boy says.

"I can't today. Sorry."

"But the doctor said this week, right?"

"Two more weeks." Trevor's voice sounds tight. The little boy lets out a disappointed groan, and Trevor says, "You're tellin' me."

My eyes wander to my bare walls. They're an empty canvas, waiting for me to decorate.

The boy continues, "Oh, Ma called and said to tell you to put dinner in the oven because she's going to be late."

"Okay, I'll be right there." To me Trevor says, "Sorry about that."

"What happened to you?" I ask.

"Excuse me?"

"Why can't you throw?" I think about the two purple scars down his right shoulder. "How did you get hurt?"

"Playing football."

I keep a groan from voicing its opinion. "You're a football player?"

"I was last year, before I got hurt."

"That sucks."

"Yeah, pretty much. So, anyway, I have to go, but did you need a ride to the movie or did you just want to meet us over there?"

"I don't have a car yet." Another casualty lost to the move. Even though my car is ancient, it's still more advanced than anything they have here, so I had to leave it behind. My dad promised to get me a Norm-friendly car soon.

"Okay, I'll come get you then."

"Thanks. I'll just text you my address."

I hang up and pocket my phone with a smile. I have a friend. I'm proud of myself. I spin around and nearly trip over the basket full of clean and folded laundry near the foot of my bed. The phone in my pocket vibrates, and I answer before the number has time to register on the screen. "Calling to cancel already?"

"Cancel what?" Laila asks.

"Oh! Hey!"

"You sound happy. Why are you happy?"

I start to put away my laundry. "Because I'm going out with Trevor and his friends on Friday."

"Aw, I'm like a proud mother bird watching my daughter fly from the nest. Fly, little bird, fly. Oh no! Don't fall. No, that's the ground. Addie, watch out for the ground. Man, tough luck. You'd better come back home."

I stick out my bottom lip. "Was that supposed to be encouraging?"

"No, but it amused me. And I'm ready for you to come home."

"Why?" One of the cuffs on a pair of folded jeans is sticking out farther than the other, so I refold them.

"Because you're my best friend." She sounds down.

"There's another reason. What is it?"

"It's just . . . it's just nothing. I miss you. So tell me about Trevor."

She can't get off that easy. "Laila, talk to me."

"You just keep me grounded, that's all. Now, please do your job. So this Trevor guy is my supposed replacement?"

I sigh. "Yes."

"You know that will never work. Boys and girls can't be best friends. It's impossible."

I shake my head as if she can see me. "No, that's not true. He fits all the criteria of a male best friend."

"Okay, I'll play. What are the criteria of a male best friend?"

"One: I feel completely comfortable around him, no nervousness or anxiety. Two: He's really nice. And three: He doesn't annoy me."

"Wait, are you saying a love interest has to annoy you?"

"At first. And then eventually it's realized that all that annoyance and mistrust is actually romantic tension."

"Addie, you're seriously screwed up."

I add the folded jeans to a stack in the closet and then sit on my desk chair. My other line beeps, and I pull the phone away from my ear to see who's calling. "Ugh, my mom."

"Answer it," Laila says.

"I don't want to."

"She nearly attacked me the other day at the grocery store asking how you were doing and if you were adjusting. It was pathetic."

"If she wanted to know how I was doing, maybe she shouldn't have left my dad."

"You have to talk to her sooner or later."

I bite my lip. I know she's right. I know my dad's right— I should call my mom. But just the thought of talking to her makes my throat close up. "I choose later."

I hear a knock on Laila's door. "Hey, hold on." In the background her dad asks her if he can borrow some money. "I don't have any, used the last of it on lunch today," she tells him. I can't hear his exact response, but I can tell he's not happy. She finally gets back on the phone. I can practically hear the eye roll in her voice when she says, "My dad is killing me."

"What did he say?"

"He owes some guy money. What's new?"

"I'm sorry."

"No feeling sorry for me." She lets out a long sigh and then yells, "Dad! Doorbell." To me she mumbles, "It's probably Mr. Debt Collector." There's a pause and another grunt from Laila. "Hey, I gotta go get the stupid door. I'll talk to you later."

"Okay. Be careful and don't do anything stupid," I say, but she's already gone.

CHAPTER 11

PAR•A•li•a•tion: *n.* beyond the average humiliation

I stare in the mirror, trying to ignore the nervous pattering of my heart. The strip turned out more electric blue than I thought it would. Plus it covers a larger section than I had intended. I could tell it was bad when even Laila's eyes got wide after we dried and straightened my hair.

Laila fluffs it. "Maybe you should wear it curly after all. Straightened probably brings it out more."

"No," I insist. "Rebellion requires commitment."

"I think it looks hot," Duke says. "But that's just coming from the guy who hopes to play another role in your rebellion."

Laila looks between us. "What?"

"Nothing," I say. "I'd better get home."

"Hey, Duke, can you take her? I need to check on my dad."

I throw Laila a look, but she sings, "Thanks" as she runs out of the bathroom and disappears down the hall.

Duke laughs. "I should be the one thanking her."

"I'm kicking her butt tomorrow. Come on, let's go." We walk out the door and Duke says, "I'd put my money on her in a fight."

I gasp and backhand him across the stomach. Then I blush when I realize that counts as flirting in Laila's Flirting 101 crash course she's tried to give me many times over the years. "Sorry," I say, shoving my hand in my pocket.

"It didn't hurt."

When we get in the car, Duke turns up the radio to just short of unbearable and proceeds to talk above it the entire ride, about football and how small his meditation cubicle is and how his mom makes the best peach pie that I should try and on and on. I'm glad I don't have to try to fill the silence.

"This is me." I point out my house that seems so small and plain with Duke looking at it. He lives on the edge of town with all the other large houses. He pulls over. "Thanks." I start to get out.

"Are you sure you don't want me to come in with you? Your mom probably wouldn't yell quite as loud with a witness."

I do not want him to come inside. "We can't lay it on her all at once. The hair is first. The boy is second." I have no clue why I said that.

He nods. "All right. Well, good luck. I'll see you tomorrow."

His stare is so intense, I feel like he can see right through me.

I put my hand on the center console, inches from where his rests. "Do you like to read?"

"Read?"

"You know, download a book onto your tablet and read it . . . for fun."

"Not really."

I raise my eyebrows. "See you tomorrow." I hop out of the car.

"We're like magnets, Addie," he calls after me.

I laugh. He does make me laugh. I sigh and walk into the house.

"Addie, where have you been?" my mom asks from the kitchen.

I take a deep breath and pat my hair for a moment, tempted to run to my bedroom and grab a hat. I remind myself that rebellion takes commitment.

"Addie?" my mom calls again. "Are you going to answer me? Where have you been?"

"Just at Laila's house."

"I wish you would've called. I made dinner." From the smell of it, she burned dinner.

"I already ate." I walk into the kitchen and grab a water bottle from the fridge, trying to act casual. Out of the corner of my eye, I see my mom gaping.

"What did you do to your hair?" Her voice is low and angry.

My commitment falters. "It comes out. Twenty-one washes." That's not what I intended to say. The plan was to put my hand on my hip and say, "It's my hair. I can do what I want with it."

That's what brave, angsty teenagers say after they do something rebellious. But I'm pretty sure those teenagers didn't ever have to answer to someone like my mother. I'm also sure I'm neither brave nor angsty.

"Addie, seriously?"

"What's the big deal?" Again, it is supposed to sound punkish, but I sound scared.

"Go away from me. I don't want to look at you again until your twenty-one wash cycle is complete."

I start to walk to my room.

"Oh, and no one else gets to look at you outside of school until then as well. You're grounded for as long as it takes to wash it out."

Could she be any more controlling? "No wonder Dad left." It's the first thing I say that actually sounds how I want it to and the only thing I instantly regret. I don't have to look back to know I hurt her with the words. The lights in my room come on as I enter, and I sink onto my bed with a sigh of frustration.

My cell phone rings with a number I don't recognize. "Hello?"

"How'd it go?" Duke is on the other end.

I stand up and part the drapes covering my window, wondering how he timed his call so perfectly. Did he see my bedroom lights go on? The street is empty. "How did you get this number?"

"I made a few calls, but eventually found Laila's number.

102

Then she gave me yours. I figured it wouldn't be a big deal since you were already kicking her butt."

"Are you a stalker? Because I'm not really into stalkers."

He laughs. "So, how'd it go?"

I pinch the bridge of my nose, a dull ache starting behind my eyes. "Perfect, actually. Just like I thought it would."

"What movie is she taking you to?"

I collapse back onto my bed. "Um, we're not quite that far into the reaction process yet."

"I see."

My mom knocks on my door and it slides open. "They can't hear your voice either. Off the phone," she says, and then leaves.

"What did she say?"

"Yeah, grounded."

He laughs really loud for a long time.

"Hanging up now."

"So much for the typical reaction."

"Yes. It's so funny. Bye." I hang up and then stare at my phone for a few minutes before going into Recent Calls. I find the last number listed under Received and enter it into my contacts with his name. I feel a slight thrill. Girls would kill to have Duke's cell phone number, and I just got it without even asking. He had actually searched mine out. I'm beyond flattered. But then I remind myself that Duke and I are incompatible. He loves to be the center of attention. I hate it. He is the king of the school. I do not want to be the queen.

• • •

I sit in my car longer than normal the next morning, waiting for Laila. Since I lost my phone privileges, she has no idea I'm grounded. The clock on my dash tells me I have five minutes to get to class. Did I really expect her to be on time? I get out of my car.

"So when does phase two commence?" Duke asks, catching up to me in the hall.

"Phase two?"

"Sneaking out from your prison sentence and hanging with the bad boy."

"You know, I'm actually a good girl. For the most part I do what I'm told." I'm not necessarily happy about it, but I do it.

"Only because you've been forced to live with a lie detector. Your dad is gone now. Time to hone your skills."

My dad is gone now. I haven't gotten used to that thought. "Wow, you really are trying to fulfill the role of the guy who's not good for me."

"Yes, it needs to be authentic, right?"

I stop in the middle of the hall. It's time to end this. He takes two more steps before he notices, then turns. "What?"

"Duke, I can't do this."

He bites his lip. "Really?"

My heart flutters a little, seeming to disagree with my statement. I scold it for its betrayal.

"This isn't a marriage proposal, Addie. Just a date. We don't even have to call it a date."

I have obviously hesitated for way too long because he grabs my hand and leads me toward class. I sigh and pick up my speed. "Duke, I'm grounded." We round a row of lockers, and I'm forced to stop in shock. His hold on my hand jerks it forward once before he stops as well.

"What's that?" I ask. In front of us, where the library used to be, is now just the blue sky and floating red letters that spell out: "Give him a chance."

"So, what do you say, Addie?" he asks, turning to face me completely, the letters at his back. "Will you give me a chance?"

"Make them stop." I look around, searching for the Perceptive who's creating the illusion, but it could be anybody. It's not like we wear name tags announcing our abilities. People are piling up where the door of the building should be, looking for a way in. My face is getting hotter by the second. "Duke, seriously don't. Tell whoever is doing that to stop."

He's holding my hand with both of his now and he has his standard charming face on. "Say you'll go out with me."

I look back at the floating letters. The bell rings, and I jump. "Fine."

"Really?"

"Yes. Really. Now have the building put back."

He points to someone over my shoulder and gives the thumbs-up sign. Slowly, the letters fade and the red bricks of the library come into view. It takes my face a little longer to return to normal temperature.

He squeezes my hand, then lets go. "I'll pick you up on the

corner of your street Friday at ten."

"Don't you have a game Friday?"

"Yes, but it's a home game. I'll be done by ten. And I'm always in a good mood after we win."

"And if you lose?"

"I don't lose." He smiles. "Okay, I'm going to disappear until Friday so you can't change your mind."

I rub my arms as I watch him retreat. *So much for my resolve.*

CHAPTER 12

ab•NOR•Mal: *adj.* out of the ordinary,
like zombies and certain creepy boys

Trevor opens the passenger-side door for me and I climb in. When he's in his own seat, pulling away from the curb, I say, "Sorry, my dad is kind of overprotective." My dad just treated Trevor like he was the main suspect in a crime investigation, and I know he used his ability.

"No big deal. He's never met me."

"Yeah, I tried to tell him there'd be a *bunch* of people he's never met before, but that didn't seem to make a difference."

He smiles. "I don't understand why."

"I know, right?"

"He has an intense stare."

"He's really good at telling if someone's lying or not."

"Oh yeah?"

It's the first time since I've been here that I wish I could tell someone about the psychologically advanced. "Freakishly good."

"I'm glad I passed the test."

He not only passed but even got my dad to smile and give me the I'm-impressed eyebrow raise. "Me too." I glance at my cell phone again.

He nods toward my phone. "You waiting for a phone call?"

"No. Yes. Sort of." I haven't heard from Laila in a couple days. It isn't too weird. We don't speak every day, but she seemed so sad last time we talked, and she didn't answer her phone earlier.

"Sort of?"

"My best friend from home."

"Where is home?"

I freeze, still not comfortable with the lie. I curse myself for straying from the Compound-appointed backstory. At least that would've been partly true. What I really want to say is, *Well, you see, there's this walled city in Southeast Texas. If you ever did happen upon it, which is highly unlikely, it would just look like a mountain range. But that's where I lived, along with thousands of other gifted people.*

"California. Uh, the southern part." I unzip the small inside pocket of my purse, pull out a metal container, and pop an

Altoids in my mouth. It doesn't help get rid of the bitter taste of lies.

"Cool."

"What about you? Have you lived in Dallas your whole life?"

"Yup." He reaches for the radio, but then stops. "Are you a music or a no-music kind of girl?"

"It just depends on the situation."

"For this situation?"

"Yes, music. It will hide any awkward silences."

"You already have me failing at conversation?" He drops his hand, leaving the radio off.

"Well, you just seem like the perfectly-okay-with-silence type. I'm the oh-crap-why-can't-I-think-of-anything-to-say? type."

He laughs. "No worries. The people we're hanging out with tonight have no problem filling the silence."

"Who are we hanging out with tonight?" I shift in my seat, and my foot crunches a piece of paper on the floorboard.

"Oh, sorry." He grabs it and throws it behind his seat, where it joins a floor full of others. My eyes linger on the mess. So Trevor isn't exactly the tidiest guy in the world. *Not everyone needs a perfectly organized environment to function*, I hear Laila say in my head. I force my attention back to Trevor as he says, "We're meeting the guys you met at the football game and some girls you've probably met at school."

"I haven't met anyone at school."

"Maybe you should join the land of the living at lunch."

"Point taken." And the exact point taken is that he wants me to hang out with him and his friends at lunch. Awesome. No more roaming the library in Loner Loserdom.

After a few minutes of silence, I turn on the radio. He laughs.

When we arrive at the theater, his friends are already there, hanging out by a large fountain outside. After buying tickets, we join them. He introduces everyone, and I listen so I can match some of the names I already know with their faces. They all wave and say hi, then go back to their conversation. It seems to be about how much money Rowan gathered when he jumped in the fountain last week.

"Five bucks," Rowan says, as if that amount made it totally worth the effort. I remember that Rowan was the one who tried to get me to go to the party after the football game. Without paint and the hot-pink wig, his skin is a creamy brown and his hair is black and shoulder length. He's cute, if you're into pretty boys.

A girl weaves her way through the group and arrives in front of Trevor, then gives him a hug. "Hey, Stephanie," he says, hugging her back. Her eyes look at me and say, *Back off, he's mine*, but her mouth says, "Good to meet you, Addison. We have math together."

"Yeah, I recognize you." She's tall, with ridiculously long legs, dark hair, and chocolate eyes. She kind of looks like Trevor, except his lashes are longer. Her hair is pulled back in a high ponytail, not a single strand out of place, and her outfit looks like it went straight from a magazine to her body. I take a small step away from Trevor to let her know we just came as friends. Though I'm a little surprised Trevor didn't mention her, I'm not here to steal anyone's boyfriend.

Rowan uses the newly created space to slip between Trevor and me. "Important question," he says, looking at me. "Do you scream at scary movies?"

"I'm more of an eye coverer," I say.

"Awesome. I call a seat next to Addison!" he announces, throwing his arm around my neck. Not a big fan of personal-space invasion—especially by strangers—I immediately twist out of his hold, playing it off with a laugh. It doesn't seem to faze him.

"I just barely got my hearing back from the last movie we went to." He rubs his ear and glares at Stephanie.

She rolls her eyes. "Oh, please. I don't scream that loud."

Several people surrounding the fountain shout out their confirmations of Stephanie's screaming abilities. Her scowl quiets the group.

"See," Rowan says. "I'm not alone." As if sensing Stephanie is about to implode, he changes the subject. "So, Trevor."

"Yeah?"

"I found another one."

Trevor sighs. "Give it a rest, Rowan. It's over. Come on, let's get our seats."

As we walk, Rowan still between Trevor and me, he says, "Just hear me out. His name is Neal Summers. He blew out his knee at the beginning of this season."

111

"Rowan, it's football; people get hurt. Lots of people. There's no connection."

I have no idea what Rowan is referring to, and it doesn't seem like Trevor feels like explaining—not even after I give him the yes-I'm-curious head tilt. So I just work on maintaining a comfortable distance between Rowan and me. Despite my efforts, he still manages to brush against my shoulder several times.

The boys pause at the door, and as I look over my shoulder at them, confused, I remember why, too late. My face meets the glass with a thud. "Ouch." I step back, rubbing my cheek. This place is so confusing. Why are some of their doors automatic and some not?

"Addie, door handle. Door handle, Addie," Rowan says, opening the door for me. "You two should get to know each other."

"Funny," I mumble.

"You okay?" Trevor asks.

"Fine."

Inside, Rowan holds true to his word and sits next to me. Stephanie somehow ends up on my other side, separating Trevor and me by a seat. I really want to sit next to Trevor but can't think of a good excuse to seat hop.

The lights lower.

"Do you want some popcorn?" Rowan asks, putting his hand on my forearm. I'm sure he did it just to get my attention, but my reflexes are faster than that thought, and I yank my arm out from under his, bumping the popcorn he's holding. It spills all over.

"I'm so sorry," I say.

He laughs. "It's okay. You're nice and jumpy. You're going to be more fun to watch this movie with than I thought."

"Is it buttered?" I ask. "I hope I didn't ruin your clothes." Considering Rowan is dressed nicer than I am, I really do hope his jeans aren't splotched with grease stains.

"Nah, they're fine." He stands and shakes himself off, then sits back down.

I fold my arms. "I promise to keep my out-of-control limbs to myself for the rest of the night."

"No, no, no. It's okay. Here, have the armrest." He pulls one of my hands over to the armrest and places it there, patting it twice as if it's some sort of pet he has asked to stay put. Then, much to my relief, he passes the popcorn down the aisle to Lisa and places his own hands on his knees.

I know why I'm jumpy. It's that it's dark, and the last time I was in the dark sitting next to a guy, it didn't end well. It wasn't just that Bobby got handsy and rough, although that was bad, it was that I froze. It took me several minutes to defend myself. And then several more to free myself. To be able to push him away and walk out of his house. And that reaction—my inability to react—scared me more than anything. Even though seconds later I snapped out of the Search, it still felt so real.

Stephanie looks over, and in a loud voice says, "Could you

113

two get to know each other after the movie? I'm trying to watch here."

I look at the screen, my face hot. The movie hasn't started. I want to tell her to chill, that it's just the previews, but then Rowan might think I actually want to get to know him and that I'm mad at Stephanie for interrupting. So I just say, "Sorry, popcorn dilemma."

Trevor leans forward and says, "Yes, Addison, pay attention. There'll be a zombie-hunting quiz after the movie." He smiles, then leans back.

Stephanie scowls, but I don't care; those two sentences make me feel infinitely better. That is, until halfway through the movie when Rowan's arm decides it wants to share the armrest with mine. This time I resist the urge to jerk away. Nothing is happening. It's just an armrest. People share them all the time. I once shared one with a hairy-armed old man, and I managed that just fine. I count to ten and then move my arm.

The guy is undeterred though, and he leans over me to tell Stephanie, "I haven't heard any screaming yet."

"That's because this movie is lame."

"Claustrophobic," I say.

Rowan laughs and pulls back. I lean a little closer to Stephanie, who is leaning really close to Trevor.

I put all my energy into watching the movie, which so far hasn't been too gruesome.

One of my friends at the Compound has a photographic memory. Everything she ever sees, reads, or hears, she remembers forever in perfect detail. I used to be so jealous of that ability when I took tests. I begin to realize that her ability might not be as great as I once thought. She probably has to be really careful about everything she lets enter her mind. And what about her Bobby-like experiences? Does she remember them perfectly forever?

The graphic image of a boy getting his head bit off by a one-armed zombie makes me cringe away from the screen. Next to me, Stephanie screams and grabs onto Trevor's arm, burying her face in his shoulder.

On my opposite side, Rowan chuckles and then pets my shoulder. "It's okay, Addison, it's over now."

I stand abruptly and climb my way past Rowan and down the aisle, not looking back until I make it into the bathroom. I shut myself in the nearest stall so I can hear if anyone comes in and dig out my phone from my pocket. Praying that Laila will be home this time, I dial her number. By the third ring, I can hardly breathe.

"Hey, girl."

"Hi," I say in relief. "You're there. Where have you been?"

"You're not the only one who had to get a new social life."

The words sting, even though I know she doesn't mean for them to. Of course she has to get new friends. It's not like I'm sitting at home waiting on her phone call. I am out, trying to have some sort of life without my best friend. Just like she is.

"So, what's wrong?" she asks.

"I thought we could be friends, but I don't think he likes me at all and he probably brought me here as a favor for his really creepy friend and I hate Bobby Baker," I say, my words tumbling over one another.

"What? Slow down. Who are we talking about? Bobby?"

I try to breathe deep, but it feels like the air can't get through the emotions wedged in my chest. "No. I wish you could come pick me up."

"Where are you?"

"At the movies." I sit on the back of the toilet and rest my feet on the seat.

"With who?"

"I came with Trevor, but like I said, I think he brought me here as a favor for his friend Rowan, who's like an overzealous Chihuahua."

"Aw, Chihuahuas are cute."

"Okay, fine then, a hairless cat that wants you to pet it so it rubs along your leg all night."

"Ew."

"Exactly."

"What makes you think he's setting you up with his friend?"

A long section of toilet paper is clinging by a corner to the roll. I kick it and watch it slide to the ground. "Well, the first time I met Rowan he was really adamant about me going to this party. So now I'm thinking maybe Rowan said something to Trevor about me. Trevor probably told Rowan he'd get me to come on a group date or something."

"You were right. Trevor is my replacement. I would totally do something like that."

"Set me up with a creepy guy?"

"No, Trevor doesn't think Rowan is a creep. What I mean is, if a guy I thought was cool came up to me and told me he liked you, I would definitely make it my goal to get the two of you in the same place to see if you liked him too. It's my job as your best friend. So see, Trevor thinks you're cool."

"Really?"

"Yes, for sure."

I'm finally able to take a deep breath. She's right. Trevor has no idea how Rowan makes me feel.

"Hey, I have something that will cheer you up," she says.

"What?"

"I was looking at the football schedule, and in two weeks, the Compound plays Carter High. I'm going to go so I can see you."

"Really?" I almost slip off the back of the toilet in my excitement. "That makes me so happy. I didn't realize they played schools so far away."

"That's because you don't follow football."

"You only follow it because of the hot guys."

She gasps in faux offense. "So untrue . . . sort of. *Anyway*, you aren't that far away. Your school is in our league because they have Containment Committee members stationed there to supervise and prevent leaks. It's all carefully calculated, my pet. But you're missing the point. The point is that our football team

117

is playing your football team."

"You're right. I am missing that amazing point. I'm excited. You have to come. You can stay with me, make a weekend out of it."

"I think I will. Now put your game face on until you get home. Don't let that hairless cat see you upset."

"Thanks." I hang up and exit the bathroom.

Trevor is waiting in the hall, a concerned look on his face. "You okay?"

I'm surprised by how happy I feel that he's standing there. "I'm fine. Just got a little nauseous."

He lowers his brows. *"Hmm."*

"What?"

"I don't know if you can stomach zombie-hunting after all."

It's your friend I can't stomach, almost slips out of my mouth. I'm able to stop the thought before it becomes words. "I think I can handle it." I grab his arm and pull him back toward the theater.

CHAPTER 13

PAR•A•dise: *n.* a place of extreme happiness

Friday night around eight o'clock, my bedroom door slides open and my mom walks in. I look up from the book I'm reading, then back down without saying a word. She sits on the end of my bed.

"I think I overreacted," she says.

You think? "What do you mean?"

"About your hair. I'm sorry."

I shrug one shoulder. I want to apologize for what I said too, about my dad leaving because of her control issues, but I can't bring myself to do it. Mostly because I still believe it's true. I just want everything to be the way it was a month ago. The happy front may have been a charade for my parents, but it was real to me.

"Do you want to go to a movie with me tonight? There's one that starts at eight forty-five."

Great. She picked tonight to be typical? I look at the clock on my wall monitor. Only two hours until I'm supposed to sneak out to meet Duke. "I'm actually really tired tonight."

"Are you sure?" She rubs my leg, making me feel immediately guilty for my future actions. Maybe I *should* go with her. It would probably be good for us. I look at her hand still moving along my leg and wonder if she's trying to Persuade me to go. Her voice sounded the same, but she's talented at subtlety. "Can we do it tomorrow night?" I ask.

"Of course, hon."

I nod, still not sure if she made me agree to go out tomorrow or if I chose that on my own. When she doesn't leave I wonder what else she wants from me.

"Addie? Would you be interested in a mind relaxer to help you transition through this challenging time in your life? The department has some really good programs. Some I even helped develop. I can load one onto your tablet."

Does my mom seriously think a mind-pattern program is going to make everything better again? As if it's *my* mind that needs to change. I realize I haven't said anything, but I'm pretty sure my look says it all. Just in case it doesn't, I shake my head. "No."

When she leaves I just want to pull the blanket over my head and go to sleep. I run my thumb along the keys on my phone and toy with the idea of canceling my ten o'clock meeting with Duke. Even though I know he's in the middle of his game, I text: *Make it eleven.*

At ten o'clock the doorbell rings. I leap out of bed but am not fast enough to beat my mother, who was in the living room watching television. I had been wondering if she was going to sleep anytime soon. I arrive at the door just as Duke says, "Hi, you must be Addie's mom. I'm Duke."

My mom is cold when she answers, "Yes, I am. How can I help you?"

"I know it's late, but I just got done with a football game."

Duke will be disappointed to find out that my football-liking gene—or lack thereof—comes from my mom. Only, she likes it less than I do. He can't use his star status to persuade her to do whatever it is he showed up at my door to do. Why didn't he just meet me on the corner at eleven?

"And I know Addie is grounded," he continues.

"She is."

"But I hoped we could watch a movie together." He runs a hand through his wet hair, sending off a wave of soap-scented goodness that I can smell from where I stand behind my mom.

"She can't go anywhere."

"I know. I expected as much." He produces a smile. "That's why I brought the movie here." He holds up his digital card, where he must've uploaded a movie.

Nice try. My mom shifts from one foot to another and looks back at me. My jaw almost drops, and I have to clench my teeth to keep it in place. She is wavering. My mom doesn't waver. "Well . . ."

"I promise to leave the minute it's over. You should watch it with us too. I hear it's a good one."

Because that will be fun—my mom, Duke, and me, watching a movie together.

"If you'd rather I leave with my tail between my legs, just say the word." He slowly starts to back up.

"No," my mom says, and I let out a surprised, "Huh?"

She glances back at me again, and when she does, Duke winks. I don't understand why my heart seems to think that action is so irresistible.

"Stay," my mom says. "Addie has been the perfect detainee for the last thirty-six hours; she deserves a little fun." Ah, there it is, the reason she's relenting. It's the same reason she wanted to go to a movie—she feels guilty. She steps aside, and Duke comes in. His arm wraps around my frozen-in-shock shoulders as he passes. Then he twists me until I stand in front of him, my back to his chest.

"Hi," he says, and kisses my cheek before releasing me.

My mom gives me the look that says I've been holding out on her. I'm sure the only look I'm returning is the I'm-just-as-weirded-out-as-you-are one. My mom clasps her hands together. "Okay, well, you kids have fun. There's popcorn in the kitchen if you want some, and Duke, don't forget your condition of leaving right after the movie is over."

"I thought you were going to watch it with us, Ms. Coleman."

"No, thanks."

As soon as my mom is gone, I hiss, "What happened to meeting me on the corner?"

"I had a feeling you were going to text your way out of that. And besides, sneaking around isn't a good way to start a relationship. Especially one I want you to take seriously."

One he wants me to take seriously? I walk past him to the kitchen without a word. In the pantry, I find a bag of popcorn and remove the plastic wrapping. While it's popping, I grab a couple of water bottles from the fridge and put them on the counter. When the popcorn is done, I pour it into a bowl and carry it back to the living room. Duke's card is already plugged into the port and he's sitting on the *lair*, feet on the coffee table, arms stretched along the back cushion.

"Make yourself at home." I place the popcorn on the coffee table and sit on the couch, even though he left plenty of space next to him. The lair may be bigger than a chair, but it's the smaller-than-a-love-seat part that keeps me away. He doesn't seem to notice my choice of seats or at least doesn't act like he does.

"Do you have any water?" he asks.

"Oh, yeah, I left it on the counter." I point to the island in the kitchen visible from where we sit. I don't get up because I know he can whisk it over in the blink of an eye.

"You're closer," he says with a smile, grabbing a handful of popcorn.

"Are you serious?"

"I don't want to show off."

"Since when?"

He raises his hands in front of him. "Watch closely." He stands and slowly moves toward the kitchen. "Did you see that? They came to me." He grabs the waters and throws one toward the couch. It lands perfectly next to me. "You need anything else?"

I smile at him. "No, I'm good."

When he comes back, he sits right next to me and I realize the real reason he stood. Subtle. He reaches across me and grabs a handful of popcorn.

I take the bowl and put it between us, scooting over to make room, and then say, "Play." The movie starts. His arm goes to the back of the couch, and as we watch the movie, his fingers find my blue strip of hair and gently pull on the ends of it. I have to resist the urge to melt into him. I try to pretend like I'm following the movie and I laugh whenever Duke does. In reality, I have no idea what it's even about.

When the popcorn is gone, Duke moves the bowl to the coffee table and settles in closer to me. He drapes his arm around my shoulders, and this time his fingers trace a pattern on my upper arm. Every nerve ending in my body comes to life. It doesn't even seem like he is consciously aware of his actions, because he intently watches the TV. It reminds me that he probably does this kind of stuff all the time with girls. The thought sends me plummeting off the cloud I'd been floating on for the last hour.

I stand. "I have to use the bathroom."

In the restroom, I turn off the water's motion-sensor device, then step into the tub. I pull the shower curtain closed, as if that will help muffle the sound of my voice, and dial Laila's number.

"Hey, girl," she answers.

"Remind me of who I am."

"Excuse me?"

"I hate obvious boys. Tell me that."

"You hate obvious boys. Because heaven forbid you like something that everyone else does. If you don't have to hunt for it, and carefully plan its capture, it must not be worth having."

I ignore the fact that she just made a guy sound like a prize elk and say, "No, it's not that. It's that if everyone else likes something, that something usually knows it and has a huge head because of it. The things I have to hunt for don't even realize how awesome they are." I take a deep breath now that I've remembered myself.

"Do you feel better?"

I shift and lean my shoulder against the wall. The faucet in the shower has a leak, something my dad didn't fix before leaving, and a drop of water lands on my foot. I use my other foot to dry it. "Yes. Much better."

"But there's an exception to your rule."

"What?" Another drop lands on my foot, so I move back a little.

"Not what, who. Duke Rivers. I think you're kind of into him, and he's more obvious than any boy I've ever met."

"He totally is," I say. "He's hot and the most popular guy in school and over-the-top charming. I don't think there's a single girl who would meet him and not wish she could be with him. So obvious."

"And you have to stick by your principles. I mean, sure they're based on punishing a guy just because he's too perfect, but whatever."

"No, you have to help me talk myself out of him, not into him."

"I thought you were grounded. How are you calling me?"

"I thought I was grounded too, but my mom let him in."

"Who in?"

"Duke," I say with a sigh.

"Duke's in your house, and you're talking to me?"

"Yes."

"Leaving now. Oh, next time we talk, remind me to tell you about the football schedule. And there's nothing wrong with obvious boys, Addie." The line goes dead.

I shove the phone in my pocket and walk back out.

Duke says, "Pause," and the movie goes quiet. "What did Laila say?"

I stand over him, staring at his perfect smile. I take in his eyes that I've never allowed myself to look at for very long. They're crystal blue and hold mine intently. "She said you're too obvious," I say quietly.

He runs a hand through his hair and sends another waft

of clean-soap scent my way. "I've tried subtle before. I'm not very good at it."

I laugh. He couldn't be subtle if he tried. I sit back down next to him.

He looks at the television. "Which part did you leave off on? I'll skip back."

"I—uh."

"Had the guy revealed his ability yet?"

If I confess I have no clue, he'll know he's been a distraction. I bite my lip. "No, he hadn't."

"Okay, cool. This part is really good. Scene Menu." The scenes come up in little boxes on the screen. "Scene twenty. Play." For the first time, I notice Duke's lips are quite full. "Are you watching?" He glances my way and catches me staring. I avert my gaze to the TV, but it's too late, he's already caught me. He lets out a low chuckle. "You like your guys obvious, huh?"

"No, actually, I usually don't."

"Usually?" His hand goes to my neck before I answer. Tingles spread from his fingertips all the way down my spine. As his fingers weave themselves into my hair, I try to maintain clarity.

"What about you? What's your type?" I ask.

"I thought that was obvious."

He pulls me toward him and when his lips touch mine, I try not to audibly sigh. I can't help it though, and he chuckles again, against my mouth. In the back of my mind I still wonder if we're right for each other, but the rest of my mind doesn't seem to care.

CHAPTER 14

NORM•games: *n.* strangely foreign, slightly lame, and yet unexplainably compelling rites of passage in the Normal world

Back in the theater, I let go of Trevor's arm. Our entry is accompanied by the horrified screams of really bad actors. I glance up at the screen in time to see the decaying face of the lead zombie. This movie is so dumb.

Once I've taken my seat, Rowan leans in. "Are you sick or something?"

"No, I'm okay." *And I'll be even better once I tell Trevor that he doesn't need to set me up with his friends.*

After the movie, I turn my back on Rowan to exit to my left.

I hope he follows Lisa, Brandon, and the others who are leaving the opposite way. He doesn't.

"That was the lamest movie ever," he says behind me.

"I've seen lamer," Stephanie says, and even though we're standing, she's cuddled up to Trevor's arm.

"Remember that werewolf movie we saw last year?" Trevor says. "That was worse than this."

I have no idea which movie they're talking about, so I keep my mouth shut. We get new movies way before they come out here.

"I don't know," Rowan disagrees, squeezing himself alongside me. "That had the scene where the three wolves fought the big wolf, and that totally redeemed it. Well, until Stephanie's screams ruined it all."

"Oh, shut up, Rowan," she says, with an eye roll.

I take a few steps closer to Stephanie so that she'll turn and start to walk. It seems to work, and soon we're standing outside the theater by the fountain again.

"Okay, who's up for the dessert game?" Rowan asks.

Brandon and Lisa—who are holding hands—laugh, and he says, "We're in."

Two other guys, Liam and Jason, both nod their agreement.

"Okay, you guys are one car then. Me, Addison, Stephanie, and Trevor will be another car. Katie and Sarah, which car do you want to join?"

"I'm out. My mom's making me wake up early tomorrow to visit my dad," Katie says.

Sarah grabs Katie's arm. "And she's my ride, so you guys have fun."

Rowan points both his thumbs down in disapproval. "Just stay up all night, and you won't have to wake up early."

"Whatever." Katie hits his arm. "See you Monday."

I watch them leave and wait for Rowan to explain what's going on. When he doesn't, I ask, "What's the dessert game?"

"Whoever brings back the best dessert wins."

"What's the catch?" There's always a catch.

Rowan smiles. "That car is going to tell us where we have to go to find the dessert. It has to be one of our houses."

Brandon points to me. "We pick Addison's house, because she had no idea about this game so she wouldn't have stocked up."

Rowan lets out a low grunt. "Well, we pick Jason's, because his brothers always eat everything in the house."

"Wait, we're going to my house?" I ask.

"Just for a minute to raid your fridge and cupboards. Then we'll meet back here, and whoever has the best dessert wins."

"Wins what?" This game sounds like something the guys made up to get free dessert.

"The right to be the darers and not the darees."

"Rowan in the fountain last week," Lisa says, "his team lost the dessert game."

"I still think I won that night," Rowan says. "Five bucks."

"And an amazing rent-a-cop parking-lot chase," Lisa says. "It was pretty awesome."

It did sound kind of funny. I find myself nodding.

"Okay." Brandon looks at his watch. "We meet back here in thirty minutes exactly. Pictures for proof, and cheaters automatically lose." The second he finishes his sentence everyone runs for the cars, except me, of course. I'm a beat behind, trying to play catch-up.

By the time I get to Trevor's car, it's already running and Stephanie is in the passenger seat. I climb in back and buckle in.

"So what do you have at your house? Any good treats?" Rowan asks, leaning toward me.

The fact that Rowan is about to find out where I live is just now sinking in. "No. We have nothing. Really, my dad is a health nut. Why don't we just go to the store instead?"

Stephanie turns around. "We have to take a picture with a cell phone of us inside your house holding whatever we find. If we don't, we automatically lose."

"Nobody knows what my house looks like. And we're going to lose anyway," I say. "We might as well try."

Rowan laughs. "I like this girl. She's a rule breaker."

"No. I'm really not," I say too quickly. I don't want him to get any more ideas. Trevor's eyes find mine in the rearview mirror. I'm trying to give him the please-come-up-with-a-different-plan look. Laila would know the look.

"We can go to my house instead," Trevor offers. "I think there's half a cherry pie in the fridge." I smile. Perfect.

"No," Stephanie says with a pout. "Everyone knows what

the inside of your house looks like. Come on, I don't want to be on the wrong end of Lisa's dare. She'll make me do something really bad."

Trevor tries to hold my gaze in the rearview mirror again, probably hoping I'll give him the okay. I shrug. If he wants to pacify his little girlfriend, I guess I don't want to ruin it for him.

The rest of the ride I look out the window to my right. It slowly turns white from the hot air inside the car. I run my finger along the smooth glass, drawing my standard doodle—a line that halfway up splits in two. Then I circle the pivot point. The point right before the path separates. I press my finger into the center. One little choice can make all the difference.

The phone in my pocket chimes. It's Laila. *Have you ditched the hairless cat yet?*

No, I text back, *we're actually on our way to my house.*

You've decided to make him your pet? Not exactly what I had in mind, but that works.

I smile.

"So this is it, huh?" Rowan asks, pulling my attention away from my phone and to my single-story, white house. The front porch light seems too inviting for this moment. We all get out of the car and walk the cement, shrub-lined path to my front door.

At first I widen my eyes, prepared for a scan, but then I remember the keys in my pocket. "Oh. Keys." I bring them out. There are three. One is for my dad's car, one is for the mailbox, and the other is for the front door. I know I'm staring at them too long, but I can't remember which one is which. I need to label them.

"Sorry," I say, trying to fit one into the lock and missing the slot a few times. It's so small.

"Need some help?" Rowan asks with a laugh.

"No, I got it." Finally the second key works. We need a Norm-training class at the Compound on opening historical locks. It's harder than it looks.

When we walk in, my dad glances over from where he sits in the recliner, watching what looks to be one of his criminal-interview videos. He must've been focused, because he's as surprised to see us as I am that he's still awake. He pushes Pause and stands.

"Hey, Dad. We're just playing a game. We won't be here long."

"What kind of game?" he asks.

"A game we're going to lose because we have no good food in this house."

I start to move toward the kitchen, but he stops me with: "Would you like to introduce your friends, Addie?"

"Oh, yes, sorry. This is Rowan, and this is Stephanie. You already met Trevor."

My dad shakes Rowan's hand. "You guys having a good night?"

Really? My dad is going to analyze Rowan's answer to a question about enjoyment? I give him the are-you-serious? look and he gives the I-know-I'm-overprotective-but-you-are-my-only-daughter look back. How can I argue with that look?

"Yes. It's been fun," Rowan says.

"Dad, we're kind of on a time limit here."

"Okay, I'll get out of your way." He sits back down on the recliner and my eyes drift to the television as the others head around the counter to the fridge. The man on the screen is a wiry guy with tattoos up his arms and an eyebrow ring. I wonder if this is the same DVD I had seen the other day. Poison. I'm surprised when my father pushes Play. But then I realize it's turned down very low. I join the others in the kitchen, where they've already pulled out chocolate syrup and some natural granola bars.

"Do you have a plate we can use?" Rowan asks. I hand him one, and he unwraps the granola bars and places them side by side on the plate. While he drizzles chocolate syrup over them, my eyes wander back to the TV. If I watch the lips of the criminal and concentrate on opening an energy channel between myself and the television, I can barely make out what he's saying.

"You can't pin her murder on me just because we were together. It was consensual. She was using me for the drugs anyway." There's a pause because obviously the interviewer is asking a question, which without the lip-reading addition to the sound energies, I can't hear. But the answer given to the question is, "Of course I didn't know she was in high school. I hardly knew her at all." Another pause. "I didn't kill her. Look, if you don't have enough evidence to hold me, then I'm ready to go home." He stands up, and my dad writes something in his notebook.

The voices in the kitchen are muffled because I've blocked

134

off all other channels except the one to the TV. So when Trevor taps my arms, I jump.

"What do you think?" Trevor asks. Rowan holds up the plate for me to inspect.

"Oh. Yeah, cool. Better than I thought we'd be able to find." Stephanie snaps a picture that I wasn't ready for. "Let's go."

"Thanks, Addison's dad," Rowan says on our way out the door.

My dad waves and says, "Don't miss curfew, Addie."

"I won't."

Rowan holds the plate in the air as we walk toward the car. "We may not win," he says as though speaking to a crowd, "but we'll lose with style." We climb into the car, and he punches the back of Trevor's headrest. "That should've been the theme of your last game, Trev."

"That's a horrible theme," Stephanie says. "The theme should've been 'Revenge will be ours. Cheaters never win.'"

"But they did win," Rowan says.

"I mean in the end. Karma."

"Cheaters?" I ask.

"Don't get him started." Trevor glances over his shoulder and then pulls out onto the road.

"Yes, cheaters," Rowan says. Obviously I had gotten him started. "Trevor was taken out of last season because a couple of guys sacked him after the whistle. It was a dirty play."

"Did they get punished?" I ask.

"One flag—five-yard penalty. Five yards!"

"It was actually fifteen," Trevor says.

"Whatever. It was garbage! But we'll have our revenge." He shakes his fist in the air in a dramatic fashion. "We play their school not this Friday but next."

"What school?" I almost want to take back the question because I'm afraid to hear the answer.

Stephanie turns around in her seat to face me. "Lincoln High."

My cheeks go numb and my eyes slide to Trevor's in the rear-view mirror.

"They're really good. Have you heard of them?" he asks.

I shake my head. "No."

"They're not that good," Stephanie says, patting Trevor's shoulder. "They're not as good as you are."

"Was," Rowan says. "As he *was*."

"As he's going to be again," Stephanie says.

Trevor's eyes drop for a split second before he gives her a small smile.

Rowan starts sniffing the granola bars. "Is it weird that I want to eat these chocolate-drizzled pieces of cardboard?"

Trevor laughs too loud over the not-that-funny comment. "No. Not at all." I sense that he's grateful for the subject change.

Back at the theater, when the other team shows up with half of a layered chocolate cake that has my mouth watering with a single look, I know we're doomed.

CHAPTER 15

PAR•[A]•dy: *n. a poor imitation*

Away from Duke, all the doubts creep in. I go between feelings
of elation that Duke kissed me to feelings of suspicion. Driving
to school Monday morning, my stomach tightens to knots. Since
I'm still grounded, despite my mom's thaw, we haven't seen each
other since Friday—the blue streak in my hair still as blue as
ever. I'm not sure what happens next. Does he expect me to hang
out with him? Are we together now?

I pull into a parking space, and a football hits my windshield,
causing me to jump. My car door opens before I even have a
chance to shut off the engine. I unbuckle my seat belt and reach
for my backpack. Finally I glance up at him. He grabs my hand

and pulls me to my feet and into a hug. "Hey."

"Hi." I smile. "Will you cool it with the football assaults? You're making me jumpy."

"It's kind of my signature now." He nuzzles his face into my neck, and I close my eyes and relax into him. "Besides, it's how I snagged you, so I can't stop now."

"Snagged me?" I'm not a fan of the description.

"Yeah. Heads up. Remember?" He pulls away, gives me a quick kiss, and then retrieves the football off the ground by my tire.

I shut the car door and adjust my backpack on my shoulder. "Yes. I remember. You did that on purpose?"

He nods proudly. "Of course I did that on purpose. I wanted to meet you. But I didn't mean for it to actually hit you. I honestly thought you would duck."

I smile. "Well, I never claimed to be coordinated."

He grabs my hand as we walk. "Why don't we have any classes together?"

"Probably because you're a senior and I'm a junior," I say.

Two girls leaning against the first row of lockers say, "Hey, Duke." He waves, and then the girls add, "Hi, Addie." My gaze, which had barely registered their presence before, now zeros in on them, waiting for recognition. It doesn't come.

Duke squeezes my hand, and I say, "Oh, hi," just before we pass them.

By the time we get to my locker, two more people say hi to both of us. A surge of pride fills my chest and I'm annoyed by its presence. I never cared what people thought of me before.

"I'd better go before I'm late for meditation."

"Addie, are you embarrassed by me?" he asks, pulling me close.

"Embarrassed by you? Yeah right. The hottest guy in school is hugging me, and I'm embarrassed by him."

"Why is your face red then?"

Because I'm irritated that I'm a fan of all this attention. "Because I'm not exactly an advocate of PDA."

"Well, after today you're going to have to be really vigilant to keep the rumors away." He pushes me against a locker and starts to kiss my cheek.

I don't know why my eyes sting with frustrated tears. But then his hands are on my shoulders and his kisses become soft and sweet so that by the time his lips cover mine, my anxiety has melted away. My hands go to his chest, where I grab two fistfuls of his shirt and pull him closer.

"I thought you didn't want to be late," he says against my lips.

I ignore him for a couple more blissful moments and then push him away and run, leaving him laughing in my wake.

At lunch, I meet Laila at our normal place, not sure what girlfriend protocol is. I'm not even sure I am his girlfriend.

"Well, hello, Mrs. Rivers," she says. "I didn't think I'd see you alone."

I hoist myself up onto the stage and then pull my lunch out of my backpack. The grass around the stage is purple today, one of our school's colors, but it doesn't make me feel even a hint of school spirit. The people sitting on it seem bland against the bright background. "Yeah, well, just because we kissed doesn't mean I'm going to turn into a starstruck fangirl and follow him around like a puppy would. I'm still me."

"Wait, so you're telling me that even now that you're together, you're not going to admit you have the hots for him?"

"The hots?"

"Yes, the hots. You are so into Duke Rivers that you can't even think straight. I want you to admit that out loud, and I want you to tell me that I was right all along."

I see Duke walking across the grass toward us, looking anything but bland. He smiles and waves to people as he goes. His blond hair seems to reflect the sun and create a halo of light around his face. He catches my eye, and his smile widens. "You were right," I say to Laila. "I totally have the hots for Duke Rivers."

She laughs.

"Hey, Blue Eyes," he says, when he's in front of me.

Laila clears her throat. "I'm not going to gag on my lunch if I stick around, am I?"

He turns to her. "No. And actually I was hoping you ladies would accompany me off-campus for lunch."

"But we're juniors," I say, maintaining my seat as Laila hops up, ready to go without question. Going off-campus for lunch is a senior privilege.

"Don't worry, we won't get in trouble. I have an in with the parking-lot guard." He grabs my brown-bag lunch off my lap, wads it into a ball—food and all—and sends it flying into a trash can twenty feet away.

"Hey. I could've saved that for later."

He holds up his hand. "Do you want me to get it back?"

"Gross. No."

When Duke said he had an "in" with the guard, he just meant that, like always, he could sweet talk anyone "*into*" anything. Five minutes later, Duke pulls into the parking lot of a local burger joint called Fat Jacks, and right away, through the large wall of windows, I see tables full of seniors from school.

"You didn't tell us we were meeting people," I say. It looks like the whole football team is in there, plus the cheerleading squad.

"Bring it on," Laila says softly. Like a predator, she scans the fresh meat through the window, picking out her prey. I laugh. As we walk toward the door, I notice Bobby sitting at a corner table and I immediately stop, squeezing Duke's hand.

"What's wrong?"

"Bobby's here."

"It's okay, he already knows. He's cool with us."

But I'm not cool with him, is what I want to say, but Laila is already holding open the door.

"Duke," the guy grilling burgers calls out when we walk in.

"Hey, Ernie! You comin' to the game Friday night?"

"Wouldn't miss it."

To me Duke says, "Go find a seat, and I'll order for us."

"Cool." Laila marches straight over, and I follow.

"Hey, Ray," she says, sitting at an open table next to him.

Ray looks up, seeming pleasantly surprised to see Laila. "Hey, ladies." He raises his hand, and the ketchup bottle flies off our table and hits his open palm with a loud smack that makes me jump. "Welcome." He opens the ketchup and pours it on his fries. When he's done, he looks right at me. "Clairvoyant, right?"

Duke must've told him my ability. "Sort of."

"Awesome," Ray says. "Tell me my future."

I want to tell him not to look so impressed. My ability may be rare, but it can only help me.

"I'll tell you your future." Duke sits down and sets a basket of fries in the center of the table. "It's in the end zone, gripping a football."

Ray nods. "Yes!"

I offer Duke a thankful smile, and he rubs one hand down my back, then holds up his other hand and says, "Ketchup." The bottle flies back over. After he pours some on his fries, he says, "Smile, I'm about to embarrass you."

"Please don't." But before I even finish the words, Duke stands and says, "Everyone, this is Addie, my girlfriend, and her best friend, Laila. Introduce yourselves when you get a chance." Again with the surge of pride at the word *girlfriend*. When did other people's opinions of me start to matter so much?

I give a halfhearted wave. Laila says, "Hey."

Duke sits back down and kisses my cheek, but when the guy behind the counter calls out the order, he pops back up again. I feel like I'm in an alternate universe when Bobby sits down next to Laila and across from me at the table.

"Hi, my name is Bobby," he says sarcastically. "Welcome to the group. At least for the next couple weeks."

Laila's fists, resting on the tabletop, tighten. But before she can punch him out, which I have no doubt she is about to do, Duke sits down with our burgers and sodas.

"Bobby," he says, and they do a "cool guy" fist-bump thing.

"Hey. Addie and I were getting caught up."

"Good," Duke says. "I hope everything is cool with you two."

Bobby gives a sly smile and says, "Of course."

My heart pounds in a mixture of anxiety and frustration. I pick up my burger and try to ignore my heart—it's been too opinionated lately anyway.

Between Ray and Bobby, the entire lunch hour turns into a who-has-the-best-story-about-Duke showdown. Apparently he was the king of toilet-papering houses and helping himself to people's pools at midnight.

"Telekinetics make the best TPers," Ray says. He imitates throwing a roll of toilet paper. "We get a nice arch . . ."

"And then send it even higher," Duke finishes for him.

"*Pff*," Bobby says. "But you can't get it *through* walls."

"Wait," I say. "This was recently? I thought these were little-kid stories. But these are post-ability pranks? Wow. So mature."

"Hey. We were freshmen. We hadn't quite mastered poise and sophistication yet," Duke says with a laugh.

Laila clears her throat, and I anticipate her sarcastic remark about how they still haven't, when instead she says, "Look who just walked in."

Duke and I glance over our shoulders and see Poison.

"Who is that?" Bobby asks.

"A huge loser," Laila informs him. She gets a sparkle in her eye that I don't like. "I'll be right back."

"What are you going to do?" I ask.

"If he looks out the window, distract him."

"What?" I'm confused, but she's already halfway to the door.

Poison orders food, and I watch Laila scan the parking lot, then spot his car and swiftly walk to it. She reaches up to her hair and must've pulled out a bobby pin because when she gets to his car, she kneels down and unscrews the tire cap.

Duke laughs. "She's letting the air out of his tires."

At the counter, Poison is just finishing his order. He's seconds away from turning around and having a full view of Laila at his car. I grab a soda off the table, jump up, and walk around behind him. As he turns, I slam into him and let the cup smash between us, sending ice and soda all over. I didn't think about the fact that the front of my shirt would end up soaked, but it does the trick.

He lets off a string of cusswords.

"I'm so sorry," I say.

He meets my eyes, and I don't know if he recognizes me from Laila's house or if he just realizes that I'm a teenager and undeserving of his verbal abuse, but his expression softens. "It's not a big deal," he says gruffly. "Just watch where you're going."

"Yeah, I will." Not sure if Laila is done yet, I grab a stack of napkins off the counter and start wiping his shirt.

"I'm good," he says, and storms to the bathroom.

The man behind the counter is staring at the mess on the floor.

"Sorry," I say, about to drop down and use the napkins there.

"It's okay. I'll get the mop."

My shirt is wet, and my face and arms are sticky. When I turn back around, Duke is smiling. "Good one," he says as I sit down.

"What was that all about?" Ray asks Duke.

I give Duke a look that I hope tells him not to air Laila's dirty laundry, and he says, "Oh, nothing, that guy just cut us off on the road earlier."

I pull my wet shirt away from my skin. "I'm going to need to change."

He unzips his backpack and whips out a purple jersey with the name Rivers across the back in gold print.

Not in a million years, I want to say, but he has the cutest expression on his face. I take it. "Thanks. I'll be right back."

After I change into Duke's football jersey, I stare at myself in the mirror. It's so not me. I feel like a fraud. Not only am I swimming in it, but it's like an advertisement to the world that I belong to Duke. People will think I asked him if I could wear it.

My hair only adds to my fraudulent look—I've been straightening it ever since Duke told me it looked hot that way, and I feel as pathetic as that sounds. Now my hair is sticky with soda and attempting to curl on one side. I free an elastic band from my pocket and pull it up into a ponytail. I tuck the front of the jersey into my jeans and make myself feel better with the fact that I can change into my emergency outfit when I get back to school. Suddenly I don't feel quite so neurotic for keeping (and continually replacing) that outfit in my locker.

When I exit the bathroom, everyone is filing out of the restaurant and piling into their cars. Duke and Laila are waiting for me. Even Laila knows I shouldn't be wearing the jersey, because she curls her lip when she sees it. But Duke smiles and lifts me into a big hug. "You are so adorable."

As we walk out of the restaurant, Poison is standing by his car, holding a to-go bag and staring at his tires.

"Man," Laila says, "that sucks."

I want to push her and tell her not to draw attention to herself, but that would only add to it.

Poison turns slowly, then looks her up and down. His gaze travels to Duke and then lingers on me. I lower my head and pull on Duke's arm, wanting to walk faster, but Duke just stares at him and then says, "Can we do anything to help?" in the friendliest voice ever.

Poison wrenches open his door, throws his bag inside, and pulls out a cell phone from his pocket.

"I guess that's a no then?" Duke says. Laila laughs.

As we drive away from Fat Jacks I turn around and smack Laila's leg. "You are seriously demented. That guy is going to kill you. His name is Poison, Laila, remember? And did you see those tattoos on his arms?"

She leans back in her seat and laughs harder. "He's a pathetic druggie. A hardcore loser." Her laughter trails off, and she says in a voice I'm sure she intends to be light, but I can hear the pain behind, "Just like my dad."

CHAPTER 16

NORM•trap: *n.* a device used to trap a Norm
(okay, fine, I got trapped too)

Monday at school, Trevor, Rowan, Stephanie, and I sit in Trevor's car. My notebook is propped on my knees, and all our ideas for "dare completion" are listed out.

"What happens if we fail?" I ask.

"They get bragging rights for the rest of their lives," Stephanie says. Her sour expression—which I've decided is her face's default setting—is present. "We are not failing."

I doodle a couple of split lines on the corner of the page. "I say we add a rule to the dessert game that the dare must take place the night of the loss. None of this, 'On Monday you have to steal the principal's bobblehead toy off the dashboard of his car.'"

Rowan raises one eyebrow, and one corner of his mouth rises with it. Default setting = creep. "Are you scared?"

"What?" I blow air between my lips. "No," I say, when really the thought of breaking into the principal's car ranks right up there with suffering through one of my mom's mind patterns.

"I still think me distracting the principal right when he comes back from lunch, and one of you climbing into the car before he has a chance to set his alarm is the best option," Rowan says, pointing at my notebook. "Oh, and while you're writing things down, Addison, write down the name Luis Vasquez. Look him up, Trevor. Last year he had a major back injury during a game. Does his name sound familiar? It should, because he was up for All-American, just like you."

"This isn't helping our current situation," Stephanie says.

"I agree," Trevor says. "I'm for the borrowing-the-principal's-keys-out-of-his-office idea."

"But then someone has to put them back," Stephanie says. "And that's assuming he doesn't keep them on him."

I glance at my cell. "Well, lunch is almost over, so we'd better figure it out soon."

"Okay, let's try the distraction technique," Rowan says. "Who's going in for the bobblehead?"

Stephanie's head immediately whips toward me.

Not me. "Why me?"

"Because you're the one who had the pathetic dessert."

"She had no idea about the game, Stephanie," Trevor points out.

Everyone stares at me, and I find myself saying, "No, it's fine." I close my notebook and tuck it into my bag. "I'll go in. You just better keep him occupied, Rowan." There is no way I'm getting kicked out of Norm school over a stupid dare.

"I will. I'm an expert at distraction."

"I'll help Addison," Trevor says. "Stephanie, you be backup for Rowan."

"Yeah, okay." She blinks several times, then looks up. Just when I start to wonder what someone said to upset her, she pulls down her lower eyelid and sticks her finger in her eye.

I gasp, but no one else reacts.

"My contact is bugging me." She pinches a thin, clear film out of her eye, and since nobody else finds this at all disturbing I try to control my facial expression.

I must not have done a good job because she says, "What's your problem? You don't know anyone who wears contacts?"

No, actually. A Norm lesson about subpar vision is skirting just outside my memory. I need to get a memory program fast, because I seem to have forgotten all our lessons.

"You have it back in?" Rowan asks, and Stephanie nods. "All right, break." He ducks out of the car like he thinks he's a spy. Stephanie follows.

"He needs some theme music," I say, hoping Trevor doesn't

ask about my reaction to Stephanie's contacts.

"Mr. Buford has some he can borrow."

I laugh and move toward the door, my feet crunching papers as I do. "Your car is a mess."

"You're disgusted."

"No, I'm not," I say too fast.

He laughs. "Your face says otherwise."

"*Disgust* is the wrong word. It's not like it's littered with half-eaten food or dirty socks." I reach down to pick up one of the many crumpled papers. "It's just . . ." I start to unfurl the paper.

"Negative," he says.

"Negative? Did you seriously just use that word?" The paper is crumpled up into a pretty tight ball, and I can't open it as fast as I want to.

His eyes twinkle with a smile, but he grabs my wrist. "Addison, drop the garbage."

I laugh. "If we weren't in such a hurry, I'd fight to see what caused Mr. Laidback to use the word *negative* as a command." I drop the paper with the others, and he releases his hold.

A few moments later, Trevor and I crouch behind the tailgate of a truck, waiting for the principal to pull into his spot. "Are they lists of people you want to kill?" The fact that he wouldn't let me look makes me want to know that much more. I'm really good at keeping a secret, but when I know someone is keeping one from me, it drives me insane.

He smiles, and I decide he has one of the nicest smiles I've ever seen. "Yes, pages of them."

"Okay, love letters?"

"Absolutely not." He stands and stretches his legs, then squats down again.

I bite the inside of my cheek, thinking. What would a quiet, easygoing guy like Trevor not want me to see? "You write. You're a writer."

He raises his eyebrows in the do-you-seriously-think-that's-a-possibility? look.

"Maybe your stint in the library inspired you to pen your memoirs."

"You're making a bigger deal of this than it is."

"Negative," I say, stealing his word. "You are. Anytime you make something a secret, it becomes a big deal."

He smirks. "Are you going to keep guessing until I tell you?"

I nod once. "Yes."

"So if I tell you, you'll drop it?"

"Yes."

"Okay. Here's the huge secret: I draw a little and fail at it a lot."

I thought finding out what the paper really was would make me want to see it less, not more. "You draw? What do you draw?"

He gives me the didn't-you-say-you-would-drop-it? look, then peers around the tailgate. "You ready? He's here."

I turn and see a black SUV pull into the principal's spot, Rowan already standing on the sidewalk ready to distract him when he exits the car. "Let's go."

"Principal Lemoore," Rowan says, when the principal steps out of the car and shuts the door behind him. I approach the back passenger-side door, slowly opening it. Trevor stands behind me, waits until I'm all the way in, and closes it. I crawl along the floor but pause when I see the principal's back in the driver's-side window. Couldn't Rowan have led him farther away? I hold my breath, tempted to wait, but I know I need to get it and get out before he sets the alarm. I start to crawl over the shorter middle seat and into the front. That's when I notice a briefcase sitting on that middle seat. *Crap.*

I duck behind the driver's seat just as I hear Rowan say, "Wait, what are you doing?" The front door opens. The principal grumbles and grabs his briefcase, then shuts the door again.

Another door opens and closes, and Trevor whispers, "I'll get it, Addison. You just go out the back."

Gladly. I head for the door. "Do you have it?"

"Yes." At the same moment he utters the word, the horn sounds twice.

I drop back down, curling into a ball. "Tell me that was you accidentally bumping the horn."

"It wasn't."

"Great."

Rowan's face appears at the window. "Uh. He just set the alarm. Sorry, guys. Operation 'key retrieval' in motion." Rowan disappears.

I crane my head back to look at the silver door handle. "So we open the door and set off the alarm. He won't know it was us." I suddenly feel very trapped and have an overwhelming desire to get out of the car.

"If we didn't have to borrow his bobblehead, I'd say, yeah, let's bail. But we should give Rowan a few minutes and see if he comes through."

I roll onto my side and realize I can see Trevor under the seat. I focus on him and only him and try to forget where we are and what kind of trouble we can get into because of it. "Is this guy a bobblehead collector or something? I don't believe he'd notice it missing."

He laughs. "Yeah, he's a freak. You should see his office."

"Considering where we are, I think that's a huge possibility."

Trevor's jaw tightens. It's interesting to watch someone when he doesn't realize you can see him. Trevor's unguarded expression looks more concerned than his normal one.

The fact that he might be as worried as I am eases my nerves. It's like there's a certain amount of stress appointed to every situation and I'm used to being responsible for holding it all by myself. It's nice to share it with someone. "You okay?"

He looks over and smiles, the worried look immediately gone. "Oh, hey."

"So let me see this toy that's causing so much trouble."

He rolls onto his side, facing me. I can tell he's pretty cramped in the space when he brings his hand up and it's smashed against his chest. The bobblehead jiggles slightly. It's a football player, but I have no idea which team it's supposed to represent. "Here's the offender," he says.

"A football player."

"Yeah."

"Is everyone in the world obsessed with football?"

"It's pretty big around here."

It seems to be the theme of my life lately, and I don't even like the sport. "What's up with Rowan always coming up with players and their injuries?"

He rolls his eyes. "I'm surprised he didn't say it the other night. He has this theory that someone is purposefully injuring the competition."

My throat feels dry, and I try to swallow down some moisture. "Why does he think that?"

"Well, because of the nature of my hit. It was after the whistle. I wasn't expecting it, and neither was my line—which is odd, because I'm always on guard for a few seconds after each play. But that time I felt completely relaxed. And then I was hit. Hard. The ligaments in my shoulder were torn pretty bad. Which makes him think that someone tried to permanently injure me."

"But you don't think that?"

"No. Football is all about smashing into other people as hard as you can. Of course players are going to get hurt. And how could someone know how badly I would get hurt anyway?"

I clear my throat. "And these other players who have been

hurt too . . . The ones Rowan's been telling you about. Did they all get hurt while playing that same school as well?"

"I don't know. I try not to take Rowan too seriously. It's been my downfall many times." He pauses. "But he's a lot of fun. He lives off adrenaline. You'll never be bored with him around."

I'm not sure if that statement was made specifically for me or if he was speaking in generalities, but it's time to make my feelings for Rowan clear. "Adrenaline is overrated." Okay, so that isn't the clear-cut 'I hate Rowan' statement I was looking for when I opened my mouth. But I feel bad; I don't want to be rude about his best friend.

He readjusts his position on the floor, but it doesn't seem to make him any more comfortable. "I never did give you that zombie quiz on Friday."

"That's because you were too busy driving strangers to my house."

He groans. "I thought you might've been mad about that. Sorry."

"Yeah, well, you've known me for such a long time. You should be able to read my looks by now. Glaring at you in the rearview mirror, like this, means: 'You will die if you take people to my house. Come up with an alternate solution.'" I give him an example of the look.

"Good to know. I'll start a list."

My cell phone chimes, and I pull it out of my pocket. The text message from Laila reads, *I just let the air out of the tires of one of my dad's loser friends' car at Fat Jacks. It felt so good.*

I close my eyes, trying not to let this news affect me now, from hundreds of miles away. Because my immediate response is to ask her if she's crazy. *What're you doing off-campus for lunch? Shouldn't you be sitting on the stage tormenting people who walk by?*

I felt like Fat Jacks. Snuck off. Apparently the entire football team hangs out here. You should see this place. Packed. What're you up to?

I'm locked in a car with Trevor, I text back.

"Is that our rescue squad giving us an update?" Trevor asks.

Ooh, Sounds fun, Laila responds.

"Oh. No. It's my friend Laila. Rowan doesn't have my cell number, and I really don't want him to, so please don't give it to him."

Trevor's eyes dart to mine. "Wow, it was that obvious, huh?"

"Yeah, and I'm not really interested. No offense."

"It doesn't offend me. It was a best-friend favor. Sorry."

"No, it's okay. Will you just let him know?"

"Yeah, sure." He shifts his shoulders again, and I wonder if he's in pain.

"Isn't there a way to move the seat back or something? You look so uncomfortable." My Compound car immediately adjusts to my settings. Was it the same here? I hadn't paid enough attention. Maybe I just made the stupidest suggestion, because the car obviously doesn't have Trevor's fingerprint in its database. How is he supposed to move the seats in someone else's car?

"Yes, the lever is probably on the side. Can you reach it?"

"Lever?" So it was a stupid suggestion for a different reason—I have no idea what he's talking about.

"On the side of the seat. By the door."

"Oh, right." I reach to the side of the seat, hoping to find something sticking out. I do, but I still don't know what to do.

"Did you find it?"

"Maybe?"

The next thing I know, his hand is on mine. His fingertips, slightly calloused, travel over mine in search of the lever. "You probably just push it back."

Our eyes meet under the seat. The car is entirely too stuffy and hot. I take my hand out from under his. "Maybe we shouldn't move the seats. The principal will probably be able to tell."

"True."

The horn beeps, and I jump.

"We're free," Trevor says. "Let's take a team picture with this and then put it back." He starts to get up.

"Trevor?"

His face reappears under the seat. "Yeah?"

"Sorry about your shoulder."

He smiles. "No need to be sorry. Really. Rowan makes it into a much bigger deal than it is."

I nod, wondering if Trevor really had let it go. And more than that, I wonder if Rowan has a reason to be suspicious of Lincoln High.

CHAPTER 17

PAR•A•pha•sia: *n.* to lose the power to speak correctly

It's my first time standing at Duke's front door, and I'm nervous. I haven't met his parents yet. It feels like a big deal. I ring the bell and gnaw on my lip. A beautiful woman answers, and her smile is contagious, immediately putting me at ease. "You must be Addie," she says, grasping both my hands for a quick moment and then dropping them. "Come in."

"Thank you." I readjust the backpack on my shoulder and step in. The entryway is huge and ends in a wide staircase, straight ahead of me. Actually, every aspect of the house is huge: tall doors, large paintings, thick banisters.

"Upstairs, first door on your right," she says.

I begin to walk upstairs. Maybe this study date was a bad idea, but it's the only kind of date my mom would allow with my grounding still in force. The first door on the right is shut, and I knock quietly.

"Come in," Duke says, and the door slides open.

I step inside. He sits at a desk, his back to me, writing. "Give me one sec."

His room is bright, the drapes on both windows wide open. From where his house sits, on the very edge of town, the unob-structed view of the mountains is impressive. As I stare out the window, I wonder if the Perceptives change the image through-out the day. Do they elongate the shadows in the afternoon? The thought of a manufactured reality sits heavily on my shoulders from this close up, and I'm suddenly happy I don't have Duke's impressive view every day. I'm happy for my daily view of the neighbor's water-stained fence.

I turn my attention away from the windows. I expect Duke's walls to be covered with football posters or shelves full of tro-phies, but they're a clean beige, like his mom's pants. A single painting of an ocean view hangs on the wall opposite his king-size bed. As a whole, the room screams hotel—generic enough to house anyone, and yet nobody ever feels like they belong there. It is clean though, which is nice.

He finishes whatever he's working on and then stands and turns. "Hey, girlfriend."

"Hi." My heart flutters. I raise one hand, and when I lower

it my backpack slips down my arm, causing me to take a jerky step forward.

He laughs. "Aren't we past the awkward stage yet? Where is my mouthy Addie who acted like I was nothing special when we first met?"

Sometimes I wonder the same thing. "Are you someone special?"

"There she is."

He takes several steps forward and scoops me into a hug. When he puts me down, I say, "So this is your room, huh?"

"Yep, this is it. Have a seat." He points to his bed, and I take the chair he just abandoned instead.

"I thought there'd be more . . . stuff. Trophies or whatever."

"Yeah, well, my mom doesn't like holes in the walls. Plus, my dad has an entire room filled with my . . . *stuff*. It's embarrassing."

"He's proud."

"He just loves football. Has his whole life."

"So is that why you started playing?"

"Yeah, I was told my dad handed me a football when I was born."

"Is he Telekinetic too?"

He nods slowly and looks around as if noticing how bare his room is for the first time.

"Have you been to the ocean?" I ask, nodding my head toward the painting.

"Once. A long time ago. I liked it a lot." He stares at the

painting. "Are your walls plastered with posters of hot guys or something?"

"How did you know?"

"Really?"

"No. I actually have a lot of . . . um . . ." I pull on my fingers, realizing how uncool I am about to sound and how little he actually knows about me. "Painted words and book pages on my walls."

"Book pages?"

"Yeah, some are from novels; some are from graphic novels."

He raises his eyebrows. "Graphic novels? As in, comic books?"

"Yes. But it's not because I think the characters are cute or anything." Even though Laila sometimes stares at them with dreamy eyes. "It has more to do with the story lines . . . usually the parts where I felt the most tense or the saddest. I'll pin that page on my wall, and every time I read it or look at it, I get that rush of feelings I got reading it. . . ." *Holy crap, this is not normal. Why am I telling him this?* ". . . Never mind."

"No, wait, tell me. So you're saying you like to remember certain feelings?"

"Sort of." I pull up my knee on the chair with me. "It's hard to explain. In my life, I'm surrounded by people who, no matter if they are trying to or not, can manipulate me. Like my mom. She says she doesn't use Persuasion on me, but just the fact that I know she can makes me more likely to do what she asks, because I don't want her to use her power on me. So even though she's not using it, in a way she's still manipulating me. I just let her skip a step. My dad too. Since I know I can't lie to him, I don't. Does any of this make sense?"

"Yes, of course, but I don't understand how that relates to pages from books pinned to your wall."

The desk chair swivels as I shift my leg back and forth once. "When I read, I feel emotion all on my own. Emotion no living person is making me feel. To me, it almost seems more real, because I know that those characters can't influence me with any power. So I like to remind myself that I can feel without anyone manipulating me. . . . I know, it's lame."

"No, it's not lame. But you sound like a Naturalist again. You sound like you want to live in a world where people don't have powers."

My eyes drift to the view of the mountains out his window. "No. I want to live in a world where people aren't using their powers against me to fulfill their own agenda."

"You don't trust people, do you?"

"I've seen a lot of alternate futures. I guess it makes me more wary than most." I turn toward his desk. "So what are you working on?"

"Are you trying to change the subject?"

"Yes."

He laughs. "I'm working on college stuff."

"Oh." The thought stops me cold. Duke is going to college next year. I'm not. "Where are you going?"

"I haven't decided yet. I have several options, and they've all offered full-ride football scholarships. It's a hard choice."

"Yes, I'm sure it is."

"Well, it won't be for you. You can just do a little Search, and all will be well." I sense a hint of bitterness and am not sure what to say. He puts a hand to the back of his neck and rubs it. "I'm sorry. I'm just tired of thinking about it." He flops on his bed face-first. "Do it for me," he mumbles into the mattress.

I smile. "Okay." I pick up several pamphlets from the corner of his desk and slowly flip through them. "Here. This one looks nice. There's a picture of a tree on the front."

He raises his head. "Is that how I should decide? Whichever college puts out the prettiest pamphlet?"

"Totally."

"Well, that school is in California."

I drop it onto the desk. "Never mind. That one is off the list. Too far away. I still don't believe you're leaving the Compound for college."

"I know, it's weird to think about."

"Do you feel like it's going to affect your ability progression?"

"Sometimes. But I'm committed to keep it up. I'll practice. And I'm hoping Ray comes with me, so at least we can push each other."

"That would be good." I turn back to the stack of pamphlets. "Okay, so no to California. See, this is easy. One down . . ."

"Twenty-five more to go."

"Twenty-five? Jeez, you are someone special, aren't you?

I wish you would've told me."

He shifts onto his side and props himself up on an elbow. "Come to my game this Friday."

"What?" I say, even though I heard him perfectly.

"I have a game this Friday."

"Home or away?"

"Here."

"So that means you're playing one of the other Para teams?"

"Does it matter? I'm playing."

"Of course I'll come to your game, if my mom lets me. I can't promise I won't fall asleep, but I'll come."

He rolls off the bed, lowers his shoulder, and barrels toward me.

"You told me to be mouthy!" I scream, and run for cover.

CHAPTER 18

NORM•vid: *n.* captured footage
with no special effects added to enhance quality

"I think guys on Lincoln High's football team use their abilities even when they're playing Norm schools." I hold the phone to my ear while I use my other hand to scrub the grout on the kitchen counter with the rough side of a sponge.

Laila laughs. "You think?"

"But that's wrong."

"Why? Are you telling me your dad doesn't use his abilities in his new job?"

"That's different."

"How? He's using his abilities to get ahead at work. He lives in the Norm world. You don't think his ability gives him an edge on a coworker up for the same promotion? It happens all the time. Sports are no different. Our football players want college scholarships. They're going to use their abilities to be the best they can and edge out Norm players."

"It just seems wrong." I rewet my sponge and move on to a new section.

"You've never had a problem with it before."

"I guess I've never met anyone on the wrong end of an ability."

"Addie, are you cleaning?"

I pause in my scrubbing efforts. "Yeah, why?"

"Because you're out of breath. Stop getting so worked up unless my bedroom is the benefactor. Speaking of, it's a mess since you've been gone."

Is that what I'm doing? Getting worked up? I do feel agitated and annoyed that someone or, more likely, several someones are abusing their abilities like this.

"Who do you think was responsible for Trevor's injury then?" Laila asks.

I throw the sponge in the sink and walk into the living room. "I don't know. I guess a Mass Manipulator, for one. They're the only ones I think who could tear muscle like that." I pause suddenly as I remember something else Trevor said.

I must've gasped as well, because Laila says, "What?"

"A Mood Controller."

"What? The ones who work the football games? I'm pretty sure they only influence the crowd."

"No. Not someone on the staff. Someone on the football team."

"What makes you say that?"

"Because Trevor said right before the injury, he was off guard, relaxed. Someone soothed him on purpose, got his defenses down."

"You think?"

"I don't know. I'm just trying to make sense of it all. Are there any Mood Controllers on the football team?"

"I don't know. I just assumed all the guys on the team were Telekinetics."

"So did I, but they must not all be. How can we find out?"

"I guess I can ask."

I'm touched that she'd do that for me when I know how much she hates asking people what their abilities are. There has to be a way we can find out without her having to ask every member of the football team his ability (although that might be the only perk for her). I think about it for a moment. "The school has to have a record of it. I mean, when we registered they recorded our claimed abilities. There's got to be a master list or something."

"School office, then?"

"Kalan," we both say together. She works in the front office. She could probably get her hands on a list like that.

"I'm on it," Laila says.

"I just feel terrible for Trevor."

"He could've gotten that kind of injury whether someone was using an ability or not. Football is a contact sport, Addie."

"Yeah, I know." And for now I need to cling to the idea that it was all just an accident blown out of proportion by Rowan's overactive imagination.

I'm now standing by the TV, holding my dad's DVD. It must be calling to me. It's the third time inside a week that I've picked it up just to stare at it.

"Hey, I gotta go. I'm on my way to the football game," she says.

"I swear that's the only thing you ever say anymore. Are you crushing on some football player? The quarterback? What's his name?"

"You're kidding, right? You honestly forgot his name?"

"It just slipped my mind." I search my memory. "Oh, Duke! Jeez, I thought I was going crazy for a minute there." I haven't been gone that long, and yet it already feels like I've let a portion of my old life go. This new life fits comfortably.

"Forgetting Duke is the equivalent of losing your mind."

I roll my eyes. "Yeah, whatever. Well, have fun staring at boys smashing into each other."

"Believe me, I will."

I hang up the phone and look at the DVD in my hand. Before I talk myself out of it again, I open the case and put it in the player. "Sorry, Dad," I whisper as I sit on the couch to listen to the interview.

The screen starts off blue, and then a shot of a Bureau employee and his name card—too small to read, clipped to his dress-shirt pocket—comes into view.

He clears his throat. "The following is an interview of Steve

Paxton, brought in as a suspect in the Freburg murder—first murder in the Compound in"—he consults his tablet—"seven years, four months. Recommended course of action upon positive Discernment results: brain scan, incarceration with rehabilitation program."

My heart is pumping fast. A murder in the Compound was rare and always solved. The video cuts out for a moment, and when it comes back the same wiry guy my dad had been watching the other night sits at a metal table.

"Mr. Paxton, state your full name for the record."

He runs a hand through his greasy hair. "Poison."

"Your real name," the voice behind the camera says.

"Steve Paxton, but you can call me Poison."

"Mr. Paxton, where were you on the night of September sixth between the hours of eight and twelve p.m.?"

"I'm not sure. I'd have to consult my calendar." His voice is sarcastic, like this is all a big joke.

"It was a Friday night, three weeks ago," the voice says.

"Fridays I normally hang out at the club."

"Alone?"

"No. I'm rarely alone."

"Who can verify your whereabouts?"

"Anyone who saw me at the club."

"Mr. Paxton. Were you with anyone that night?" The voice indicates its owner is losing his patience.

"I was with a club full of people."

"Give me a name."

"Whose name would you like?"

"Do you recognize this girl, Mr. Paxton? She's sixteen." The table in front of Poison lights up, and he looks down. As if I'm watching a movie I expect the camera angle to change so that I can see the image too, but it doesn't. I'm stuck staring at the top of Poison's greasy head as he looks at the picture on the table screen. I wonder if I know the girl he's looking at. Freburg, he had said. Did I know any Freburgs? There are only three high schools in Jackson.

"No, never seen her before."

"That's funny." A paper slides into view. "Her phone records indicate she called you at least twice a day for the last month."

He leans forward, obviously pretending to inspect the picture further. "Oh, yeah, I guess I do know her."

"She's dead, Mr. Paxton."

Even though I already know, I flinch with the announcement, but he hardly reacts at all. "I'm sorry to hear that."

"It was made to look like she killed herself." The table screen flickers, probably changing the image, but Poison doesn't even glance at it. He looks straight at the camera and says, "Maybe she did."

I fall back a little. His eyes scare me. They're hard and unafraid. He's sitting at the Bureau being interrogated for a murder, and he's not scared. Is it because he's innocent? But if he was, wouldn't he ask for a scan to prove himself? They'd need more proof to force a scan on him. It's obvious why they sent this tape to my dad—he'll know if Poison is lying.

"We think you did it, Mr. Paxton," the voice says.

"You can't pin her murder on me just because we were together. It was consensual. She was using me for the dr—"

The sound of the garage door opening rumbles in my feet. I jump up, turn off the television, and shove the DVD into its case and back on top of the TV just in time for my dad to walk in.

"Hi, Daddy," I say too enthusiastically. He'll know I'm up to something just by the tone of my voice. It's his ability. I pull out my phone and pretend I'm reading a text. I've tried lying to him before with no success.

"What're you doing, kid?" he asks.

I want to ask him about the interview, about Poison and what his conclusions are. But I know he can't tell me. I remind myself to ask Laila tomorrow about any missing girls on the news. "Oh, just texting with a friend." Really? I had to actually admit to something? I could've just shrugged my shoulders and said, "Nothing," which would have been the truth in that moment.

My dad stops midstride and lowers his brow. Unfair. I quickly type, *Lie detectors suck sometimes,* and hit Send. Laila will get a kick out of that. I hold up my phone for him to see. "Just texting," I repeat. This time it's the truth.

"Sounds exciting." He resumes his walk toward the hall. "I'm going to go change."

"Okay."

My phone chimes, and I look at it. The text is three question marks, and it's from Trevor. How did that happen? Then I realize that I just assumed Laila was the last person to send me a text. But she wasn't; Trevor was. He had texted me last night to ask what the homework assignment in Government was and we ended up texting the rest of the night.

Sorry, that was supposed to go to Laila.

What did you mean by it?

It's what we call my dad.

Oh. Your dad giving you problems?

Yeah.

I'm inviting the gang over to my house tonight. You up for it?

Am I one of "the gang" now?

You did successfully complete the bobblehead retrieval mission. I think you're in.

Let me ask. I walk down the hall to my dad's room. His door is not quite shut, and just as I'm about to knock I hear his voice through the crack. He must be on the phone.

"How did you get this number?" A pause. "I don't take kindly to threats, Mr. Paxton."

My breath catches in my throat.

"Just tell the truth, and you won't have to worry about my input." Another pause. "No, actually it's not a subjective ability; my findings are conclusive and binding. Good-bye, Mr. Paxton, and this will go in the report."

I count to ten, trying to return my breathing to normal, and then knock.

"Come in."

I start to pretend like I didn't overhear what I just did, but my heart is pounding and I'm sure he can read fear all over my face. "Are you okay, Dad? Who's threatening you?"

"Eavesdropping?" His voice is perfectly calm, but for a moment I see tension tighten his eyes.

"I'm sorry."

He lightly brushes my hair with his hand. "It's okay. And I'm fine. Nothing I can't handle." Sometimes I wish I were a lie detector too, so that I could determine if he were telling the truth. But, I remind myself, my dad doesn't lie to me. His eyes drift down to my cell phone clutched in my hand. "Did you need something?"

"Oh, yeah. Trevor invited me to his house for a movie. There'll be a bunch of us."

He loosens his tie. "Like a party?"

I plop onto his bed and lie back. "No, like ten of us."

"Are his parents going to be there?"

"I don't know."

"If they are, you can go."

I feel lame asking, but I know my dad will know if I don't. I hold the phone above me and type, *My dad wants to know if your parents are going to be home.*

My dad's tie lands on my face. I wad it up and throw it after him as he retreats to his closet. It doesn't make it very far, uncoiling and snaking to the ground. He laughs at my attempt.

My phone chimes with Trevor's answer. *Yep. And my little brother too.*

He'll love that. Text me directions and I'll see you in a while.

"His parents and little brother will be home," I tell my dad.

"Okay, have fun."

As I leave I give my dad one last look. He's already unbuttoning his shirt and pulling out a replacement. I hope, like he claimed, that Poison really is someone he can handle.

CHAPTER 19

dis•PA•RAte: *adj.* distinct, different, dissimilar

My heart races, and my head pounds. The screams of cheering fans surround me. The band's music pulses in my ears, and I feel lost in a cloud of haze. "This is so crazy!" Puffs of white breath accompany my words. The whistle blows, and Duke runs onto the field again.

"I know, right?" Laila rubs her arms, which are covered by a too-thin jacket. She was obviously more worried about fashion than warmth. "Why can't the Perceptives make us think it's *warm* too?" She nods at the lightning that has been streaking across the sky since the game started. "I'm freezing."

"Because an illusion is an illusion. Reality always exists despite the facade." An exceptionally bright flash, unaccompanied by thunder, bursts in time with the snap of the ball.

Duke drops back for a pass. When he releases the ball, it zig-zags across the sky, tugged first one way and then the other by all the Telekinetic players trying to direct its motion. Number seventy-six on our team catches the ball, and I start jumping up and down squealing.

Laila gives me a sideways glance. "Okay, the Mood Controllers are laying it on thick tonight."

"That's my problem, right? Because I feel super-weird."

"Go get us some sodas. When you're out of the stands, the excitement wears off."

"Good idea." I climb over cheering teens and down the cement steps to the back of the stadium, where the food vendors are. Once in the open air, I immediately feel better. My heart rate slows and my brain stops buzzing. I take a sigh of relief. I had no idea I was that susceptible to influence. It makes me feel better when I think about how many Mood Controllers work the football game.

"Well, hello."

I turn and see Poison leaning up against a cement support pillar. My heart rate immediately picks up again, but I try to pretend nothing is wrong. "Oh, hi. Um, soda guy, right? Sorry about that again."

He blows air between his lips, and a puff of white smoke

blurs his sharp features for a moment. "Don't pull that on me. You know who I am." He takes a step closer. "I know who you are. And next time you and your friends want to play a prank on someone, you might want to stick with your little high school buddies."

"I don't know what you're talking about."

"I'm talking about the fact, Addison Coleman, that you do not want to be on my bad side."

He knows my name. "You don't scare me," I say. He terrifies me.

"I may not be a Discerner, but I'm going to say that's not true. I wonder if my findings would be conclusive and binding."

Conclusive and binding? "I don't know what you're talking about."

He takes another step closer, and I fall a step back. We walk this way for several steps and just as I'm about to turn and run, he says, "Do you know what it feels like, Addie, to have zero control over your own actions? To have someone make you do something?"

"What do you mean?" I ask. If he's a Mood Controller, he's not making me feel at ease. I feel only tense and terrified. Maybe he wants me to feel that way.

My leg lifts and takes me a step toward him. I panic and try to back up, but I'm frozen there. Literally. No matter how hard I tell my leg to move, it won't.

"Give a message to your little friend's daddy," he says in a scratchy voice that makes my blood curdle. "Tell him that if he doesn't pay me back, I have other ways of collecting. One way or another, I will get that money."

I nod slowly, and he turns and walks away.

CHAPTER 20

NOR•Ma•po•late: *v.* when normal people
try to solve a mystery without extra help

I knock on Trevor's door, and a little boy answers. He looks like
a mini version of Trevor, with big brown eyes and longer-than-
life lashes. I can't resist the urge to reach out and ruffle his hair.

"Hey," he objects, smoothing it back into place. "Who are you?"

"I'm Addie. Is Trevor here?"

"Addison," Trevor says, coming around the corner, "is the bodyguard refusing you admittance?" Trevor pats him on the back,
and he straightens up.

"No. I was about to let her in before she messed up my hair."

"Sorry, he's just so cute."

Trevor laughs. "Addison, this is Brody."

"She said her name was Addie," Brody accuses.

"Only special people can call her that."

"Like who, her boyfriend?" Brody asks.

I stare at Trevor, surprised at his reasoning. Here I thought he didn't realize Addie was my nickname, when really he just felt he hadn't earned the right to use it. It takes me a moment to notice he's staring back with his normal casual expression that seems to portray more than laid-backness in that moment. But what, exactly, I can't decide. Embarrassment? Amusement? I look away first, remembering Brody's question and now feeling awkward that I had locked eyes with Trevor after Brody's mention of a boyfriend. "Exactly, only my boyfriend," I say, looking at Brody. "So will you start calling me that?"

"*Ew.* No." He runs away.

My cheeks heat up, and I don't know why. I try to talk my way through it, hoping Trevor won't notice. "He's adorable. I could squeeze him all day long."

"When he was three, he might've let you. But he's a tough eight-year-old now. Girls are disgusting."

"I know, they are."

"Did you want to come in or just hang out on my porch all night?"

He leads me into a room with a pool table and a couple of couches. A television is mounted to the wall, and a couple guys stand in front of it, pointing remotes at the screen. I've heard about Norm video games, but it's funny to see one in person.

These guys would die to play the virtual-reality games in the Compound—no remotes required.

I can see why Trevor's friends hang out here a lot—it's like a rec room. Lisa and Brandon sit on a couch drinking sodas, and Rowan and Daniel play a game of pool. Rowan looks up when I walk in, and I feel guilty. He probably hates me after Trevor told him I wasn't interested. But if he does, it doesn't show.

He smiles and waves. "You want to play the winner, Addie?"

"Uh, sure."

"Now I have some motivation to beat you, Daniel," Rowan says.

My head immediately whips over to Trevor. "I promise I told him," he says quietly. "He's just persistent. He thinks he can wear people down."

"So is that why—"

"No," he interrupts, "that's not why I invited you tonight."

"It better not be, or you would be on my list."

"What list is that?"

"People-to-kill-when-I-gain-superpowers list."

"How many people are on that list?" he asks.

"You'd be the first."

He laughs. "Nice." He gestures toward a table in the corner where food is laid out, and I follow him there. "What would your superpower be?" He grabs a handful of chips and eases into a chair.

Even though I'm the one who brought it up, the question catches me off guard. "I'd, uh . . ."

"Bore people to death with your knowledge of ancient litera-
ture?" he offers.

I pick up a chip and throw it at his face. "Shut up. No. I
would definitely have Telekinesis."

"You'd want to read people's minds?"

"No, that's Telepathy. I'd want to move things with my mind."

"Yeah, I guess that would be pretty cool. I was referring to
real superpowers though, like flying or superstrength."

I'm sort of offended but can't show it, or he'd wonder why.
"You don't think mind powers are extraordinary?"

He shrugs one shoulder. "Yeah, I guess."

"So if you could have a mind power, which one would you
want?" I ask, curious.

"I'd want to be able to tell the future."

I curl my lip. "It's not that great."

"Are you judging my fake superpower?"

"No, it was a good try, but it's not the best one." Not even close.

He throws a chip back at me, and it bounces off my cheek.
"Well, it's the one I want. Then I could warn you that Rowan
is heading your way and will reach the table in approximately
three seconds."

I take a handful of chips and shove them into my mouth.

"Addie, I won. Your turn to get crushed," Rowan says.

I turn and point at my mouth. "I'm eating. I'll be right there,"
I say through my mouthful, but I can tell he doesn't understand
me because his brows go down and he leans closer. I scoot back.

"Give her a sec, Rowan. She's eating," Trevor says.

"Okay, I'll be waiting over there."

The chips scratch my throat going down, and I cough. "Thanks."

"If you don't like Rowan so much, why did you come?"

"Because you're my only friend." I point at myself and say, "New girl here."

"So when you find some new friends, you're bailing on me?"

"Probably." I have to shield my face as a handful of chips fly at me. "Hey, do me a big favor? Will you hang out with Rowan and me while we play pool? Just pretend you're watching. The last thing I need is for him to try to teach me how to play or something."

"Sure thing."

The first half of the game goes smoothly, with Trevor acting as my buffer. It's actually pretty fun. We laugh and joke around, and for the first time since moving here I feel like maybe I'm part of this group, not an outsider. Rowan is on pretty good behavior tonight too, not extra flirty. Just when I start to think I belong here, Stephanie walks into the room. She takes in the scene, then slowly walks to the food table. When she sits down, she says, "Trevor, can I talk to you?"

He looks to her, then back to me. "You're good now, right?" he whispers, and starts to walk away.

"You are officially on the list. Just wait until my super-powers come."

He turns and smiles that amazing smile. "First zombies, now

superpowers. I think you actually might be trying to kill me off." But he doesn't stop and joins Stephanie at the table.

"He is still so whipped," Rowan says. He takes a few steps toward me, and I grab my pool stick and put the table between us, pretending to study the ball positions.

"Do you like him?" Rowan asks.

The change in his tone surprises me. It went from player to nice guy with the single question. "Trevor?"

"Yeah."

"No, we're just friends." I think I'm being truthful, but Rowan raises an eyebrow like he's suddenly gained the ability to detect lies and he finds my answer false.

"Then what is it about me that you don't like?" he asks.

"Honestly?"

"Yes, of course."

"You come on too strong, very touchy. It's uncomfortable. And you remind me of this not-very-nice guy from back home."

"That's not good."

"No, it's not. But just this conversation is making you less like him. This is what girls like, sincerity and honesty."

"So you're saying you like me now?" he says, his cocky smirk coming back onto his face. I sigh, but then he adds, "Just kidding."

I laugh. "Good. Now whose turn is it?"

"It's mine."

He hits a blue ball into the corner pocket.

I pick up the square piece of chalk and twist it between my

thumb and forefinger, my gaze drifting to Trevor and Stephanie. She has a sour expression on her face (surprise, surprise) and is talking with big hand gestures. Trevor is staring at the chip bowl, his normal relaxed posture replaced by a rigid back and tightened jaw. Are all relationships just a series of fights strung together?

I've never had a boyfriend and have kissed only one boy, not counting Searches. Joey Turner. I met him at the bookstore when I was fourteen and assumed we were made for each other, brought together by our common love of books. Turned out his mom had dragged him to the bookstore. Of course, I didn't find out any of this until several days and several kissing sessions later.

"For what it's worth," Rowan says, standing by my shoulder and bringing me out of my memory, "he seems much happier since you've started coming around."

"What? Who?"

He nods his head toward Trevor. Obviously I had been caught staring. "This last year has been hard on him. With his shoulder and everything. Then you show up and . . . I haven't seen him smile and laugh so much in a long time."

"Really?"

"Really."

I smile. I'm glad Trevor enjoys himself around me, because I enjoy being around him too.

Rowan lines up his next hit, and I ask, "So all these injured players you've been telling Trevor about, did they all get injured while playing the same school—Lincoln High?"

"Yes. That's why it's so suspicious. Am I the only one who finds that suspicious?" he asks the ceiling.

"No. It's definitely odd." That confirms it for me—some football players at my old school are purposefully thinning the competition. But who? Is it the whole team or just a few rotten players? It's one thing to use powers to do better at something, like Laila had said, but to me it's completely different to get ahead by hurting someone else.

A few more people show up during our game. Rowan does end up crushing me, but at least he doesn't try to give me a conciliatory hug.

"Do you know where the bathroom is?" I ask Rowan.

"Yes." He points. "It's down the hall, third door on the right."

"Thanks."

On my way back from the bathroom, the sound of someone humming the theme song to *Star Wars* comes out of a slightly open door on my right. I peek in and see Trevor's little brother, Brody, sitting on his bed looking at a book. The door creaks a little when I bump against it, and Brody stops humming and looks up.

"Hi, again," I say. "What are you reading?"

"Star Wars comics." He holds up the book.

"Awesome. That's Episode One, right? Have you gotten to the part where Anakin enters the race yet?"

His eyebrows shoot up. "I just passed that."

"Can I look and see what else you have?" I point to a book-case in the corner.

"Sure."

The bookcase is a disorganized array of graphic novels. Some are stacked sideways, others with their bindings toward the back. The sideways ones are one thing, but bare pages to the front make my teeth hurt. I turn several around. There are a few books I've had my eye on so I take them out and study the covers. "Are these any good?"

"I don't know, I haven't read those. You should ask Trevor. They're his."

I pause halfway through flipping a page. "Oh, is this Trevor's room?"

"Yeah, I come in here to read his comics."

I look around and realize it's nothing like an eight-year-old's room. There's a large bed with dark bedding against one wall, a desk topped with stacks of paper against another, and several pairs of big shoes spilling out of a messy closet—the boy needs some serious organizational intervention. I put back the books in my hands, resisting the strong urge to organize them. On the wall above his bed is a large eye painted in shades of black and red. The pupil has the scene of a city in it. "That's cool."

"It's the cover of the comic book he's drawing." He points to the desk, and I walk over. Next to his desk a garbage can overflows with crumpled paper. Above it, pages are pinned up on the wall. They're obviously pictures he's drawn of the characters from his comic book.

"He's really good," I say, my finger running along the edge of one of the pages. I reach down and grab a paper out of his trash. It's a redheaded girl in a cape, jumping between two buildings. I have no idea why he threw it away. If he thinks this is garbage, Trevor must be really hard on himself. "Do you think he'd let me read his comic?" I ask Brody.

He laughs. "He doesn't let anyone read it."

"Not even you?"

"He lets me see the pictures."

"Addison?" Trevor says, from the doorway behind me.

I whirl around like I've just been caught snooping, holding his trash . . . which I have. "Sorry, I . . . ." Pocketing the paper, I swallow down my embarrassment. Trevor scans his room, probably deciding how embarrassed *he* should be.

I point to his bookcase and quickly say, "You told me you didn't like books."

He smiles. "Those don't really count."

"Those totally count. I have *Ninja Wars* and *Elementals* myself." I nod my head toward his desk. "And it looks like you succeed at drawing a lot more than you think you do."

"Sometimes I get lucky."

"You must not understand the definition of luck."

He meets my eyes then, and I think he's about to say something when Rowan's loud voice yells down the hall, "Trevor!"

"Oh, I forgot. Rowan has some sort of presentation for all of us." He gives me a yes-I-constantly-humor-Rowan look.

I don't want to leave this room and rejoin the party. I could spend the rest of the night parked in front of Trevor's bookcase (or his trash, for that matter), discussing the novels on his shelf. He must sense that too, or maybe it's my longing gaze at the books, because he says, "You can come back later. My bookcase is all yours."

I walk toward the door. "I've just decided those are my favorite five words in the world."

He laughs, and as I pass him he grabs hold of the corner of the paper that's sticking out of my pocket, freeing it.

I scrunch my nose. "You were just going to throw it away."

"Exactly." He wads it up and tosses it across the room. It lands on top of the others in the trash.

I'm more disappointed than I should be that I can't keep his drawing. It would've looked good on my wall. I make it a goal to acquire at least one of his drawings. It shouldn't be too hard, since the floor of his car is littered with them, but then I realize I want him to willingly give me one. Better yet, I want him to draw one for me. That is my new goal.

When we get back into the game room, Rowan says, "Okay, everybody. Come over by the couches. I have a surprise for Trevor."

Trevor glances at me like I should know what is about to happen, but I'm clueless. Rowan stands in front of the group.

"This next weekend is the first anniversary of Trevor's injury. It also happens to be the weekend that Lincoln High dares to show their faces again in our stadium."

Heat slowly creeps up my face.

"I was able to get my hands on a poster of this year's Lincoln High football team." He runs to the corner and comes back with a rolled-up poster. He unfurls it and lays it on the coffee table in front of us. My eyes travel over all the familiar people, stopping on the smiling face of Duke. "We all know how impossible it is to get information on any of these people. It's like their school is some sort of national secret. But I say we each pick two members of the starting lineup and find out as much as we can about them when they're here this Friday."

"Mr. Buford would be proud," Liam says with a laugh.

Rowan points at him. "Exactly. We know something weird is going on at that school. Trevor's injury was not an isolated incident—there have been players at other schools. Trevor was on the road to college stardom, and they took him out. We can't just sit back and let them get away with it." He jams his finger onto the poster. It lands right on Duke's face. I flinch.

Rowan will never find out anything. It's why the Compound has a Containment Committee. Information never gets very far. But I find myself wishing he could discover who's behind the injuries. I wonder if Laila has gotten the list of abilities from the front office and if it will shed any light on who's to blame.

Trevor laughs, but it sounds forced. "All right, Rowan. That's enough. How about if we just hang the poster and throw darts at it." He stands.

"I'm dead serious. We have to do surveillance. Some of their students come and watch the game. We can place spies in their student section."

Trevor grabs the poster, rolls it up, and whacks Rowan on the shoulder with it. "Sounds like a plan."

CHAPTER 21

preP•A•RA•tion: *n.* precautionary measures taken
to be ready for future events

Duke, Laila, and I sit in his car after the football game. I haven't stopped shaking since Poison showed me his power, but I'm trying to keep it under control because I've never seen Duke angry before. The muscle in his jaw twitches several times as he clenches and unclenches it.

"So, what do you think Poison's ability is then?" Laila asks. "I've never heard of anyone who can take over a nervous system."

I've been trying to figure out his ability since the moment

he walked away from me, finally allowing me to control my own movement again. Taking over a nervous system is an ability I had never heard of either. Is it something that can be learned, like Thought Placement and Light Manipulation, or is it something a person is born with? "Maybe people can do it, but we've never met anyone who *would*."

"So you think he can manipulate mass then, like Bobby?" Laila asks.

"It was definitely manipulation, but I had no idea Mass Manipulators could do *that*." I free my phone from my pocket. "I should call my dad. This is crazy."

"No." Laila's voice stops my finger just before I hit the call button. "Your dad is going to ask questions. He's going to wonder how we know him. You're going to have to tell him about my dad. They'll take him in."

"I'm pretty sure my dad already knows about your dad's drug problem."

"Yeah, but this has gone further than that. What if this guy does something to my dad because we talk to the authorities?" Her voice is hard and confident, but the look in her eyes is sadness mixed with desperation. "Please, Addie, let's just see if we can figure out something first."

After coming face-to-face with Poison behind the stadium, I have no doubt he can make good on a threat. I put my phone away. "Okay."

"I'm going to kill him," Duke finally says.

"Oh, don't be dramatic," Laila says. "We all know you're the type to defend Addie's honor. Now let's think of serious ideas, not extreme ones."

"I *am* serious."

I reach over and grab Duke's hand. He tenses again before he relaxes. As he exhales I relax as well. "He didn't hurt me, Duke. He didn't even threaten *me*. It was Laila's dad he was making threats against." I turn toward the back. "How much money do you think your dad owes him?"

She rolls her eyes. "Who knows? But no matter the threat, my dad can't produce something he doesn't have. It would be like trying to pull an ability out of a Norm."

"So what are we supposed to do?" Duke practically yells. "Ignore him?"

"Maybe we should." I squeeze his hand. "Ignore him and avoid him. And leave his car alone," I throw back for Laila.

"Yeah, yeah," she says. "I'll leave his car alone, but that doesn't mean we shouldn't try to find out all we can about this guy. I want to know who we're dealing with. We'll do an investigation."

"I happen to know a whole team of guys who could use a new punching bag."

It's weird to see Duke like this. I'm used to his ever-present smile. "No, Duke, don't. Please don't do anything to him. It'll just make things worse."

He turns toward me and grabs both my hands in his. "We're going to practice Thought Placement. If you're ever in trouble, we need to make sure you can let me know."

"You can do Thought Placement?" Laila asks, which is the same question I was about to ask. "I thought that was nearly impossible if your ability is related to manipulating objects and not other minds."

He gives an irritated glance back to Laila before looking at me again. "The word *nearly* is used for a reason, isn't it?"

"I'm not good at doing it over long distances yet," I say. "What's the point of telling you I'm in trouble if you're standing right next to me?"

"We'll practice. We need to learn each other's energies. Be in tune with each other." He puts a hand on the back of my neck and pulls me toward him until our foreheads touch. *We'll practice*, I hear in my mind. The thought comes in my own voice, but I know he placed it there.

"Gag," Laila says. "Please practice when I'm far, far away."

My cheeks go hot, and I back out of his hold. "Let's not forget that I'm not the only one in trouble here. Laila is in just as much danger as I am. Maybe more, since it's her father he's after."

They both laugh.

"What?"

"Addie, my ability alone puts me at an advantage." Then her eyes travel over me. "And that's just the first thing."

"You think you're tougher than me, is that it?"

"Know."

"Fine." I fold my arms and sink back against my seat. "Whatever."

"But if you want to give the bad guy the two paths he can

196

take, I'm sure he'll be impressed," Duke says with the first smile I've seen since we got in the car.

I roll my eyes and try to stay irritated, but his smile makes it impossible. "Funny."

"She can't tell the bad guy *his* two paths. Only her own. So she'll be able to tell him if she dies or not."

"You two are a regular comedy duo. I think I liked it better when we were all worried about me."

Duke's smile disappears. "That hasn't changed." He turns back toward Laila. "Okay, let's find out all we can about this creep."

"Can't we just wait until tomorrow?" We're standing in the dark hall of Laila's house. Our first step is to get Poison's number from her dad's cell phone. His snores echo down the hall.

"No, he's a more predictable sleeper at night," Laila says. "Just wait here." She tiptoes into her parents' room.

Duke, who's standing behind me, slips his arms around my waist. "Are you nervous?"

I relax back into him, and his breath tickles the hair on my neck. I can feel his heartbeat against my back. "Not anymore."

"Good. We'll fix this. He probably just gets a kick out of scaring people. Especially pretty young girls."

"I guess."

Laila comes back out and motions for us to follow her to the living room. The cell phone is in her hand, and she scrolls through his phone book.

"Addie, put his number in your phone."

"Okay." I wait, phone ready.

She tells me the number, and I enter it into my contacts attached to the name Freakshow.

"More like Dead Freakshow, if I ever see him again," Duke says, looking over my shoulder.

I elbow him.

"Okay, I'm going to put this back." She leaves, and I stare at the numbers on my phone. This all seems so pointless.

"What's wrong?" Duke asks.

"We have a number, but now what? It's not like we can call him up and ask him to tell us all about himself."

"No. But my best friend happens to know how to hack into computer systems. It's one of the perks of his ability."

"Really? Who?"

"Bobby."

I groan. "Bobby? Are you serious? I don't think we should share this with him. I don't trust him." I still haven't told Duke about what Bobby did to me in my Search. I wonder if I should, if he'll think I'm overreacting. It's hard for people to understand how real my "memories" are. Laila's the only person who knows what Bobby did . . . would've done . . . to me. The night I told her, she held my hand and asked me if I wanted her to wipe his memories and turn him into a drooling vegetable. I said no, but just the thought made me feel better.

Duke pushes a button on his cell phone, then spins it once

before pocketing it. "Well, I trust him. And right now, we could use his help."

"Right now?" I look at my phone. It's past eleven.

"Yep, I just texted him. Bobby stays up late."

Laila walks back out, and Duke says, "We're going to Bobby's to see if he can dig up any information on this guy."

Laila's eyes dart to mine. "We are?" She searches my face, probably looking for any signs of resistance.

I want to give them, but I just shrug and say, "Yes, I can't think of a better idea, or believe me I would."

"Okay then, let's go."

We pull up in front of Bobby's house, and my blood runs cold. I've never been inside except in my Search. As I stare at the large oak tree in his front yard the memory of Bobby's eyes boring into mine while we sat in his car comes into my mind. I remember wondering how we had ended up in front of his house in the first place when he was supposed to drive me home.

"My mom wanted to meet you," he had said.

"Oh, okay." But no one had been in his house. It was dark, and I felt uncomfortable. "Where is your mom?"

A smile crept onto his face, and he sat down on the couch and patted the cushion next to him.

My instincts told me to leave, but his green eyes softened.

"Come sit next to me."

I didn't want to be rude, and the dance had been fun. I sat down, and his arm snaked around my neck, his hand instantly finding my collarbone, tracing a slow line along it and then lower.

"I don't think so," I said, grabbing his hand and using it to remove his arm from my neck, then hanging on to it for good measure.

"What's wrong? You don't like me?" His free hand went to my thigh, where his fingers dug into my skin.

"Ouch, Bobby. Knock it off." I tried to stand, but he held on to my leg and pinned my shoulder with his.

For a moment I was frozen in shock, unable to believe what was really happening. His mouth found mine, rough and uncaring as his hand continued to travel upward. The sound of the skirt of my dress ripping and the feel of his hand brought me out of my shock, and I kneed Bobby hard. Holding together my ripped dress, I ran out of his house, my eyes stinging.

Now, in the car with Duke and Laila, those feelings are back. I try to push them aside as I step out of the car, not wanting Duke to think I can't handle this. I can handle this. Bobby doesn't control me. Laila must sense how I feel, because she's at my side immediately, grabbing hold of my hand.

Bobby opens the front door before we even knock. I don't like the way his eyes travel over me as if he, too, remembers the Search and enjoys tormenting me with it. But I know he doesn't remember; only I get that privilege.

Bobby leads us into a back room, which I'm glad isn't as familiar as the family room we passed. "I got started with the number you gave me. His name is Steve Paxton." In the corner of the room, computers light up the wall.

"Your house is like a tomb," Laila says. "Don't you have sensors?" She waves her hands over her head, but nothing happens. "Bobby," she says in exasperation, and he points at the wall. She finds a switch and flips it on. When the overhead light flickers to life, the breath I didn't realize I was holding slowly seeps through my lips.

"It's after eleven," Bobby says. "It's not like I traipse around the house with all the lights on. Especially when I'm the only one home."

"So, what did you find out?" Duke asks, pointing to one of the screens, where a seedy-looking picture of Poison fills one corner of the monitor.

Bobby sits down at the desk. "Not much. He's been arrested a few times for enhancers, but that's about it. What exactly were you hoping to find out about him?"

"If he's dangerous," Duke says.

"He seems fairly harmless," Bobby says.

So does Bobby, but I know what he's capable of. "Are you sure? Is that the only place you looked?"

Bobby narrows his eyes at me. "I think the police station is a pretty good place to look. But I guess I can check the library to see if he has any outstanding late fees. Knowing you, that would help."

"You don't know me," I say quietly.

"No need to be a jerk," Laila says. "She was just asking. What about his address? Were you able to find that?"

"Yeah." He pulls out a piece of paper from the desk drawer and writes down the address, then hands it to Duke.

"Thanks." Duke slaps him on the back.

My eyes have found the screen again and can't look away from the image of Poison. My mind goes back to the way he had forced me to step forward, held me there without hands. I don't understand that kind of power. It's nothing like my mom's, who Persuades me to do things. If I try hard enough, and recognize what she's doing, I can fight against her influence. But with Poison, I hadn't wanted to move forward, and yet he made me. I was totally at his mercy.

"Did you want to hang out, or are you going to leave with your boyfriend?" Bobby asks. I look around the room and realize Duke and Laila are on their way out. I whirl around and head for the door.

"What did I do to you?" Bobby asks from behind me.

I stop.

"What did you see me do that changed the way you look at me?"

"I saw who you really are."

"Then why did you come here tonight?" He sounds far away and small.

"Because for some reason Duke trusts you." I run out of the

room and catch up with Duke. He slides his arm across my shoulder and kisses my temple. I cuddle into him.

"So what are we doing now?" I ask.

"Surveillance."

CHAPTER 22

phe•NO[R]M•e•non: *n.* someone who thinks
his existence is an impressive occurrence

I've been staring out the window for the last two hours, even though Laila told me she probably wouldn't get here until six, just enough time to freshen up and get to the football game. It's been almost a month since I've been gone, but it feels like I haven't seen her in an eternity.

When a truck pulls up in front of the house, I race out the door. She's halfway up the walk by the time we reach each other. Neither one of us is a squealer, but we embrace and proceed to jump up and down screaming.

She pulls away.

I point. "You're wearing sunglasses."

"That's because it's insanely bright here. Crazy story. I stopped at a gas station, feeling mentally tired, and like an idiot I asked the guy behind the register if they had any Brain Food. He looked at me all weird, and I remembered that huge lecture we got before leaving the Compound about not letting things slip, so I Erased a minute of his memory."

"You did not."

She laughs. "Totally did. I thought I was going to have to zap the whole store, but there was only one other woman, and she was distracted putting this nasty-looking hot dog into a bun. There was a rack of sunglasses next to the register, so I grabbed a pair and bought them. Hopefully feeling them on my face will make me think more like a Norm."

I smile. "Have I told you how much I miss you yet?"

"I miss you too. When are you coming home?"

"Come on, let's get your stuff, and I'll show you around." I help her pull out a bag from the truck bed. "You rented a truck?"

"Yeah, sure, me and all my money. No. I borrowed this from that guy who rebuilds useless Norm crap."

"Obviously not so useless after all."

"Funny. That's what he said when I was scanning over the rest of my monthly allowance if he let me use it. I mean, I know we can't have Para-tech out here, but seriously?" She pounds the tailgate.

Inside my dad hugs Laila. "Good to see you again. How is life at home?" He grabs the duffel bag off her shoulder and slings it over his own. I smile, loving that my dad treats Laila like a daughter. I hope that in some small way it makes up for the fact that her father doesn't.

"If I said fine, you'd know I was lying, so I'll just say same as always."

"Keep your chin up."

"Yes, sir."

"Let's go get ready," I say.

"Where are you girls going?" my dad asks.

"Remember, I told you we're going to the football game?"

"Oh, that's right." He leads the way down the hall, deposits the bag in my room, and leaves us to get ready.

"For an older guy, your dad is hot," Laila says, staring at the door he just shut.

"Gross." So much for thinking of him like a father.

"I'm just saying." Laila moves her bag onto my bed, opens it, and pulls out several papers. "Tell me you love me," she says, presenting them to me.

"What is . . ." I start to ask, but then realize it's an alphabetical list of all the kids at school. Next to the names are their abilities. "You are awesome."

"I've highlighted the football players," she says.

I meet her eyes. "And?"

"There aren't any Mass Manipulators on the team, if that's who injured his muscle. And if someone was making him relaxed to catch him off guard for the injury, there's only one Mood Controller." She takes the papers back from me and flips through a few pages. "This guy . . . Andrew. But he's not a starter. In fact, he's a freshman. Didn't you say Trevor got hurt *last* year?"

"Yeah. He did." I glance over her arm to look at the page. "Maybe their Mood Controller from last year graduated. Maybe Andrew is the replacement. What's a freshman doing on the varsity team anyway? He could easily soothe the opposing team's emotions from the bench."

"True." She tosses the papers onto my bed. "We'll have to keep an eye out. Come on, let's beautify ourselves."

We walk through the parking lot on our way to the stadium. Laila stops at a car, pulls out her lipstick, and bends over to use the side mirror. She growls. "I can't see a thing." She yanks on the mirror, and the car alarm screams at her.

"Come on, let's go," I say, glancing around to see if the owner is nearby.

"No, I got this." She holds up her hands, clad in lacy fingerless gloves, and the car goes silent.

My mouth falls open. "What the crap was that?"

"Okay, so don't get mad."

"Why would I get mad?"

"I've been hanging out with Bobby, and he taught me how to extend my ability."

"Extend your . . . what is that supposed to mean?"

"You know, kind of like advanced ability control."

My mind flies through all the lectures my mom has ever given me about the dangers of untested mind experiments. "Are you crazy? Do you want brain damage? There's a reason we're not supposed to push our abilities until our minds are fully developed." I know I sound a lot like my mother, but in this case my mother is right.

Laila snaps her gum. "What reason is that? So adults can maintain control over us? They just don't think we can handle the extra power. They think we'll abuse it."

"I don't know why they'd think that," I say sarcastically, pointing to the car whose alarm she just disabled. "How?"

"I mentally find the car's electrical board and Erase the last thirty seconds of its 'memory.'" She finishes with air quotes.

I glance between the car and her several times.

"And there's more," she says. "Watch this." She holds up her hands and closes her eyes. I'm not sure what I'm waiting for. The car has already been wiped. But then suddenly, with a jolt that radiates through my body, the car wails back to life. I throw my hands over my ears, my shoulders going up as well. She smiles wide and then quiets the car again. I don't move.

She points at me. "Why are you doing that? Why didn't you just mentally muffle it?"

Why *did* I do that? Out of practice? "I don't know. I was surprised, I guess. . . ." I lower my hands and stare at the car. My mind races. "Did you just . . ."

"I restored its memory."

My mouth opens and closes twice before I'm finally able to

say, "I didn't know you could do that."

"I couldn't. Advanced. Ability. Control." She laughs. "Come on." She tugs on my arm, and we start walking again.

"You've been hanging out with Bobby?" I ask, the rest of her admission finally catching up with me. How did *he* of all people end up in her new pool of friends? "Bobby."

"I know, I know." She waves it off like it's no big deal. "But I had to. I wanted to be able to defend myself. My dad has this creepy friend who keeps coming around the house, threatening my mom and me, and I found out Bobby is really good at enhancing abilities."

We cut through the dark baseball field, toward the football stadium. "Some guy threatened you? Is everything okay?"

"Yeah, it's fine. He's a loser who gets off on scaring girls. It probably makes him feel tough. Nothing I can't handle."

I hook my arm in hers. "Be careful, okay?"

"Yeah, I will."

"Speaking of, have you heard about a murdered girl around our age in the Compound?"

"What? No. Why?"

"It's something my dad is investigating, but if you haven't heard about it, I guess that means they haven't released it to the public yet."

"A murder? In the Compound? Are you sure? Who did it?"

"They're interviewing suspects. It might not be a murder at all. They think she may have killed herself."

"That would make more sense. That sucks. So does this mean you've been snooping in your dad's things? You naughty girl."

I kick at the dirt as we head toward the lit-up ticket booth. "I know, he would be so mad."

"I'm surprised you've been able to keep it from him."

"He just hasn't asked the right questions yet. Let's hope he doesn't start."

We hand our tickets to the lady when we reach the booth and then enter the stadium. The sound of the band playing and the noise of the crowd immediately make my heart pound.

"Look at you grinning like a fool," Laila says.

"I'm excited for you to meet my new friends. And for them to meet you. And don't forget . . ."

"Yeah, we've never heard anything about Lincoln High."

"Thank goodness we've never been to an away game before, or they might've recognized us."

"Your lack of school spirit has proven useful. Where exactly does Trevor think you're from?"

"California."

"They made you a California girl?"

"Not technically. But I claimed it. I've been there. Once."

She rubs her brightly colored lips together. "So, what—do you describe It's a Small World when he asks about your home?"

"I usually just change the subject." I grab hold of her arm. "Come on, there they are."

"We should mess with some Norm minds tonight," she says, with a mischievous smile. "Make them do funny things."

"No." I squeeze her arm, forcing her to look at me. "Don't. They're really nice and smart and . . . just don't, okay?"

"Okay, okay." We continue our walk toward the group. "Which one's Trevor?" she asks. I notice they're all dressed normally tonight, no painted bodies or wigs. It must be for the "surveillance mission" we're on.

"Wait, let me guess." She slows her walk. "Who would Addie be drawn to? Cute, but understated. Shy, but confident. The dark-haired guy with his boot on the bench in front of him." She points directly at Trevor.

The group hasn't noticed Laila and me yet, but Trevor is the only one who isn't moving—his eyes are fixated on the field. Rowan is climbing over Jason and reaching under the seat. Jason is attempting to push him to the ground. Daniel is blowing up a beach ball. Katie and Lisa have their cell phones out and are texting, and Brandon is trying to get Lisa's attention.

"And where is Trevor's girlfriend?"

I point to the field. "She's a cheerleader."

"And yet Trevor's not watching her; he's staring at the boys throwing around a football."

"I didn't say that was Trevor."

"Is it?"

I laugh. "Yes."

"That's what I thought." Laila fluffs her hair, laughs, and then says, "Let's do this."

We arrive at the group. "Hey, guys," I say.

"Addison." Rowan jumps up. He's holding a foam hand, and

he pokes my shoulder with it. "Who's your hot friend?"

"You must be Rowan," Laila says.

"Rowan, this is Laila, my best friend from back home."

Rowan raises one eyebrow at me. "Welcome, best friend from back home. You can sit next to me."

I shake my head. "Rowan, have I taught you nothing?"

His fake smile turns into a real one. "I'm a slow learner."

I point out everyone else, saying their names, and they each give Laila a wave.

"Holy crap, Addie, you have friends. Lots of them." We work our way down the aisle, past Daniel, Katie, Lisa, and Brandon to Trevor. He stands. "Hey, Addison."

"Hi, this is Laila."

"Good to meet you, Laila."

Laila takes his outstretched hand and shakes it. "I heard you're my competition."

Trevor looks at me with a furrowed brow.

I throw her the thanks-a-lot look. "I told her you were my *future* best friend. But with a mouth like hers, that future is getting closer."

"Oh, I see," he says. "I didn't realize I was competing for *that* title." His emphasis on the word *that* makes me give him a double take. When he maintains his normal expression, I decide I must've imagined it.

"I still think I have the advantage, despite my big mouth," Laila says. "You may be just as good-looking as I am, but I'm tougher. Plus I've known her for ten years longer. So I don't think we need to fight yet."

"That's good."

"Are these for us?" I ask, pointing to the two empty spots beside him.

"Yeah, I didn't want to be put on any more death lists, so I thought I'd save you seats."

We all sit down, Trevor on my left, Laila on my right. Laila leans forward. "Don't worry, Addie is more bark than bite."

When Laila leans back, Rowan is there, squatting by her legs and looking at the three of us with a serious expression. "Operation Lincoln High School is about to start."

Next to me, Trevor sighs as if he honestly thought Rowan wouldn't go through with this and just realized he thought wrong. I try not to laugh and nudge his shoulder with mine.

"We will be infiltrating their student section in shifts," Rowan continues. "So, Addie, work on your flirting, it's lacking."

"Hey," I object, even though it's true.

"Laila," he continues, unfazed, "just walk over there, and any male with eyes will notice you."

Laila laughs. "I like this one." She takes his face in her hands and kisses his cheek. "He's adorable."

When she lets go, Rowan loses his balance and lands on his backside, a goofy grin on his face, and a red lip print on his cheek. "So we'll start after kickoff." Instead of taking a seat next to Laila, like I expect him to do at this point, he scurries off.

"Speaking of all bark and no bite," Trevor says.

"Well, Laila is both, so he'd better watch out."

The band starts to play, and I turn to Laila and say in her ear, "Rowan may want to do his infiltrate-the-student-section mission that we both know is going to result in nothing. . . ."

She nods.

"But I want to do some real digging. Later I'm going to sneak into the locker room and spy on some conversations. You think you can cover for me?"

"Of course."

"Thanks." The band's tune changes to a marching beat, and the football team runs out.

Laila claps her hands and whispers, "Duke's almost here."

After our team runs through a banner and the tunnel of cheerleaders to loud cheers from the crowd, Lincoln High's football players barrel out. Duke runs to midfield, points up at the stands like he's some sort of rock star, and then bows. Bows!

"Oh, brother," I mutter.

"Not a fan?" Trevor asks.

"Not at all."

"He's actually a pretty nice guy."

My head whips toward Trevor. "You know him? I mean, off-the-field know him?"

"Yeah, we were both at this All-American awards banquet thing. They sat us at the same table. We spent like four hours together making fun of all the awards. To ourselves, of course." He nods down to the field. The teams are now at their own benches, getting ready for the first play of the game. "He's really good. I understand why he'd bow."

No amount of greatness can make me understand that level of cockiness. "Did you ever bow?"

"I was never that good."

"But you were at the same awards banquet. You must've been one of the best. Maybe this year you would've been better than him."

He shrugs. "Doesn't help to waste my time thinking about would've-beens."

Laila whispers, "He says to the girl with a mind full of them."

CHAPTER 23

in•com•PA•RA•ble: *adj.* unequaled in greatness

My dad looks older than I remember him looking. Tired. Even his smile seems strained. "Hi, baby. I've missed you." He gives me a hug.

"Is everything okay?"

"Work is just keeping me busy."

I tilt my head, trying to decide if "busyness" is a good enough excuse for the stress he's trying to hide with a smile.

"I'm glad you're here." He turns me sideways and grabs my blue strip of hair. "So this is what has your mom worried?"

"Yeah," Laila says, coming up the walk with our bags, which my dad immediately takes from her. "Isn't it awesome, Mr. C?"

"*Awesome* isn't exactly the word I was thinking of, but it's far from Future Crime Lord."

"Exactly," I say with a sigh. "She grounded me over it."

"As she should've," he says with a smirk, making me know he just has to say that as a responsible adult but doesn't really mean it. I've missed him so much.

"We hate to show up and then run, but we're going to catch the football game."

"No worries. I know you came for the game. You're all mine tomorrow though."

"For sure."

He shows me to a room that looks more sterile than a hospital and says, "I know it's kind of plain, but it's yours for whenever you visit, so feel free to put up your comics pictures and stuff."

"Thanks, Dad. I will." He starts to leave, and I stop him with, "Are you sure you're okay?"

He chuckles. "I'm fine, Addie."

As Laila and I get ready in front of the cramped bathroom mirror, she asks, "Did you and Duke do any more surveillance last night at Poison's house?"

"No, we didn't have time. Why, did you?"

"Yes. But it was nothing different from last time. Just druggies going in and out. Is it weird to you that half the druggies are teenagers?"

I go over my hair with a straightener, wondering if I should've reverted back to curls for the wetter air. It's already a little frizzy.

"I know. I found that odd as well. I don't know why, but I guess I thought our classmates were smarter than that."

She adds some black eyeliner under her eyes. "You know what it has confirmed to me, though?"

"What?"

"That we've been worried over nothing. Duke feels the same, right?"

"Yeah, he does. There is nothing but extreme-brain-cell-deterioration going on at Poison's house."

At the game, I wish I had brought an extra layer of clothing—it's pretty cold. I blow on my hands and then rub them rapidly across my thighs. Laila is bouncing up and down next to me, and I can't tell if it's in an effort to stay warm or if she's excited. She solves the mystery when she says, "I don't believe we've never been to an away game before. What's wrong with us? This is fun."

"Yeah, exciting."

"The Norms seem so . . . normal."

"Here they come." I point to where the team, led by Duke, runs out of the tunnel as the announcer says a drawn-out version of our school name.

Duke runs to center field and bows.

I sigh. "I wish he wouldn't do stuff like that. It makes him seem more cocky than he is."

"It's just Duke having fun. If we were closer, you'd see the teasing twinkle in his eye."

Teasing or not, the whole stadium probably thinks he's full of himself. Why doesn't that bother him? To our left is the other team's student section. I notice Laila looking over.

"What?" I ask.

"Norm boys are pretty cute."

I scan them as well. They seem like the guys I see on a daily basis at my own school.

"We should mess with their minds."

I laugh. "How?"

"Okay, pick out one of those boys and I'll get him to come over here."

"How?"

"He'll think it was his own idea. You should do it too, since you're supposed to be practicing Thought Placement. How is that going anyway?"

Not well, and I'm tired of practicing. Whenever we have free time, it's all Duke wants to do. "I think I'm getting better."

"Prove it. We'll have a race. Whoever gets her boy to come over first wins."

I roll my head to the side and groan. "Fine."

"Okay, name your boy, so we're not trying to call the same one over."

This time I study them closer. "The one with his hands in his pockets. Cowboy boots. Dark hair." He looks sort of familiar to me, but I can't place him.

She rolls her eyes. "Of course, typical Addie boy. I pick the guy with the foam finger."

"Which one?"

"The one jumping all over the place. Shoulder-length hair, beautiful skin."

I zero in on him. Just when I think I've figured out Laila's taste in guys, which for a while I thought was just any male between the ages of sixteen and twenty-two, she surprises me by picking someone completely different. Like this guy, for example; he's cute enough, but thin and too dressed up for a football game. I thought Laila liked to have the upper hand in the style department.

"Ready?" she asks.

I nod.

"Go."

Without trying to be obvious, I take several glances at my guy and concentrate. *Go talk to the girl with the blue stripe in her hair,* I say in my mind and then try to push it into his. He meets my eyes once and then looks away. I try again, but by this time Laila's guy is already walking toward us. I let out a low growl, and she laughs. "Ha! I picked a guy with less impulse control. You have to look for the wild ones, Addie, not the conservative ones."

Ah, so that was her criteria this time.

He takes a seat two rows behind us. Does he think he's being subtle? Poor guy is being told he wants to come over here and has no idea what to do now that he's here.

220

"I told him he wanted to sit by us. That's not really by us." Laila turns around, looks up at him, and says, "Really? Are you that much of a wimp?"

"He's probably intimidated by you," I say, but he walks down the cement steps.

"What's your name?" Laila asks, when he sits down next to her.

"Rowan."

"I'm Laila. This is Addie."

"Hi," I say.

"You guys here with the visiting team?" he asks.

"That's kind of why we're sitting in this section."

"This is a long way to come for a game. You must be friends with some of the players."

"As a matter of fact, that's Addie's boyfriend." She points to the field, where Duke is dropping back for a pass.

"The quarterback?"

"Yeah, his name's Duke Rivers. Have you heard of him?"

"He's up for All-American this year, isn't he?"

I shrug my shoulders, but Laila says, "Yes. Is he up against any of your players?"

"No. Our quarterback sustained a major injury."

"That's too bad," I say.

"It really is. He was awesome. He might've beat Duke this year." He points back to where he had been sitting. "That's him right there—Trevor."

Laila laughs, and I know exactly why she's laughing—Rowan's pointing at the guy I had done Thought Placement on. Was that

221

why he looked so familiar? Had I seen his picture in some of Duke's football albums?

"What's so funny?" Rowan asks.

"Nothing, my *friend* just thought he was cute. And my friend swears she doesn't like football players."

"Ah, well, he's sort of taken." He points to a gorgeous cheerleader waving her pom-poms around down on the field. Just the kind of girl I would expect a guy like Trevor to be with.

"How can someone be 'sort of' taken?" Laila asks.

"He broke up with her about a month ago, but she keeps coming around, and he's too nice to tell her not to."

"Wow," Laila says. "We just have to put a quarter in you, and you spit out all kinds of information."

Rowan's face reddens. "What about you guys? What's your school like?"

Laila shrugs. "Just your average high school."

"Then how come you never host sports there?"

"Because our stadium is a piece of crap. And our school would rather spend the money busing us all over the place instead of fixing it. The school is run by a bunch of idiots." We had been trained by the Containment Committee the day before on what we were and were not allowed to say to outsiders. This is an example of an acceptable answer. Well, close to acceptable. Laila probably found the irony of her last sentence hilarious.

Rowan tilts his head and seems to be studying her sincerity.

"Wait?" she says with a gasp. "Has our real secret been blown?

222

This guy's good. He found out we're all superheroes-in-training and that we're hiding out so no one will know our secret identities."

I barely hold back the laugh that wants to exit through my nose.

"Funny." He laughs.

"You're adorable," Laila says. "I bet you're feeling the desire to buy me a soda right about now, aren't you?"

His eyes widen a little and I know Laila had probably made him think that right before she said it. "Yes. I'd love to."

"You going to be okay for a minute alone, Addie?"

"Yeah, of course. Be nice to the boy." When she leaves, I turn my attention back to the field and notice Duke on the sidelines looking up at me. He waves, then blows me a kiss, and my cheeks go red. A few girls behind me let out a dreamy sigh. I lift my hand in a half wave. When Duke goes back to his game, I self-consciously glance toward the Norm student section. Trevor is gone.

CHAPTER 24

NO[R]M•i•nal: *adj.* being true in name only but not in reality

After doing our round in enemy territory—Lincoln High's student section—and finding nothing except some friends to chat with, Laila and I settle in for the second half of the game. When the whistle blows, indicating the start of the quarter, I'm surprised Trevor isn't in his seat, watching intently. I scan the sidelines to see if he's talking to Stephanie. He's not. Stephanie's in the middle of a high kick.

"Hey," I say to Laila. "I'm going to see if I can find Trevor. I'll be right back."

"Okay."

Now that the game has started again, the blacktop behind

the stadium is deserted. The lights from the lone building—the snack hut—create a glowing island in the otherwise dark alley. I immediately see the broad back of Trevor, standing at the counter, giving the cashier some money. When she hands him his soda, he turns away from the stadium steps where I stand and walks into the darkness. I have to run to catch up to him.

"Trevor," I call, breathless.

He turns. "Oh, hi, Addison."

"What are you doing? Aren't you going to watch the rest of the game?"

"I . . . no, actually."

"Why not?"

He takes a swig from his soda. "I just feel a little stiff. Thought a walk would help."

"That's a good excuse, but what's the real reason?"

He smiles. "Did you inherit some of your father's lie-detector genes?"

"Maybe," I say, even though the only bit of Discernment I have has to do with manipulating time. The reason I know he's lying is because he's not acting like himself. He's been even quieter than normal all night, which isn't saying a lot, because he's pretty quiet all the time.

"I guess even though I'm usually good at not thinking about 'would've-beens,' I'm having a hard time tonight. I'll blame it on the team we're playing."

"Let's just blame everything on them."

"Sounds good."

I wait for him to say more, but he doesn't. He just quietly drinks his soda. I know the would've-been that he's having a hard time not thinking about—his injury. But I wonder if there's more to it. "What are you thinking about?"

He rubs his shoulder. "The doctor says I can throw again next week, but I realize I'm never going to play competitively again."

I nod.

He takes another long drink from his soda, finishing it off. He seems to be stalling, maybe waiting for me to leave, but I don't want to. I want him to talk. I want to be here for him. "It's not that I'm not strong enough," he finally says.

"Of course not," I agree too quickly, then laugh a little. Technically I shouldn't know that, but I just happened to have seen him with his shirt off and took plenty of time appreciating the evidence of his statement.

"I am."

"I know. I just agreed."

"But you're laughing. You don't think I am." He looks at the soda can he's holding, turns it sideways, and then crushes it between his hands.

I laugh harder. "Was that meant as proof?"

He smiles. "Yes, actually."

"You totally got that out of *Ninja Wars Two*. I remember that. Naoto's eyes are like bugging out of his head while he crushes a soda can." I bite my lip to stop my laughing. "You're such a nerd."

"You're the one who remembered the comic. You can't call me a nerd."

"Total nerd."

He grabs me by the wrist, pulls me toward him, and somehow lifts me up and is holding me off the ground, his arms wrapped around my thighs, before I can blink.

My heart is immediately in my throat. "Okay, that's much better proof of your strength," I say, patting his shoulders. "I believe you. You can put me down now."

He doesn't move. His face is serious again. "It's not that I'm not strong enough to play. It's just that specific motion."

"Throwing?" My hands are gripping his shoulders, their solidness further proof of his claim.

"Yeah."

So a Paranormal precisely targeted his throwing muscles? It's hard for me to believe someone would do that on purpose. But what else could it be? I have to find out who. Trevor loosens his hold, and I slide gently to the ground. A little light-headed, I take a few wobbly steps back.

"Tonight, watching Duke play, was hard." He pauses for a long moment, and I don't want to push him into continuing, so I hold my tongue. "Do you ever feel like you do something or are something for so long that it defines you?"

If only he knew. "Yes. I know exactly how that feels."

"Really?"

"Yes. Sometimes I feel like I'm slowly floating away. I'm

constantly looking for something to grab on to so I don't lose myself." Mostly because without my ability to define me, I'm not sure who I am or how others see me.

He nods like he understands exactly what I'm talking about. "I know I was only a junior last year, but I had my whole future planned. Now I feel like I'm still trying to hold on to what I was, even though the thing that made me that person is gone. And everyone else seems to be hanging on to that person too . . . man, are you sure you want a future best friend who is such a whiner? Just ignore me. I'll be back to pretending tomorrow."

His thumb is hooked in the front pocket of his jeans, and I have an overwhelming desire to hold his hand. To comfort him. But I know I can't. He has Stephanie for that. I'm supposed to punch him on the shoulder and tell him to buck up or something. I settle for a speech. "Whining is definitely something best friends are allowed to do in front of each other—it's in the handbook. And you don't have to pretend with me, Trevor. You are more than a football player to me. I didn't even know that version of you. I only know who you are now—a great friend, easy to talk to and be around, an amazing artist, an awesome brother . . . a total nerd." I smile. "And that's just what I've learned in the last few weeks."

The distant lights from the stadium mask half his face in shadows. "Thanks, Addison. And for the record, whatever you left behind, whatever has you feeling like you're floating here, doesn't define you either."

I want to ask him what does define me. Who he sees when he looks at me. But I can't get the words out. They sit in the back of my throat for fear he won't know the answer to that question either.

"But," he continues, "if you need something to hold on to until you feel grounded, I make a pretty good anchor."

An unexpected feeling of warmth fills my chest and makes me want to hug him or cry. I can't do either. "Yeah, you proved that."

He laughs. "Do you want to go watch the rest of the game?"

"Not really, but I left Laila up there."

"Okay, I'll see you Monday then." I watch him until he disappears into the blackness.

When I get back, Laila gives me a sideways glance. "Where's your boyfriend?"

"He's not my boyfriend."

"Oh, right . . ."

"What did I miss?" I ask, changing the subject. When Laila gets an idea in her head, no matter how off base it is, it's best not to try to talk her out of it.

"Only Duke being awesome," she says with a smile. "But I'm sure he'll do it again."

Fifteen minutes pass, and she leans toward me. "Told you."

I glance up at the scoreboard—21 to 3. Five minutes left.

We're getting our butts kicked. "Are you ready to cover for me? I'm going down to the locker room."

"Yeah, go already."

In the locker room I position myself behind a bin of soccer balls and wait. It feels like it takes forever, especially since the grass/sweat combination isn't a pleasant smell. Why am I doing this?

A couple years ago Laila showed up to lunch holding the janitor's golf-cart code and a skateboard attached to a rope. "We won't get caught. Search it," she said, when I refused. I did. Even though the skateboard path led to one of the best days ever, it also led to the principal's office. I chose the other option. The safe one.

My knees scream out in pain from squatting behind the soccer balls for so long. I am doing this because I have to know . . . for Trevor. Just as I stand to stretch them out, the hollers and stomping feet of a large body of people echo through the halls. I push myself farther into my hideout.

Before I had the brilliant idea to inject myself into this situation, I hadn't thought about the logistics of what would actually happen in the locker room. But when I hear water running, I turn all the way around and press my face against the wall. Slowly, some of the players trickle into the rows of lockers, where I can pick up on conversations. Nothing interesting is being said. I don't know what I had hoped to hear.

Obviously no one is going to come out and say, *So who should we purposefully maim next week?*

"Duke, great game," a loud voice says. Several others agree with the comment and give an appreciative *whoop.*

"Thanks, guys. You too."

"That was some great soothing out there tonight," a guy I don't recognize says.

Then Duke says, "Just a little influence is all it takes to make the other team as docile as little girls."

I peer around the soccer balls to see if I can see the Mood Controller—I'm assuming Andrew—who Duke is talking to. I recognize one of the guys standing next to him—Ray—they were constantly together. The other guy is scrawnier; maybe he's the freshman. These were the people who ruined Trevor's career—Duke, obviously the mastermind, and his minions. But who did the actual injuring? Laila had said there weren't any Mass Manipulators on the team. The only Mass Manipulator I know is . . .

Bobby? Could he be involved somehow? And why? Did he even know Duke? Did he go to the football games? I'd have to ask Laila.

I stand by the soccer balls until the locker room has emptied out. I feel like my brain has been emptied out as well. Disappointment is slowly filling in the curiosity of before. Deep down I thought I would prove Rowan wrong, not right. I sink to the floor. Is this really the kind of people we have become?

The kind who can use their powers to hurt others without any remorse? I wonder what the locker room sounded like after Trevor's injury had been successfully administered—did they congratulate one another that night? The thought makes me sick.

When I don't hear anyone, I abandon my hideout and walk toward the exit. Apparently I should've walked faster, because Duke rounds the corner and slams right into me, sending me flying backward.

"Oh, jeez," he says, startled. "I'm sorry." He holds out his hand to help me up. "Are you okay?"

"Yes, I'm fine." I ignore his offered hand and push myself up off the ground.

"Hey, you're Addie Coleman."

"Yes. I am."

He flashes me a killer smile. "Clairvoyant, right?"

It catches me off guard to hear someone say my ability out loud like that again. I look around. "Yeah, sort of." I rub at my stinging palm.

"Are you hurt?" He takes my hand in his and inspects it. A chill goes through me as he traces a finger over the tiny scratches on my palm.

His hair smells good and seems to freeze me in place for a moment. I finally regain my senses and take my hand back, wiping it a few times on my jeans. "I'm fine."

One corner of his mouth goes up into a half smile, and my

heart seems to think this is the most adorable thing in the world. I remind myself of who he is and what he's been doing, and the annoyance comes rushing back.

"Laila told me you moved. Did you move here? To Dallas?"

"Yes."

"Well, you're missed."

"I know what you're doing," I say evenly.

He lowers his head with a smile and kicks at the ground. "My flirting isn't very subtle, is it?"

Flirting? "Not that. I'm talking about you and your friends using your abilities to get ahead."

He shrugs his shoulders. "And?"

Anger surges through me. "And it's wrong."

"So you're saying you've never used your ability to help yourself?"

"I don't hurt people."

"Neither do I," he says.

"That's right, you just stand back and let your friends do the dirty work while you reap the benefits. I don't get it. What's in it for them?"

Duke's perfect eyebrows lower, and I'm distracted by the notion that he must pluck them. "What are you talking about?" he asks.

I shake my head. "I'm talking about how one by one your competition is falling down around you and you'll be the only good quarterback left standing. Congratulations, your plan is working. I hope your victory feels as hollow as your heart. But at least you'll have your pick of colleges, right?"

Duke's smile has fallen and has been replaced by a look of shock. "What?"

"Don't try to deny it. I heard you telling your buddy that all he has to do is influence emotions a little."

"Yeah, emotions are influenced, but not for the reasons you're claiming. It just makes the competition less aggressive, a little more relaxed. It's not meant to hurt anyone, just to keep me from getting sacked." If my dad were here, I know he'd tell me that Duke is lying. "Listen. Let's talk about this. Can I buy you a burger or something?"

All I want to do is punch Duke in the stomach on Trevor's behalf, and he wants to buy me a burger? "No."

"Addison?" I whirl around to see Trevor standing in the wide corridor. The guys stare at each other, and I panic. I walk quickly toward Trevor.

"Call me sometime, Addie," Duke says from behind me. Now I want to punch him in the stomach for my own reasons. I keep walking, grab Trevor's hand, and lead him away. His hand is warm and strong, and I don't let it go even when we're outside.

"What was that all about? Do you . . . know him?"

If I'm ever going to tell him the truth about where I'm from, now would be the perfect time. "No. I don't. I was just trying to find stuff out, you know, spy. For Rowan."

I'm trying to walk as fast as possible, but Trevor slows down, and I'm forced to slow down with him.

"And?"

"And what?"

He squeezes my hand. "Did you find out anything?"

Only that Rowan is right. You were injured on purpose. I want to say that so bad, but how can I when I'm not allowed to talk about abilities? I hate lying to him so much that my stomach is rebelling against me with painful cramps. "I know you said Duke is a nice guy, but I don't see it."

CHAPTER 25

dis•PAR•Age: *v. to make someone feel stupid*

Duke runs out of the locker room and picks me up in a hug. "It was so good to have you here at my game. Looking up in the stands and seeing you there made me play better."

He is so full of crap, but it still makes me smile. "Really?"

"You'll have to come see some of my college games next year."

"Where will that be?"

"You tell me."

"Funny."

Two of Duke's teammates come out of the locker room. One is a smaller guy whose name I don't know, and the other is Duke's best friend, Ray. He's at least a head taller than Duke and twice as wide. He points at me, "Hey, Addie, you seen my future yet?"

I smile. "I haven't been looking."

Duke clears his throat and looks over my shoulder. I turn to see the Norm guy Laila and I had seen before—Trevor. He looks sad? Angry, maybe? "Hey, man," Duke says. "Are you checking out my girlfriend?"

It's dark outside, but Trevor's face deepens a shade. "No, not at all."

"Why not? She's hot."

"Stop it, Duke," I say.

"I'm just messing with you, man."

Trevor looks among the four of us, probably wishing he could disappear. I have a similar feeling. "I didn't mean to interrupt," Trevor says. "I just wanted to say great game tonight."

Duke puts his hand on his own chest and says, "Thanks, man, that means a lot. How's your shoulder doing?"

"It's all right. Anyway, good to see you."

When he leaves, Duke's two teammates exchange a look and a laugh that I'm sure Trevor hears. "That wasn't funny," I say.

"It was a little funny," Duke says.

They laugh again and the two of them start to walk away. "See you two later," Ray says, over his shoulder.

"Bye, Ray," Duke says. "See ya, Andrew."

I stare off into the distance, where I can barely make out the dark shadow of Trevor's retreating form. "How do you know that Trevor guy?" I ask Duke.

"Is that his name? I had completely forgotten. Was it obvious?"

"No, you pulled it off pretty well."

"Good." He pulls me close again. "We were up for the same award last year."

"Who won?"

"Is that even a real question?" He smiles at me, and I roll my eyes.

"Do you always get everything you want?"

"Pretty much." He kisses me. His lips are soft, and I try not to forget myself. He pulls away. "So where's Laila?"

"I'm not sure. She went and had a soda with some Norm boy and never came back. I think she was just toying with him, practicing Thought Placement. I'll text her." I pull out my phone. *Hey, are you ready to go? My dad said we can all stay the night at his house.*

Duke's reading over my shoulder and he asks, "Is your dad going to like me?"

"Doesn't everyone like you?"

My phone chimes. *I'll meet you at the truck in ten minutes.*

Duke and I have been waiting for Laila for so long that the parking lot has completely emptied out. We even waved goodbye to the team bus heading back to the Compound. And now Duke's giving me a play-by-play of the entire game. I lower the tailgate on the truck my mom rented for us and sit. "You do realize I was there, right?"

"Yes, but you weren't watching half the time, and I know

you're dying to know what you missed."

If by "dying," he meant that it was bad enough watching from the stands and hearing it now without the action is making me die of boredom then, "So true."

He positions himself between my knees, his back to me, and I rest my head against him. His voice vibrates my cheek as he continues to talk. The long day catches up with me and I feel myself drifting.

"I'm coming," Laila yells from across the empty parking lot. "Sorry."

I sit up, shaking my head until I'm fully awake. "How was Normville?"

"Rowan is funny. He is so curious about us. He kept asking the weirdest questions."

"Like what?"

"Like why our school doesn't have a website and why our football players never get injured."

"Did you tell him it's because we're made of steel?" Duke steps away from the tailgate and helps me down.

"No, I just kissed him. That got his easily distracted mind off things."

"You kissed a Norm?" Duke's expression seems stuck between surprise and disgust.

"Yeah, I did."

Duke draws his brows together like he's about to ask a scientific question. "Was he any good?"

I laugh so hard that I have to steady myself against the truck.

"It's not that funny. I'm just curious. She kissed a Norm, Addie. As in no abilities whatsoever."

Laila's lips purse, and her fists tighten—probably because I'm still laughing and Duke still looks partially disgusted. "Okay, Mr. Mover, how does Telekinesis help you kiss?"

"It doesn't help, but when I kiss, I heighten all my senses, so I can anticipate every move, hear every noise . . ." He trails off when I stop laughing and widen my eyes. "You don't?" he asks me.

"Uh . . ." I turn toward Laila. "Do you?"

"Yes. So there, Duke. You've been kissing a Norm and didn't even realize it."

"I'm not a Norm," I say defensively.

Duke shuts the tailgate. "Don't worry, I never would've guessed."

"I wasn't worried. You guys quite obviously think too much when you kiss. Some things don't require extra thinking. Maybe you're the ones doing it wrong. How are you supposed to feel anything when you have to concentrate so hard?" I know the more I talk, the more defensive I sound. But I can't help it. It's not often you get told you've been kissing wrong. "Let's go."

"My turn to drive," Laila says. I drop the keys into her upturned hand and walk to the passenger door.

"I'm sure you're a great kisser, Addie," Laila says, unlocking the door. I get in.

Duke climbs in next to me. "She is."

The middle seat belt is loose and I tighten it to fit. "Okay, stop talking, both of you. I don't need to be reassured."

Laila puckers her lips as she slides behind the wheel. "Maybe I just wanted to kiss you."

The engine rumbles to life and Duke leans across me, his hand reaching toward the dash. It stops a few inches away from the radio. "How do you turn this thing on?"

"Uh . . ." I study the knobs and buttons, trying to remember. "This one." I push the knob that says Power, and the radio blares to life.

At my house, Duke grabs my hand as we walk up the path. "I'm nervous."

"Really? Why? You're so at ease with my mom. Just tell the truth, and my dad will like you."

He nods and squeezes my hand. We walk inside, and my dad is sitting in his chair watching what looks to be one of his criminal-interview tapes, but I can't tell because he turns it off too fast.

Duke drops my hand and extends his toward my dad. "Nice to meet you, Mr. Coleman. I'm Duke."

"Duke. Hello. How did the game go?"

"We won, so I guess that means good."

"You guess?" My dad doesn't like halfhearted statements. He thinks everyone should be able to answer definitively.

"There are always ways to improve," Duke clarifies.

"I hear you have your choice of colleges next year. Any closer to picking one?"

Considering how many times people ask him about college when I'm around, I can't imagine how much Duke has to deal with that question. It has to get old—I know I'm sick of it. Maybe because it reminds me that he'll be gone next year.

"Yes, sir."

"You're closer to picking?" I ask.

"Getting closer."

My dad stares at him for a long time, and I wonder how he could think there is something to analyze in that question.

I grab my dad's forearm, and he turns his attention to me. "Well, Dad, we're pretty tired. Where do you want Duke to sleep?"

His face is hard when he says, "The room across from mine."

I wait outside the bathroom, toothbrush in hand, for Duke to finish. The doorknob rattles, but he doesn't come out. Soon the door is banging against the frame.

I take a step forward. "Are you okay?"

The door goes silent. "I think I'm stuck."

I laugh. "Just unlock it."

"I'm trying." The door shakes again. "Stupid Norm doors," he mutters.

I lean my cheek against the frame. "See the little lock in the center of the handle? Just turn it a hundred and eighty degrees. It's old, so it kind of spins. Don't turn it a full circle or it locks again."

The door swings in, and he's suddenly right in front of me. "I'm free," he says. "How'd you know all that? Are you a Norm-relic expert?"

I smile. "I got trapped in there earlier."

He bites his lip. "You look cute without makeup." We trade places, crossing in the doorway. He lets his hand slide across my waist. "Good night."

When I get back to the room after brushing my teeth, Laila is already in the trundle bed, texting.

"Are you talking to your make-out partner?"

"Rowan? No. It's my mom." She tucks the phone under her pillow. "What do you think of Rowan anyway?"

"I think he lives too far away to put any effort into analyzing him." The minute I say that though my mind drifts back to Trevor. "What was with all his questions? Why do you think he's so curious about our school and stuff?"

"I don't know."

I stare at the wall, where moonlight, projected through the blinds, stripes the darkness with white. "You know who Duke kind of knows?"

"Who?"

"Trevor."

"That guy you tried to do Thought Placement on?"

"Yeah." I prop myself up on my elbow. "And he was kind of a jerk to him."

"How so?"

"Trevor came all the way to the locker room to tell Duke that he did a good job, and Duke and his buddies laughed at him. Duke couldn't even remember his name."

Laila laughs. "Are you feeling protective of the cute Norm boy?"

I collapse back down onto my pillow. "No," I say without conviction. He was cute though.

CHAPTER 26

ig•NO[R]•Mi•ny: *n* public shame

Ever since Friday night, I feel terrible. I can't even look Trevor in the eye. I feel like I'm partially responsible for what happened to his shoulder just because my old school is to blame.

Rowan runs up to me in the hall at school and grabs me by the arms. "Addison, Addison," he says, out of breath. "I've been looking for you."

I nearly drop my notebook but manage to keep it in my grip despite Rowan's hold on my arms. "What's up?"

"Stephanie's throwing a party for Trevor tonight. You have to come."

"Is it his birthday?"

"No, this is even better. Today he can throw again."

"Oh, yeah, that's right. And he wanted a party?" Considering what we talked about the other night, how he realized he would never play football competitively again, a party seems like the last thing he would want.

"No, of course not, it's a surprise."

"Rowan, I don't think that's a good idea."

"No, it's a great idea." He looks around and then lowers his voice. "So how's your friend Laila doing? Has she asked about me yet?"

If Rowan thinks Laila kissing him on the cheek is a big deal to her, he is going to be sorely disappointed. "Um . . . no?"

He scans the hall. "There's Katie. I gotta go invite her." He starts to leave but then turns around and writes on my notebook cover. "That's Steph's address. Six o'clock. Don't be late."

At five forty-five I show up at Stephanie's house. I know I have to talk to Trevor about my old school, about the fact that I'm not actually from California at all. If I don't, I might be eaten alive by the guilt that is now in the process of gnawing a hole through my stomach. I vow that I'll find the right time tonight.

Stephanie answers the door, and her smile disappears. "Oh, hey, Addison."

I look her up and down. "You're wearing your cheer uniform."

"The whole cheer team is here. It's supposed to remind Trevor of how we first met."

"Oh." I wonder if Trevor wants to remember that. Okay, not

completely true—what I really wonder is if *I* want Trevor to remember that.

"Come in. The party's out back." She leads me through the entry and then to an enormous kitchen, where she grabs something out of the cupboard and continues on through some French doors into the yard.

The backyard is big and set up like a mini football stadium—lines painted across the grass and everything. In the tiny end zone is a bin full of footballs. My eyes slowly drift, following the lines, to the opposite end zone a good fifty feet away, where an empty bucket sits waiting. We join a couple of other cheerleaders.

"Are we going to play a game and see how many of us can land a football in that bucket?" I ask, hoping Stephanie will say yes.

"No. That's for Trevor. He's going to give us a show." Stephanie sweeps her arm through the air and points to the lawn chairs set up on the side.

"This is his first day. You probably shouldn't push it too hard."

She exchanges a glance with the girl next to her. The kind of glance that says they talk about me when I'm not around. "This is the day he's been looking forward to for a year."

"Him or you?" I try to say it nice, but her sour expression indicates I may have failed.

"What's that supposed to mean? All of us have been excited for this day. You don't know because you weren't here." The girls nod their heads in agreement. Stephanie starts to put her hands on her hips, but then must remember she's holding something because she looks down and says, "Oh." She hands the small plastic bottle she had retrieved from the kitchen to the girl on her right. "We only had Tylenol. Will that work?"

Before I think better of it, I say, "What's that?" They all freeze and look at me. My brain races, searching through the Norm Products unit we had to take in school.

"What, people don't get headaches in California?" Stephanie asks with a sneer.

We get headaches; we just don't need a pill to cure them. And for injuries too serious to self-cure, we have Healers. "Tylenol? Oh, I thought you said Lionel." It's the lamest cover-up ever. I blame my inability to tell a decent lie on my dad and his power.

"You're from California?" one of the girls asks.

"Yes."

"I have family there," she says. "What part?"

It might be my guilty conscience making them look like a pack of velociraptors ready to devour their meal, but it's also possible they suspect my lie. I clear my throat. "Near Disneyland." I point to the ice chest on the patio. "I'm just going to get something to drink."

"Yeah, okay. Rowan should be here soon," Stephanie says, like that's the only reason I came.

I sit on a lawn chair sipping water while the backyard fills up with people. The more crowded it gets, the more nervous I get for Trevor. When Rowan arrives, I try to express my concerns to him, but he's too busy being the life of the party and at one point turns to me and says, "Addison, relax. Have fun. We're at a party." I realize it's pointless.

Eventually the music is turned down and several people start shushing everyone. "He's here. He's coming."

When Trevor walks through the back door and everyone yells, "Surprise!" he looks genuinely shocked.

"Wow, Stephanie, thanks," he says. "What's the occasion?"

She blushes and gives him a hug. "We're just all so excited for you. Today is a big day. The first day of getting back on track to your future." She gestures to the grass, and a couple big spotlights come on. I watch his face. What starts off as a genuine smile tightens to a forced one.

"What's all that?"

"You're going to show us what you've got."

I want to scream, *You don't have to, Trevor,* but I know he's a big boy and can make his own decisions. Stephanie takes a few steps back and yells, "Give me a T!" The other cheerleaders jump up and fall into formation behind her while they finish spelling out Trevor's name. I have to keep myself from laughing out loud when Trevor meets my eyes and gives me the are-they-really-doing-a-cheer? look.

When the cheer ends and Stephanie says, "What's that spell?" The whole party starts chanting Trevor's name. I instantly feel like the worst friend ever. I should've called him, warned him about this, but I was too busy worrying about myself. Even *I* hadn't realized how many people would be here, how much pressure Stephanie would put on him.

He raises his hand, and the crowd quiets. I think he's going to give a speech about how flattered he is but how he can't do this. Instead he says, "Looks like I have some footballs to throw." There's another loud cheer. He walks slowly over to the bin, his normal casual swagger gone. There has to be at least thirty footballs. He picks one up and spins it between his hands.

"There's your target," Stephanie says, pointing to the other end of the yard. Her giddy look of anticipation makes me want to rip her hair out. He brings back his arm, takes a step, and releases the ball. It spirals beautifully through the air and lands inches from the desired target. A deafening cheer from the crowd assaults my ears because I'm too anxious to mentally muffle the noise.

Stephanie picks up another ball and tosses it to him. He throws again. His fifth ball makes it into the bucket, but not without its cost; he's in pain. His whole body has tensed. His face looks painted on for how fake his smile is. And Stephanie keeps handing him ball after ball.

I can't stand it any longer. I'm feeling nervous and guilty. I jump out of my seat, ready to yell, when Trevor says, "I can't do this, Stephanie."

A low muttering of exchanged comments ripples through the onlookers.

"Of course you can. You're doing it."

"I can't. I'm sorry. Thanks for this though."

Considering how many kids are in the backyard, I'm surprised at how quiet it has become. I grab Rowan and pull him to his feet. "Rowan wants to try throwing some footballs. He thinks he can get way more than one into the bucket." When Rowan doesn't move, I elbow him in the ribs.

"Yeah, I totally can."

Stephanie shoots me a look of such rage that I'm surprised I'm still standing. I raise my eyebrows and then say, "Brandon." He's sitting next to Katie and looks up when I call his name.

"Yeah?"

"You versus Rowan. Loser has to do a dare."

Brandon laughs. "Okay, you're on, Rowan." This suggestion seems to loosen up the crowd, and soon everyone is talking and laughing again. Stephanie stomps off, and Trevor goes after her without a single glance back. I wonder if he's mad at me for my attempt to take the pressure off. When Stephanie comes back, alone, she walks straight up to me and in a cold voice says, "You may think you've won, *Addison*, but when he remembers who he is, he'll come running back to me."

"He left?" It's a stupid response to what she said, but it's the only thing I care about. I don't even care if it looks like I'm running after him, since that's what I'm doing. I turn on my heel and run through the house and out the front door, where I see the tail end of his car disappear around the corner.

CHAPTER 27

ir•reP•A•RA•ble: *adj.* something that
can never be how it was

I knock on the door. Duke's mom answers. "Hi," she says. Duke must've inherited some of her charm, because her smile makes me feel just as at ease as Duke's.

"Hi. I'm supposed to meet Duke here." I hold up my backpack. "Homework." It's the excuse I'm going to use with my mom when I get home as well—I haven't asked her permission, but I really want to see him.

"Oh, Addie, he's not home yet, but feel free to wait in his room."

"Okay, thanks."

Up in his room, I pull out a book and start reading. When

I'm done with the chapter, I glance at the digital clock on his wall monitor. It's been half an hour. I know I can't stay much longer.

My phone is in my pocket and I fish it out and dial his number. On the floor between his bed and nightstand, the song that corresponds to my phone call starts playing. I sigh and reach down the crack, fishing out his singing phone. "Very helpful," I mutter, and press End. "Where are you?" Guess I'll have to leave him a message the old-fashioned way.

I move to Duke's desk to get paper. In the middle drawer I dig through some pages to find a blank sheet. As I grab a piece, a group of stapled pages comes up with it. I pull it free and start to put it back, but a bright yellow mark catches my eye. It's an alphabetized list of all the kids at school and their abilities. It looks like it was printed off the school computer. I find my name at the bottom of the page: Coleman, Addison. The word *Clairvoyant* next to my name is highlighted yellow.

That was the word I was directed to write on my registration papers when I signed up for high school. Clairvoyant. I remember my mom arguing with the dean, telling him that wasn't my ability. *It falls in the same class,* he said, *and our computers don't recognize the term Divergence or whatever you said her ability is called.* Here my mom sighed. She hates it when people act like I'm the only one in existence with this ability. My ability may be rare, but I'm not the only one.

It's just a technicality anyway, he assured her, *to make sure she gets put in the right classes for her tendencies. This isn't her official government record. When she passes her ability markers, you can take up her title with the Bureau.*

I will, my mother assured him. And she would.

In the meantime my school records show Clairvoyant. The word that is now bright yellow in front of me.

Duke's phone chimes, causing me to jump. I look to where I had set it on his desk. It just takes the slightest movement of my hand across the screen to bring the text message up. It's from Ray.

We're meeting Thursday night @ Fat Jacks to talk about football game strategy. 7 o'clock.

I close the message and look back to the paper, a surge of anger working its way up my chest as the implications of this highlighted word sink into my mind.

The door behind me shuts, and I whirl around, the paper fluttering to the ground with my movement. "Duke, you scared me."

He smiles. "You weren't expecting me to walk into my room?"

"No, it's not that, it's just that I was about to go because my mom will be expecting me. You left your cell phone, so I was going to leave you a note."

With those words his eyes move to the paper on the floor, and a look of panic flashes across his face, then is gone just as fast. It's the only confirmation I need.

"You're using me." Anger stings my eyes.

"What? No. That's not true."

I point at the paper. "Then explain that?"

254

"Okay, maybe at first I thought you could help me out, tell me my future, which college I'd do the best at. But then I got to know you. It hasn't been about that in a long time."

Tears attempt to fill my eyes, but I push them down, frustrated by their presence. "Well, you should've done your homework better, because I can't tell your future, only mine."

"Exactly. See, don't you think if I were using you, once I learned the exact nature of your ability I would've been gone?" He holds up his hands and takes a step toward me.

The edge of his desk presses into the backs of my legs. "I don't know."

"Of course you know, Addie." He reaches me and runs his hands along my shoulders, then kisses my cheek. My suspicion starts to waver.

He takes my arms and wraps them around his waist. My anger melts to uncertainty as his hand moves softly down my hair. "Addie, I don't need to be Clairvoyant to see you in my future. I want you there. I need you there. If you can't trust me, Search it. You'll see me there too." He tucks a section of my hair behind my ear and then kisses my jawline.

"That's not how it works. I can't just Search my future."

"I bet you could if you tried hard enough. And when you see me there, you'll have to apologize for all this mistrust."

I meet his eyes and when they're full of sincerity I feel guilty. "I think I'm just waiting for reality to hit. I don't understand why you'd want to be with me. We're so different."

"Different is good. Right? I wouldn't want to date myself."

He kisses me softly. "I'm falling for you, Addie. Don't break my heart."

I lay my head against his chest, and he holds me tight. My eyes find the paper on the floor. The black letters of my ability stand out bold against their yellow background. He must sense my gaze, because he picks up the paper. "Look." He drops it into the slotted recycle bin next to his desk. It sizzles as the solution disintegrates it. "Gone," he says, and pulls me back against him.

CHAPTER 28

aNO[R]M•a•ly: *n. a deviation*
from the (agreed upon) arrangement

I end up on Trevor's front porch, holding a heating pad and a graphic novel from my house. I hope he's not disappointed to see me after I didn't warn him about Stephanie's party. Brody answers the door. "Hi, Addison."

"Hi, is your brother here?"

"Yeah, he's in his room, but he shut the door and when he shuts the door that means he doesn't want anyone to talk to him."

"But I brought him a book. Do you think I could just give it to him and then leave?"

He shrugs one shoulder. "Okay."

"Trevor," I say, outside his door with a small knock. "Are you decent?" There's no answer. I knock again and try the handle, but it's locked. "Trevor, please." I rest my forehead against the door. Never before have I wished I was Bobby, but his ability to manipulate mass and walk through solid objects would come in handy right now.

Brody comes to my side, holding up a key. "Don't tell him I gave it to you."

I hug him. "You are a little angel."

He blushes and runs away.

Trevor's room is dark; only the light from the desk lamp is on. He's bent over his desk, drawing. "Trevor?"

"You might not want to stay. I'm busy feeling sorry for myself." He throws a smile over his shoulder.

The cord to the heating pad slips down my arm and sways by my legs. I look around, remembering all the things about his room that make me cringe a little but at the same time are so him: his messy closet, his unorganized bookshelf, his overflowing trash. I walk forward, searching the wall by Trevor's desk for an outlet. When I find one, I plug in the heating pad and turn the dial to hot. It takes a few minutes to heat up.

"What are you doing?" he asks, when I drape the pad over his right shoulder.

This was a tip from my dad on how Norms heal sore muscles. "I thought you were probably sore from your performance tonight. And I brought you this too." I set the book on the corner of his desk.

He stares at the cover without saying a word, then puts his left hand on top of the heating pad and closes his eyes with a wince.

"Too hot?"

"No, it feels good."

I take the opportunity to study his face. The tips of his lashes nearly touch his cheekbones. His dark hair falls across his forehead and curls up at the ends. His nose is strong, with a knot on the bridge. I wonder if it's another football injury. And his lips are thin, but smooth, no cracks or dryness. He probably drinks a lot of water, or maybe he puts on lots of lip balm.

When I look back up to his eyes, he's looking at me. I blush. "Well," I say, "I'll leave you alone now. I just wanted to say that I'm sorry I didn't warn you about Stephanie's plans for tonight. That was a major best-friend failure on my part." I turn and walk toward the door.

"Addison. Can I show you something?"

I spin back around. He's sitting sideways now, holding up a piece of paper. I move back to the desk. It appears to be a page from his comic. I take it and read through several panels. It's obviously the middle of the story, but the drawings are great and the conversations interesting. It surprises me that he's letting me see it after his brother said he doesn't show it to anyone. Why would he show this to me? Have I really earned it?

When my lungs start to burn, I realize I'm holding my breath. I suck in some air. There's a tug on the bottom of my shirt, and I look down to see a section of it wrapped around his finger. My eyes dart to his, and he's staring at me with intensity. My whole body feels like it's turned to liquid, and I barely resist the urge to melt to the floor.

He takes the heating pad off his shoulder and sets it on the desk. "You want to be best friends?" Has his voice always sounded so smoky?

I nod. No matter how I might feel, I know we can't be more than that. It's too complicated. I am lying to him. I can't have a relationship here when no one will ever know the real me. Plus we're good as friends. Really, really, g—

He grabs hold of my hips and pulls me forward. "You didn't fail me tonight. You saved me. I must've looked like the biggest idiot."

I shake my head no, his hands on my hips making my breath come in shallow sips.

"What's wrong?" he asks.

"You're confusing me."

"Really? And here I thought I was making things more clear." He tightens his hold, and a chill goes through me. I hear footsteps running down the hall. Trevor releases me, and I take two steps back just as Brody bursts into the room. "Mom says I have to say good night and go to bed now."

"Night, little man," Trevor says. Why does he seem perfectly relaxed? My breath still hasn't returned.

"How come it's so dark in here?" Brody asks, looking up at the ceiling. I hadn't noticed since I first walked in, but now it seems pitch-black and suspicious.

"We just forgot to turn on the lights," I blurt out. "It didn't look so dark because the desk lamp is on, but now it does." I practically run to the light switch and flip it on. When I walk back over, Trevor's eyes have a teasing smile in them.

"Say good night to Addison," Trevor says to Brody.

"Good night, Addison."

"Good night."

"Brody," a woman's voice calls, followed by the woman herself. "Let's go." She's pretty: long hair, dark eyes, curvy. She's wearing a pair of jeans and a T-shirt and has a pair of fluffy red slippers on her feet. She meets my eyes. "Oh," she says in surprise. "I didn't realize you had company, Trev."

"Mom, this is Addison."

She comes into the room and holds out her hand. "I'm DeAnn, good to meet you."

I shake her hand. "You too."

"I don't know if Trevor warned you about me, but whenever I meet one of his friends, I like to get the basics so I feel like I'm in the loop. I know it embarrasses Trevor to no end, but that's what moms do. So tell me a little about yourself."

"Um." *Is she serious?* I look at Trevor, and he nods as if to say, *Yes, she's totally serious, and I'm sorry.* "Okay, well, I go to Carter

261

High with your son. I'm a junior. Uh . . ." I freeze up, because this is the part where I would normally say where I'm from and I can't bring myself to once again tell that lie. I search my mind, but the first things that pop into it are weird, random facts. Somehow I don't think Trevor's mom is asking for the story of my first kiss or wants to know that I have a sensitive gag reflex.

"She loves to read, Mom. Like these really old, boring books. The ones Dad likes." He points to the graphic novel on his desk. "Plus lame ones, like I do. And she's not a huge football fan. I think she only tolerates it for our sake. She's supersmart, my main competition in Government. And since coming into my room, she has probably had to stop herself several times from cleaning up the shoes spilling out of my closet."

His mom laughs. "Maybe you can teach Trev some organization, then."

I nod dumbly. Tears prick the backs of my eyes, and I tell myself very forcefully that I'm not going to cry over the fact that Trevor just listed off several things about me like it was the easiest thing in the world.

Brody tugs on his mom's arm impatiently.

"Oh," Trevor continues, "and remember how I always used to get detention for being late to sixth period?"

His mom shakes her head in disapproval. "Yes."

"Well, Addison is so anal about being on time that she forces all of us to get back to campus after lunch."

262

"I do not." My voice comes out a little wobbly and I wonder if he noticed.

"Yes. You do."

His mom smiles at me. "That's not a bad thing. I, for one, am grateful that someone can get this boy back to school on time. I think people as easygoing as Trevor don't worry about small things like the *concept of time*."

"Yeah, yeah, Mom, I know, I'm always late. No need for a public-service announcement."

After another tug on her arm from Brody, she says, "I'm sorry, I'd better get this kid to bed. It was so good to meet you, Addison."

"You too."

"And thanks for indulging me. See, now I feel like I know who you are." And with that she leaves.

I'm standing a little in front of Trevor, my back to him. The silence stretches out, and I try to think of something to say to dispel it. *Thank you* seems like too little . . . or maybe too much, since he couldn't possibly understand how much I needed to hear what he just said. How much I needed to know that even without my ability, I am someone worth knowing. That every little and ridiculous quality I exhibit makes me who I am.

"And right now," he says, "you're dying because no one is saying anything."

I bite my lip. I will not cry over this. "I'd better get going too."

I walk toward the door as fast as I can.

"Addie. Stay."

It's the first time he's ever called me Addie, and I know I'm reading way more into it than I should. I stop by the door, hand gripping the frame for support. "You're confused. You need time to think."

He laughs a little. "What am I confused about?"

"You just broke up with your girlfriend."

"I broke up with Stephanie over a month ago. She finally got it tonight."

I don't know what to say.

"I'm starting a new comic. With all the reading you do, I thought you could help me with the writing." He opens his top drawer and pulls out a sketchbook.

I take a deep breath. I am in perfect control. "Really? What's it about?"

He nods me over with his head, and I go to his side. He starts with the character's eyes and by the time he moves to her hair, a mess of blond curls, I realize he's drawing me. "Superheroes. You can finally have those powers you want. As long as you don't kill me with them."

"Of course I will. You have to make yourself the villain."

He laughs. "Okay, that could be fun." He moves on to draw my body. He glances at me a few times, studying my shoulders and neck.

I self-consciously shift my weight from one foot to another. "Uh, excuse me," I say, pointing to the drawing. "That outfit is a little tight. I can't fight crime in that. I don't think I can even breathe in that."

"Superheroes have to have tight outfits so their clothes don't get in the way when they're fighting crime." He adds an *A* on the chest.

"I go by my real name? I don't even get a secret identity?"

"How do you know that stands for Addison? Maybe it stands for Amender or Ax Maiden or Apple Thrower."

"Apple Thrower?"

"I couldn't think of any more A names."

I smile, glad our awkward moment is over. "Okay. So what's my power?"

"What's that one you wanted? Telekinesis?"

A lump moves up my throat. "No. I think I like the one you wanted better."

"Telling the future?"

"Yeah." I have to tell him. I know I do. My father can't ask me to keep such a big part of who I am from someone I like so much. The Containment Committee will never even know, because I'm sure Trevor can keep a secret. "It's called Clairvoyance."

"It's a cool ability. So we'll make it so you can see terrible things that are going to take place and then try to change them before they happen."

"Well, it doesn't really work that way."

"What doesn't?"

"One person can't change the future. Do you know how many people and things are involved in every major event that happens? Sure, you might be able to change some of the minor aspects of a day, but ultimately things that are going to happen, if you go along a certain path, do happen."

Trevor stops drawing and looks at me. "Telling the future is only a cool power if the future can be changed."

"I know. That's why it's kind of a lame power." I put my hand on his desk for support, because I feel like I'm going to pass out.

"The way you're portraying it is." He adds a few finishing touches to the drawing of me and then holds it up to inspect. One of his fingers starts to twitch, and I quickly say, "Don't you dare crumple up that drawing."

"Your hair isn't quite right."

I touch my head, patting down the craziness that is my unruly curls. "Maybe you should make it straight. I've thought about straightening it before, and it would be easier to draw."

He looks up at me as though deeply offended. "Why would you ever straighten your hair? Your hair is perfect."

I blush with the compliment and look back at his drawing. "Trevor, you're an amazing artist." *And I really am Clairvoyant. Divergent, to be exact.* That's what I need to say, but I can't bring myself to. "You gave me too many muscles," is what I actually say. Why is this so hard to tell him? It doesn't help that my school is responsible for his shoulder. If I explain who I am, I'll have to explain that as well, and how can he ever have a good opinion of a group of people who could do that to someone?

I grab the picture and study it. He got my eyes just right.

"The cool thing about mind powers is that if someone has an advanced mind, they've usually learned how to do other cool things with it as well."

"Like what?"

"Like improve their hearing and sight."

"I like that. We should write that into the plot."

"Okay." That's exactly what we'll do. We'll write the book of my high school and when it is all done, I'll say, *That's my life.* Then he'll know that there are more good guys than villains. He'll see that in every place there are people willing to do anything to get ahead, but the majority of my people are good. And he'll know why I had to keep it all a secret. He'll understand. He has to.

He stands and is only inches from me. "I'm going to get some water. Do you want something to drink?"

"Yes, I do. I'll come with you." I turn to go, but he pulls me back by my arm.

"Don't best friends hug before they go anywhere?"

I smile. He thinks he's being funny, but I can play this game. "As a matter of fact, they do." I slide my hands past his ribs and under his arms.

He wraps his arms around me, and I relax into him with a happy sigh. But then he starts rubbing my back, and tingles spread down my spine. "Best friends don't rub each other's backs," I tell him.

His hands stop moving, but then they press me closer to him.

I can't decide which is worse, because my whole body is on fire now.

"Will you let me read the handbook so I know all the rules?"

"Yes. I will."

He bends down and rests his forehead on my shoulder, his breath warming my skin. Why haven't I pushed him away yet? "Does the handbook cover this?" he says.

I nod.

His lips tickle my neck as they move along it. Is he trying to drive me crazy? "It says definitely no."

His lips come to rest against the soft spot below my ear. I can no longer think straight. It's then I realize I have a fistful of the back of his shirt. I clutch it tighter. He must consider this encouragement because he takes my face in his hands and presses his lips to mine. They move over mine softly, his breath seeping into my mouth. My heart feels close to bursting. I want to rip up the fake handbook and throw it in his overflowing trash can. Holy crap, Trevor the nice guy is an amazing kisser.

He pulls back slightly and meets my eyes. "So when can I get a copy of this friendship handbook?"

"Friends? Who said anything about friends?"

He looks back and forth between my eyes. "Are you okay with that?"

With my fist still full of his T-shirt, I tighten my grip and pull him back to me.

CHAPTER 29

PARA•noia: *n.* extreme distrust of others

I want to trust Duke, but when he's away, suspicions start to enter my mind. What if he lied to me the other day? What if he really is still using me because he hasn't gotten what he wants out of me? What if all he wants to know is the future? A future I can't tell him.

"Earth to Addie," Laila says, waving her hand in front of my face. "What's up?"

I stare out at the sea of grass and the students surrounding the stage where we sit. My thumb rubs at the plastic paper around the water bottle in my hand, causing it to wrinkle. "Do you think Duke really likes me?"

Her brows lower. "Is that a real question? Because I thought he had made that pretty clear."

I tell her about the list of students and their abilities I found in his room the other day and his explanation for it. "That's adorable," she says, when I'm done. "That's a story you can tell your grandchildren."

"Jeez, Laila, not even I think that far in the future. Let us get through high school first." I set my water bottle next to me and face her. "So you don't think I should be worried?"

"I'm starting to wonder if *you* really like him. Is this why you didn't want to go off-campus with him for lunch today?"

"I just wanted some space to think. When I'm around him, everything seems perfect."

"I swear, you're the only person I know who would complain about something being perfect." She sighs. "You know what your problem is, Addie?"

"What?" I ask, as if what she's about to tell me will solve all my doubts about Duke.

"You like to assign roles to the people in your life. And when they don't play their parts right, you have a hard time accepting that. You assigned Duke the title of egocentric jerk a long time ago, and even though he's proven it's not the right part for him, you're quick to believe anything that will restore him his title."

I look down at my lap. Maybe she's right. It sounds like me.

There's a dull ache behind my eyes, and I rub at my temples and attempt to ease the pain with a memorized mind pattern. I just need to stop thinking so much.

The bell rings. I stand and put my empty water bottle onto the plate with the crust of pizza and drop it in the trash. "What's today?"

"The thirteenth."

We start walking toward our next class. "No, I mean day of the week. Is it Thursday?"

"Yeah, why?"

It bothers me that I'm having this much trouble focusing on my schedule. I used to know it backward and forward. "I feel like I'm forgetting something. Did we have plans tonight?"

"Aren't you still grounded?"

"Yeah, I guess. My mom's been so weird about that. It's like she wants to be strict, but every time Duke asks her if I can go somewhere with him, she caves."

"I say take advantage." She squares her shoulders. "Check out the eye candy."

I follow her stare and see Duke heading up the sidewalk from the parking lot. I smack her arm. "That's my boyfriend you're lusting after."

She laughs. "I know. He's hot."

He stops to talk to someone. "Who is that?" I ask, only able to see the back of the guy's head.

"It looks like Bobby."

Stringy hair, frayed jeans, hunched shoulders. "Yeah, you're right, it is."

"You're not going to say hi to him?" Laila asks, when I keep walking.

"I'll see him later."

When we're almost to class, a tug on my backpack pulls me to a halt. "Hey, girlfriend," Duke says, from behind me.

Laila waves and keeps walking. "See you later."

"Bye." I turn around.

He slides his legs out to the sides until we're standing eye to eye and then pulls me against him. "You were just going to walk by without even saying hi?"

"You were busy with Bobby."

"I'm never too busy for you."

Our relationship feels different. Like someone has taken my favorite sweater and thrown it in the dryer and it doesn't fit right anymore. I want to pull and tug on it until it feels comfortable again. *He is my boyfriend,* I tell myself. I didn't have a problem giving people new roles when they earned them. He had earned it. Hadn't he? I finger a button at the top of his jacket and then meet his eyes. "Do you want to hang out with me tonight? We can get a movie or something." As I say it, I remember the text Duke had received in his room the other day when he had left his phone behind. Ray and the football players were getting together at Fat Jacks tonight. That's why it felt like I was forgetting something, it was *his* appointment.

He looks up, biting his lip. "Tonight? I have something tonight, what is it?"

I start to remind him, but he continues. "Oh, yeah, I have to go to this work party with my parents. It's going to be so boring. Believe me, I'd much rather hang out with you. Maybe you can come with me." He smiles and then his smile falls. "Oh, that's right"—he pulls on my blue strip of hair—"you're still grounded. I guess I'll have to suffer through it on my own." The second bell rings, but I don't move. He kisses my cheek and then my lips. "You'd better get to class. I'll call you after the work thing, okay?"

"Okay." He walks away, and I clench my fists. He lied to me. And over what? A date with Ray? Couldn't he have just said he was going out with Ray? Guys night or something. Did that mean he was hiding something from me? What did they need to talk about that I couldn't hear? I hate myself for turning into the untrusting girlfriend, for proving Laila right, but I have to go to Fat Jacks tonight and see what their meeting is about.

CHAPTER 30

au•to•NO[R]M•ic: *adj.* having no control over
my spontaneous actions

Trevor lies on his stomach on the floor, his notebook open in front of him, penciling several characters I had already written for the comic. I sit next to him, gnawing on the end of a pen, trying to find the easiest way to explain the Compound in story form. It's turning out to be a lot harder than I thought. I lean back against his bed and stare at the ceiling for a minute. Unlike my own ceiling, there are no words of inspiration there.

I set my pen and notebook aside and slide down next to him, resting my chin on his shoulder so I can watch him draw. The steadiness of his hand gliding across the paper, creating shapes where there were none, mesmerizes me for a moment. "You're amazing. You know that, right?"

He flips the page of his sketchbook to a blank one, takes my hand, and places it on the page. Then he slowly traces around each finger. A shudder goes through me as the pencil grazes the side of my palm. I haven't done this since I was five, but it certainly didn't make me feel like this back then.

After circling my hand twice, he asks, "Writer's block?"

It takes me a moment to remember I was trying to write the story. I roll onto my back and shake out the tingling sensation in my hand, hoping to regain my thoughts. "Yes."

He turns on his side, propping himself up on one elbow and draping his other arm across my waist. "So we already have the characters."

"Yes. The Amender who can tell the future." I point to myself. "Lola, the Memory Eraser. Robert, evil villain number one who can walk through walls."

"And myself, evil villain number two. Who can . . ."

I still haven't figured out who to make Trevor in the story. At first I thought it was funny to make him the villain, but now that I'm mirroring real life as much as possible, I don't want to assign him to be one of the "bad guys" in my life. When I look at him, I don't see evil at all. I thought about making him Bobby but couldn't bring myself to do it. I should've made him the hero, but it's too late now. He'll wonder why I'm making such a big deal about it. "Who can . . . kiss really well."

He pulls me close. "I didn't realize that was a superpower."

My heart races. "Neither did I."

He gives a breathy laugh and proves my point. After fully taking my breath and my thoughts away, he resumes his position and says, "Maybe we're going out of order. Let's figure out the rules of the Superpower Compound first."

"Rules?"

"You know, things our characters can and can't do. Kind of like my mom walking by a little while ago and reminding me that I'm not allowed to have the door shut when there's a girl I like in my room." He nods his head toward the wide open door. "Rules."

"What? You like me? When did this happen?"

"It started with the zombie note. How could I resist that?"

I smile and use my finger to trace the line across his bicep made by the shadow of his T-shirt sleeve. "I started liking you when we got trapped in the principal's car together."

"Really? So the whole best-friend talk?"

"Me in denial."

He smirks. "Okay, rules."

"Yes, rules." I start listing off the things he needs to know about the Compound. "They can't leave without permission. Nobody on the outside knows about them."

"Nobody?"

"Well, only the other people with abilities. There are people with superpowers living outside the Compound, but they have to keep their identities a secret. Let's make some really smart famous people in history have superpowers too."

"Like who?"

I pretend to think of some, even though I already know the famous Paras who lived in the Normal world throughout history. "Like Steve Jobs, Henry Ford, and Einstein."

He laughs. "Okay. They'll be fun to draw. We can make them plot in super-secret meetings."

I'm pretty sure they don't plot together, even if they were all still alive, but it didn't matter. "There are representatives in almost every government agency and in high-powered positions in the world, keeping the Compound informed and helping to keep it a secret."

"Spies, then."

"Yes. I guess you can call them that. But there are also the people who work on the Outside whose job it is to check up on those living Outside. Let's call them the Containment Committee."

"So maybe that's the conflict then. The villain, me, wants to tell the world about the Compound."

"Why? Then he'd expose himself too."

"Maybe he wants to show everyone how important and special he is."

"But people fear what they don't know. The world wouldn't embrace him; they'd want to destroy him or study him." Saying that out loud makes me question again my intentions to tell Trevor about me. How is he going to feel? "The Compound may be full of powers, but its people are still very much outnumbered."

"So we need internal conflict then. How about we make it so that a child is born without any superpowers within the Compound. And he spends his whole life trying to hide it."

"That doesn't happen. Everyone has powers."

"Everyone?"

"Yes."

"You've thought a lot about this. What if someone wants to marry a Normal person?"

I sigh, my heart hurting a little bit when I say, "They risk not only their children being born without any special skills but also their residency in the Compound."

"They get kicked out?"

I nod.

"Well, that's our story then."

My heart thumps an extra beat when my brain takes too long to process that he's speaking about the story we're writing, not the story we're living.

"Those are some harsh rules you made up."

"Are they harsh though? Without the rules, there'd be chaos. We can't let the people come and go as they please, risking the safety of everyone."

"If you say so." He moves to his back, putting both hands behind his head. His bicep twitches, and my gaze is drawn to the sharp line that defines it. It twitches again, and I meet his eyes. There's a teasing gleam in them.

"I also want to be able to fly," he says.

I shake my head. "You can't fly. They only have mind powers."

"I think my mind should be able to control gravity."

I laugh. "Don't worry, everyone will know you're strong. No need for your character to fly or throw buildings . . . or girls . . . around."

He laughs, and it is such a genuinely happy sound that my heart flutters to life. I can't help myself, I have to kiss him.

He hugs me close. "Want me to pick you up for school tomorrow?"

"Yes."

I didn't really think about the fallout that would happen with Trevor and his friends as a result of us being a couple and Stephanie realizing she and Trevor were finally finished. The girls in the group sided with Stephanie, and because Katie and Brandon are still together, Brandon followed them as well. Rowan was miffed about something and I couldn't figure out what.

Outside school, everything seemed perfect, and while Trevor drew, I finally got into a rhythm with the plot of the story. Sticking to the mirroring-reality-as-much-as-possible theme, I decided to make the villains responsible for purposefully injuring a group of Containment workers in order to release information into the Norm world. Not that Duke Rivers and the football team are trying to release information into the Norm world, but I needed a plot for my story, and I couldn't say that the evil villains wanted to thin the competition in a football game; that would be a little too obvious.

By Thursday though, it's clear I have made some mortal enemies, so when Stephanie plops down in the seat in front of me in Calculus, I'm instantly nervous. She sets a bobblehead on my desk. "It's a gift for you. I got it from the principal's office."

My chest tightens.

"Do you know what it is?" She picks it up and puts it close to my face. "It's a football player. See the number on his back—fifteen? That was Trevor's number. Mr. Lemoore has a bobblehead for every quarterback who's played since he's been the principal here. Kind of creepy, huh? Anyway, I thought you might like it."

I push it away from my face. "I don't want it, Stephanie, so you can put it back."

She ignores me. "Do you know what's ironic? This specific bobblehead was sitting on the file cabinet where I also found your transcripts."

"My transcripts?" An icy chill runs through my veins. Guess there was a really good reason I should've stuck to the Compound-appointed backstory after all. My transcripts will not only confirm that I'm not from Southern California, they will let everyone know I'm from Lincoln High.

"Yeah. I made a couple copies of it. I gave one to Trevor before class. That was my gift to him. I thought you could each have a little piece of each other's past." She sets the bobblehead back on my desk. "To remember each other by." She stands and adjusts her miniskirt. "You two make the cutest couple, by the way." She walks to her desk on the other side of the room. I stare at the toy, its head bouncing slightly.

I am so screwed.

At lunch Trevor isn't where we had been meeting. I call Laila. "Hey, are you in class?"

"No, it's lunch. What's up?"

I sink onto a cement bench and explain to her what happened with Trevor. "What should I do?"

"Tell him the truth. It's not as bad as you think it is. It's not like you helped injure those players. He'll understand."

I toe the edge of the grass with my shoe. I may not have helped injure him, but I did lie to him. "You think?"

"Yes, now go."

In the background I hear a guy's voice say, "Who is it?"

"Who is *that*?" I ask.

"Bobby."

"Bobby? You're still hanging out with Bobby?"

"Yeah, well, turns out we get along."

I squint, making the trees on the edge of the grass go blurry. "Laila, run away. That guy's a creep."

"I've met your definition of a creep, and it wasn't even close."

"Rowan is not Bobby. Bobby really is a creep."

"Addie, don't pretend like you know what's going on here when you no longer live here and haven't talked to me in days."

The impatience in her voice catches me off guard, and I don't know what to say. "I'm not pretending I know what's going on there. I'm just reminding you of what Bobby did to Trevor."

"You can't prove that."

My mouth opens then closes. "Then how about what he did to me?"

"He didn't do anything to you."

"He was going to. Same thing."

"No, it's not the same thing. Not even close. It's sort of like fiction, Addie—not real."

I wait for her to laugh, to make some sort of joke. But everything is silent. "Are you being funny?"

"Sure, Addie. Is that what I am in your book? The comic relief?"

In the background I hear Bobby laugh.

"Go find Trevor." The line goes dead. I stare at my phone in confusion and then stand and walk. But I don't know where I'm going. Someone bumps into my shoulder and then mumbles an apology. I lift my phone, scroll through my phone list, then push Call.

"Hello?" my dad answers. His voice sounds tense.

"Dad, I don't feel good. Can I go home?"

"Of course," he says. Him agreeing with me so fast confirms

the truthfulness of my condition. Someone in the background makes a comment, and he answers back. Then to me he says, "Do you need me to come get you?"

I want to say, *Yes, please come get me,* but it's obvious he's busy. "No. It's lunch. I can find a ride." That's a lie. I can't find a ride. Even though home is within walking distance, I hope he calls me out on it.

He doesn't. "Okay. Feel better. Call me if you need me." The phone goes dead.

After the long walk home, I crawl into bed and shove my head under my pillow. When the doorbell rings, I realize I had fallen asleep. My face is sticky with sweat, and I smooth my hair while I head for the door. It's just the mailman, and he hands me another padded envelope, which I sign for.

After he leaves, I stare at it. Why is the Compound still sending my dad interviews? They need to leave him out of this mess. He seems busy enough as it is. I know it's wrong, but I can't help myself. I grab a butter knife from the drawer and wedge it beneath the sticky tape. Slowly, I pry it open and pull out the DVD. I shove it in the player and sit on the couch. Maybe I can do something to help. Maybe I can do a Search for him and tell him what he needs to know to break this case so he can move on.

It's Poison again.

After the initial introduction from the detective, where he

recommends the same course of action—brain scan, rehabilitation—Poison is seated in the metal chair. The table screen lights up. "Do you know this girl?"

"A new girl, huh? You really need to get to know more people, detective. You can't call me in here every time you need a name."

"Mr. Paxton, answer the question."

"She looks familiar." He leans closer to the picture. "You know, I think we did business a while back."

"What kind of business?"

"Watercolors."

"Watercolors?"

"I'm tired of you asking questions you already know the answers to. What do you want from me?"

"We want the truth."

"It doesn't matter what I say. You have someone telling you what to believe, so listen to him."

Poison must be talking about my dad.

"Her body was recently found by some campers. She was reported missing three months ago. Did you murder her, Mr. Paxton?"

"You tell me."

"We believe you did."

"Then arrest me." He stands and leans his fists on the table, knuckles cracking as he does. "Oh wait, you can't, because the evidence shows she killed herself, right? Don't bring me in again unless you plan to offer room and board."

I swear my heart has stopped beating. Poison walks out of the shot, and all that's left is an empty metal chair. I put the DVD back into its package as best I can. In my dad's room, I search through his dresser and desk for his notebook and find it in the side drawer. Under the title Poison my dad has written three findings: "Drug dealer—yes. Intimate relationship with victim—yes. Murdered victim—inconclusive."

I stare at that word, wondering if my dad ever used it before in his entire life. He always knows. It is either true or false. Yes or no. Inconclusive is the same thing as saying maybe, and my dad never says maybe. This word seems scarier to me than if the answer to the murder question had read "yes."

I pick up my phone and dial Laila's number. No answer. I send her a text: *We need to talk. Something big is going on there. Scary.*

I wait ten minutes, pacing the floor. There's no answer. Why is she being so difficult? Is she really going to choose Bobby over me? I shove my phone in my pocket and go outside.

I walk, not sure where I'm going or why, but knowing I need to walk to clear my head. What choice can I Search to help my dad? I have to be involved somehow or it won't work. So maybe I can Search what would happen if we return together to the Compound so he can investigate versus what would happen if we stay here. Hopefully I'd be able to see who's responsible at the end. I make it four blocks before I realize it's cold outside and my toes, not well-protected in flip-flops, feel like ice cubes. I head back home with new determination.

The first thing I notice when I'm almost home is Trevor's car parked in my driveway. I slow my steps. Today has been bad enough already. I don't want to have to face Trevor and try to explain why I lied to him.

By the time I get to his car, he's stepping off the porch. He locks eyes with me. I'm the first to drop my gaze, and that's when I see the paper clutched in his fist.

I stop, not able to take another step.

CHAPTER 31

seP•A•RAte: v. to force apart

I park at the quickie mart next door to Fat Jacks and then walk down the alley behind the restaurant. My plan is to hide out there until Duke and his friends arrive and then sit beneath whatever window their table is closest to. With advanced hearing, I should be able to listen through the window without having to read their lips.

The problem is, Duke never shows up. I stand, my back to a stinky Dumpster, looking around the corner for a good fifteen minutes. The smell emanating from the large bin is assaulting all my senses and making me gag every two minutes.

I decide to take my place under the window because three

other guys are there, Ray being one of them. I sit against the wall, so to anyone driving by or walking up to the restaurant it looks like I'm just waiting for someone. If that someone ends up being Duke, I hope he's not too mad. The guys are talking about some assignment for Biology. For a while I think this is a waste of time, but then Ray says, "Where's Duke?"

"He had something with his parents tonight. He couldn't come."

I put a palm to my forehead. I am an idiot. An idiot who is spying on my perfect boyfriend over nothing. I move to stand up when Ray continues, "We're playing Jefferson High tomorrow. We need a game plan. I've had my eye on this guy all season. He's the last one standing between me and the 'most yards rushed in a season' record. He needs to go down."

"I sense some knee trouble," one of the other guys says.

"I was thinking shoulder, like that kid from Dallas."

"No, save the shoulders for the quarterbacks; this guy relies more on his legs," Ray says.

"Duke's still in, right? We can't do it without him."

"Why wouldn't he be?"

They all laugh at this point, just like evil villains in books. My mind is stuck on 'that kid from Dallas' they mentioned. A quarterback. Was it possible they were referring to Trevor? Duke had asked him about his shoulder that night. What is going on? I need to talk to Duke. I need answers.

The laughter stops, and I strain to hear, but the normal voices of before have turned to quiet mutters. I move to my knees and inch toward the window, raising my head slowly until I can see inside. The guys are huddled around a table, watching Ray draw something on a piece of paper. Probably their plans to take some poor guy down.

Now is a good time to leave, while they're distracted. I stand, put the hood of my hoodie up, and walk through the parking lot toward the quickie mart. The bells on the door behind me ring, and I take a quick glance over my shoulder. It's just a couple going inside. I let out a breath of air and turn back around, finishing my walk to the car.

On the drive over to Duke's, I feel terrible. What is wrong with me? Why couldn't I just trust Duke? He had been exactly where he said he was going to be tonight. And I'm sure he'll have an explanation for what I just overheard. He'd *better* have an explanation for what I just heard.

At Duke's, I watch him and his parents pull into the garage from where I parked several houses down the street. I don't want his parents to see me. It's a school night, and I'm sure his dad will want him to go straight to bed and rest up for the game tomorrow. From where I'm parked, I can also see Bobby's house, across the street from Duke's, and as I give Duke ten minutes to get inside and up into his room, Bobby drives up.

I grit my teeth as he walks inside. I pick up my cell phone from the center console. When I see Duke's light go on in his bedroom, I dial his number. It rings twice before he answers, "Hey, girlfriend."

"Hi. I need to talk to you about something that happened tonight. Can you come see me?" I have a conspiratorial smile on my face as I get ready to tell him I'm right outside. He'll be surprised.

"Man, I wish I could, believe me I do, I'm so bored. But I think this party is going to last all night. The old people are rockin' out."

My smile freezes in place. A new set of headlights coming down the street blinds me for a moment. But when the car parks in front of Duke's house and the headlights dim, I wish they had blinded me for longer, because I can now see it's Laila's truck.

"I'll see you tomorrow, though, right?" Duke's voice in my ear reminds me I'm still on the phone. "Can we talk then?"

Laila steps out of the car, her long legs glowing in the streetlight. I pray for her to walk across the street to Bobby's house. But she doesn't. She bends over to check herself out in her side mirror, fluffs her hair, and then walks the path to Duke's front door.

"Addie? Are you still there?" Duke asks. "We can talk tomorrow, right?"

"Yeah." I don't know how I manage to choke out any words, but I do. "Sure."

Laila reaches over and rings the doorbell.

"I have to go, girlfriend. Sleep good."

"Bye." I hang up and stare at my phone as if it were the one who betrayed me and not my best friend. I want to start the car and drive away, but apparently I'm a fan of self-torture, because I force myself to watch Duke answer the door, hug Laila, and then take her inside.

CHAPTER 32

NOR•Mo•ther•mia: *v.* the process of returning
my body temperature back to normal

"You went to Lincoln High?" Trevor asks me this from across
the yard. My eyes sting with the question. I just want to disappear with my dignity, but he's standing between me and my only
escape—the house.

I must've been staring at the front door, because he steps aside
and gives the don't-let-me-stand-in-your-way gesture. At this
point, much to my dismay, my body starts shivering from the
cold. With my eyes focused on the door, I walk toward it as fast
as possible. "I'm sorry," I say as I pass him.

"Addison, wait. Don't I get an explanation?" His voice is low and hard.

I know he deserves one, but I lied. It's as simple as that. I'm still lying. And according to my dad, I have to keep lying. Nobody can ever know who I am. I stop on the porch, my back to him, and take the anger I feel toward the Compound for making me keep their secret and let it swell inside me. It's the only emotion that's going to let me survive looking at him.

I turn and his eyes are pleading. "Do you want one?" I ask.

"Yes. You lied to me. And for what? Were you worried that I hated your old school because of my shoulder?"

"Of course. Why wouldn't you?"

"I don't. It's just part of the sport. Why would I judge *you* for that?"

"Because it's more than that. There's more." So much more.

"Can we talk?"

I nod and lead him into the house. We sit on opposite ends of the couch, and he won't even look at me. I have to tell him. . . . I want to tell him. The problem is that I don't know if the truth is going to make everything okay again. His shoulders look stiff, and I hate that I've done this to him. I want to reach out, hold his hand, rub his shoulder, anything to help him relax. I inch a little closer, and he shoots me a warning look, sending me right back onto my cushion. I take a deep breath and dive in. "Rowan was right. Our school is top secret, and your shoulder wasn't an accident. But I promise I didn't know that until after I met you."

He doesn't respond for a long time. "The pain didn't come until after I was tackled. It felt like someone was ripping out my bone. For a year now I've tried to talk myself out of that memory. I don't understand. How did they do it? Special technology?"

I bite on my lip. "I'm not supposed to tell you. My dad would kill me. You can't tell anyone."

He nods.

"Aside from the fact that you gave me way too many muscles and I'd never wear an outfit like that in my life, I am the Amender."

He stares at me, probably waiting for the statement to make sense.

"The story we're writing—that's me, that's my high school."

His eyes that were starting to soften put up their cold barrier again. "Is this a joke to you?"

I shake my head, then stare at the window over his shoulder for a moment, concentrating on bending the light so I can change the color of my eyes. It's one of the things I had made the comic book version of me capable of. When I look at him again, he jumps off the couch and backs away.

"I'm sorry," I say, quickly letting them change back and standing as well. I hold up my hands. "I didn't mean to freak you out. Please don't freak out. I'm still me."

He's quiet for a long time, lingering between the couch and the front door.

I stay where I am, not wanting him to retreat any farther.

He's already looking at me like I'm something out of a sideshow. I rub my arms, the chill from outside still clinging to my body. "I can't read your mind or anything, so help me out here. What are you thinking?"

"I think I'm dreaming," he says.

"Good dream or nightmare?"

"I haven't decided yet." He studies my face as though he can find the answers written there. "How?"

"There are a lot of theories. Some say the psychologically advanced have just always been a percentage of the population. Others think that we are descendants of demigods (that's the only theory Laila chooses to acknowledge). And then there's the idea that we are the next step in evolution. Whatever the case, it's definitely genetic—something we're born with."

The phone in my pocket vibrates, and I check the screen. It's a message from my mom: *Call me. We need to talk*. My heart flips, and I write back, *Is this about Laila? Is she okay?* My mom responds, *Laila? No, this is about us*. I sigh and set my phone on the coffee table. Trevor follows my every action, and I can't tell if it's from shock or if he thinks I'm about to evaporate him with my mind powers. I point at the phone. "Sorry, it was my mom." As another chill goes through me, I realize I forgot to turn on the heater when I came home. It's so cold in here.

Trevor crosses his arms in front of his chest, and I want to run over and tug them down, tell him not to close up on me. To give me a chance. My eyes blur with tears, and I look up at the light to keep them at bay. "Will you just . . ." My shoulders shake with a sob that I'm trying my hardest to hold in. "Will you just please sit down? I'm not going to zap you or anything."

He drops his arms to his sides before running one hand through his hair. "I know. It's just . . ." He walks to the couch and sits back down. "It's just a lot to take in."

I slowly sit down as well, again on the farthest cushion from his. My phone vibrates, and from where it sits on the coffee table I can see that it's my mom. I sigh. "While you're deciding if you're horrified or not, can I ask for some advice?"

"Sure."

I tell him about the argument I had with Laila over Bobby.

"So this Bobby guy hurt you?"

"Was going to hurt me."

"So you *can* change the future?"

"No. I can only take the opposite path. For all I know, Bobby ended up doing the same thing to a different girl."

"So Bobby is one of the villains in the story, right? The guy who's purposefully injuring . . ." He trails off, as if finally connecting the story to real life. "He did this to my shoulder?"

"I don't know . . . maybe, or someone like him. He has the ability to manipulate mass. I think he could probably separate muscle from bone even from a distance. . . ." I cringe. "I'm sorry that sounds horrible."

Trevor doesn't say anything, but his expression has softened considerably.

"He sounds like a prick." It's the harshest thing I've ever heard

Trevor say, and it makes me smile a little because I can think of so much worse.

"He is."

"And Laila is hanging out with this guy despite all this?"

I nod my head.

"She's either a horrible friend or has no common sense."

"She's an amazing friend. It's not like her. I mean it's like her, but it's not. What should I do?"

"Just give her some time, Addison. She's probably feeling defensive because she knows she shouldn't be hanging around a guy who did what he did to you."

I remember Laila's words and repeat them out loud. "He didn't do anything to me."

"But he would've."

"It's not the same thing."

"To you it is, right?" He presses his palm against one eye, then turns toward me. "Am I understanding that right? To you, it feels exactly the same as if it had happened."

It's hard for me to admit it out loud. For some reason I'm embarrassed, because I think what Bobby did to me was partially my fault. If I hadn't followed him into the house, if I hadn't sat so close, maybe I led him on . . . "Yes, it feels exactly the same."

"Why didn't you have Laila Erase that memory? She is the Mind Eraser, Lola, from the comic, right?"

I nod. "Some memories I don't want to forget. A lot of times because they're so good, but sometimes, like in Bobby's case, because I need to remember."

"That makes sense," he says. "I'm sorry that happened to you."

I look at my hands, suddenly very interested in my fingernails. "It's not your fault."

He turns again, sliding his feet to the ground, and lifts his arm. The action is most likely a result of pity, but I'll take it. I crawl forward, across the cushion separating us. Wrapping my arms around his chest, I sink against his side, determined to never let go.

He runs a hand down my hair and then softly pulls on the ends. "It's not your fault either," he says quietly. "You know that, right?"

I nod and squeeze my eyes closed as hot tears fill them. It takes a few shaky breaths before I get myself back in control. I play with the zipper on his jacket as we sit in silence, moving it up and down a few inches. He's wearing a black V-neck shirt beneath it. On his collarbone is a single freckle. I run my finger over it. "You're warm."

He rests his cheek on the top of my head.

"I'm so sorry. I shouldn't have lied to you. I didn't mean to hurt you."

His deep, even breaths and the steady beat of his heart lull me. My breath has warmed the little cocoon I've created against him. He smells spicy, like cologne and salt. The skin on his neck is soft on my nose and I push it farther into him until my lips rest against him. My finger traces back and forth over his collarbone, and my mouth brushes along his neck until it finds the skin right behind his earlobe, which is even softer.

I realize Trevor has gone perfectly still. Even his breathing has stopped. I sit back and look at him, gauging his reaction. "I don't want to lose you over this," I say. "I didn't—"

He presses his lips to mine, stopping not only my sentence but my breath in my throat. He takes my face in his hands and moves his mouth slowly across mine. Every nerve ending in my body is electrified.

He pulls away and searches my eyes. "You haven't lost me," he says, before bringing me back to him. Just when I decide that I could kiss him all day long, he says, "Addison?"

"Yeah?"

"What if this is a Search?"

I stiffen. "What?"

"Have you ever thought about that before? What if now, this very moment, isn't set in stone. What if you're just seeing a vision of what could be?"

"I think about that all the time." I run my hand over his chest. He feels so real.

"What if you don't choose this? What if you decide your other future is better?"

I hug him, resting my cheek against his. "Do you know what's weird, Trevor?"

"What?"

"In the six years I've had this ability, nobody has ever asked me that question. Nobody has ever thought they were negotiable."

He takes a deep breath. "I want you to choose me, Addie," he

299

whispers. "I want this to be real."

"Don't worry. It is. I always know when I'm in a Search."

"How?"

"Because I can't Search within a Search."

"So you've Searched since you met me then?"

"Yes . . ." I trail off, thinking back. Thinking to all the times I thought about Searching. Just today I was going to do a Search for my dad. But I never actually did. "I . . . no. But I can. I will. Right now."

"No." He stops me just as I'm formulating a simple Search. "Don't. Not while I'm here. Just promise me something. If this is a Search and you don't pick me, don't pick this path, for whatever reason, promise me you won't Erase me."

That's a very serious promise, one I can't make lightly. Because even though right now, if this was a Search, I can't imagine not picking him, if for some reason something major happens and I can't be with him, remembering him and this would be sheer torture.

His eyes seem dark again, which makes his stare more intense. "I promise."

He breathes me in and then closes the space between us.

CHAPTER 33

PA•RAl•y•sis: *n.* unable to move

A numbness starts at the crown of my head and seeps slowly down my body. I want to cry, but every feeling inside me has been nullified and replaced by an overwhelming sense of emptiness. My phone rings, and a glimmer of hope flutters in my chest. Maybe it's Laila, calling to explain what's going on. To tell me why she just walked into my boyfriend's house as though they have been doing this on a nightly basis. I raise the phone. Across the bottom of the lit screen it says, *Mom calling* . . .

I pick up. "Hello?"

"Addie, where are you?"

"I'm out . . . studying." For the first time, I don't feel bad lying to her. I don't feel much of anything.

"Why are you lying to me?"

Obviously I'm still not very good at it. "Don't worry, I'm coming home."

"Yes. You are. This is ridiculous. I don't know what has gotten into you lately. You know you're still grounded, right? The Addie I used to know would have respected that rule."

The Addie she used to know did a lot of things differently. Saw a lot of things differently. Or maybe I just didn't see things that were obviously right in front of me. It's possible I said goodbye, but I don't remember saying it. Either way, I had hung up the phone. So when it starts ringing again, I'm not surprised and prepare myself for a lecture about how rude it is to hang up on people. But when I pick up the phone, glowing across the bottom of the screen are the words: *Freakshow calling* . . .

The air in my lungs leaks out. The phone stops ringing and becomes eerily silent. How did Poison get my phone number? I look around, weighing my options.

The phone rings again. I answer. "Hello."

"Addie, just the girl I was looking for. I need a favor."

I reach my thumb forward to start the car, and my hand comes to an abrupt stop, a foot away from its goal.

"No," Poison says. "You can't leave. I need you here."

I throw my phone onto the seat beside me and use my now free hand to try to move the other one. It doesn't budge but instead reaches for the door handle. I try to fight against it, to tell my fingers to turn on the car and drive away. They don't listen.

They are following someone else's orders.

I step out of the car, and that's when I see Poison standing like a dark shadow under a streetlight, twenty feet away. Screaming is my best bet, but as I open my mouth to do so, my throat constricts.

Not a good idea, he says inside my mind.

I claw at the invisible hand squeezing my neck. Then I walk again on mind-controlled legs. My lungs burn, and the street sways.

When I stand in front of him, he says, "Don't scream. I just want to talk."

I nod, and my airway clears. I cough and gasp for breath, steadying myself against the dizzy nausea.

"I need you to make a phone call. Just one little phone call, and you can be on your way."

I don't believe him for one second, but in order to buy some time I say, "To who?"

"No questions. All you have to say is, 'Hello, this is Addie.' That's simple enough."

"Why should I?"

"I thought I just showed you why you should. Do you want me to show you again?"

"No. Fine. I'll do it."

"That's a good girl." He pushes a button on his phone and then hands it to me with a reminder: "When he answers, just say, 'Hello, this is Addie.' No more, no less."

I nod, trying to plot my escape when this is over because I know he's not just going to let me walk away, but then the man answers, "Coleman here," and all thoughts of escape are gone.

I almost whisper, *Daddy*, but bite my tongue. If I say anything, my dad will think I'm in trouble. Technically I am, but I don't want my dad doing whatever Poison is going to demand of him. Not if I still have a chance at escape.

"Hello?" my dad says again.

I slip my thumb up to the End Call button and push it. The line goes dead. "Dad? Is that you? This is Addie." I try to say it with panic in my voice, which isn't hard, since my heart is thumping in my throat.

"That's enough," Poison says.

I bring the phone away from my ear, and before he can take over my body again, I push End, pretending to hang up.

"No, you idiot," he says. "I needed to talk to him."

"What do you want with my father?"

"He's telling lies about me. He needs to know I won't stand for that. I thought I'd give him a little incentive to stop." He holds out his hand for the phone. I start to give it to him, but I let go before it reaches his hand. It drops to the sidewalk with a clatter. I pray that it broke. As he bends down, cursing, I turn and run toward Bobby's house, screaming at the top of my lungs. I only get through the sentence, "Help me" one and a half times before my throat is constricted again and my whole body is frozen in place.

Just when I think I'm going to die, Bobby walks out onto the porch and glances wide-eyed between Poison and me. Never have I been happier to see him.

"Addie?" he says, and suddenly I can breathe again. My body drops to the ground, and I land on my palms.

"Bobby, help me," I croak.

"What's going on?" he asks.

I stand on my own accord, keeping an eye on Poison while I walk toward Bobby. "Just leave me alone," I tell Poison. "And my father too."

Once at Bobby's side, I grab on to his arm, my legs feeling like jelly beneath me. He protectively takes a step in front of me. "Get out of here, or I'm going to call the Bureau," he says to Poison.

Poison lets out a low laugh, shoves his hands in his pockets, and then walks away whistling.

Bobby turns toward me. "Are you okay?"

I shake my head no.

"Come on, I'll get you something to drink. Do you want me to call Duke and have him come over?"

I shake my head no again. "I just want to sit for a minute, and then I'll go home."

Bobby leads me inside.

I am overwhelmed by a sense of gratitude toward him. He just saved me.

"Was that the guy you and Duke had me research?" Bobby asks.

"Yes. Thanks for helping me."

"No problem." The door shuts with a *swoosh*, and he slides the security bar across and punches a code into the palm pad.

CHAPTER 34

NORM•less: *n.* absolutely no normalcy in given situation

I sit up in a cold sweat. My sheet is wrapped around my legs, making it hard for me to move. I untangle it and swing my feet to the ground, looking around my dark room. Something woke me, and I try to remember if it was a bad dream or a noise. Just when I'm about to lie down again, thinking a bad dream was the most likely culprit, my phone chimes. I search the blackness for the lit screen, blindly groping the top of my nightstand. It's not there. Then I remember I shoved it under my pillow before going to sleep. I pull it out.

Both messages are from Laila. The first reads, *Help*. The second, *Forgive me*.

I stumble to my dad's room. "Dad," I sob, grabbing hold of his shoulder and shaking him awake. "Dad, I need your help. It's Laila."

He sits up, groggy, his hand going to his hair first and then to the digital clock on his nightstand. "What?" he says, when he finally looks at me.

"I should've Searched, but I didn't. I was going to, but Trevor left too late, and I was tired. I might've seen something—"

"Addie. Calm down. What's going on?"

"Laila's in trouble."

"What kind of trouble?"

"I don't know. She's been hanging around this horrible kid from school." Then my memory latches on to something she had mentioned as we were walking through the parking lot to the football game. "Or there's this guy, one of her dad's drug buddies, who threatened her. Maybe it has to do with that. I don't know. I just know she's in trouble, and I'm scared."

My words seem to wake him up even further, and he rolls out of bed. "What's his name? The drug friend."

"I don't know," I say.

"Is it Poison? Was his name Poison?" My dad takes me by the shoulders. I gasp when I remember one of my dad's notes about Poison: *Drug dealer—yes.*

"Oh no. You have to do something."

"It's okay, baby, just calm down, okay?" He grabs his phone and dials a number. "Hi, it's Coleman," he says into his cell. "I know it's late. I apologize. I may have another missing teenager to report." He pauses. "You ready? Her name is Laila Stader." He spells it out slowly, each letter like a jab to my heart. "And get someone over to Mr. Paxton's house immediately . . . yes . . . no . . . Okay, let me know as soon as you have any information. Thanks." He hangs up and then looks at me. The pain that fills his eyes is terrifying. It's like he already thinks the worst.

I climb into his empty bed. The place he had just abandoned feels warm against my shivering body. The mattress behind me sinks down a little when he sits and places a hand on my back. "It's going to be okay."

"You can't say that. You don't know that. I shouldn't have left. She needs me, and I'm not there."

"What could you have done, Addie? You being there wouldn't have changed things."

I had seen too many alternate futures to be comforted by those words. "It might've. She has to be okay." I curl into a ball. It's not too late to Search now. Maybe I can see something. My brain is jumbled, and the anxiety in my chest makes it too hard to relax. Unless I can concentrate, it won't work.

"Addie, there's no need to worry before you know."

The black screen of my cell phone taunts me. I dial Laila's number again. No answer.

"I'm going to make you some warm milk," my dad says, standing and moving toward the door.

"I don't want warm milk," I snap.

He's quiet for a long time. "Do you want to call Mom?"

The suggestion rips a sob from my chest, and I pull a pillow against me. "I don't want to talk to Mom."

"She told me you aren't returning her calls. Why are you taking this divorce out on her?"

The question is a valid one, but I'm angry with him for pointing it out right now.

"The decision was mutual. You know that, right?"

"I don't want to talk about it. My friend is in trouble. That's all that matters."

"Yes, right now that is all that matters. But later you need to talk to her. Your mom misses you."

This is the last thing I need right now—him making me feel worse than I already do. I'm scared and sad and I just want him to be scared and sad with me, not try to tell me how to make my *mom* feel better about a decision *they* made. "I don't care about her."

I can tell that was the wrong thing to say because his face pales. "It was me, okay?" With the one statement he seems to age a hundred years. His shoulders droop forward, and his mouth pulls down into a deep frown.

"What?"

"I wanted to leave. I couldn't live there any longer, watching you surrounded by semirealism. And she couldn't bear to leave and risk the proper development of your ability. We fought about it for years. Maybe it would've been different if I couldn't see through lies, but I could, and they were everywhere

I turned. No matter how often she Persuaded me to stay, I couldn't do it. So hate me, Addie. Hate me for my selfishness. Don't hate her."

He leans against the dresser as if the lie had been keeping him upright and now that he expelled it, he couldn't hold himself up on his own accord. Was that speech supposed to make me feel better? Aren't parents supposed to say, *Our divorce had nothing to do with you; it was all us?* Their breaking up had everything to do with me.

I take a deep breath. I had drawn my loyalty lines early in this battle—my mom, with her overbearing personality who drove my father to escape, on one side; my dad and me, who had to put up with her all these years, on the other. I'm not sure if I'm ready to hear that I might've drawn the wrong line or stood on the wrong side of that line. But then I think about what he had actually said—living in semirealism. I didn't want that either. Did I?

"I'm sorry." He looks so tired and broken and Normal. Then, as if reading the thoughts on my face, he says, "Addie, that came out wrong. It wasn't about you. It was a fight we had for years, before it became centered on you. It was our beliefs. They were nearly opposite from each other. And then with the new mind program that's even more invasive—" He stops short, as if he had said too much. "This wasn't your fault. None of it was your fault."

I open my mouth to say something, I'm not sure what, when his phone rings and drowns any thoughts I had, replacing them

310

with fear. I throw the pillow aside and sit up.

"Coleman here . . . yes . . . I see . . ." His eyes dart to me. "Are you sure? . . . Have you arrested him? . . . There? Well, yes, I did say that, but . . . I can't leave my daughter here alone . . . No, she's sixteen, but . . . yes, of course . . . okay, an hour, I'll be there, thanks. Bye." He hangs up the phone and slowly lowers it to his side. Dread has numbed every muscle in my body, and I'm frozen as I wait for the news.

"They don't know anything for sure yet, so we shouldn't jump to conclusions."

"What did they say? Where's Laila?"

"Her parents haven't seen her since this morning. But just because she isn't at home, doesn't mean that something has happened to her. An officer is stationed at her house, so when she comes back he can inform me immediately." He goes to the closet and pulls out a duffel bag. "And I promise to keep you updated."

"Updated? Where are you going?"

He puts the bag on top of his dresser and starts loading clothes into it. "Most of the time, a video of an interview is all I need to determine if someone is lying or not. But Mr. Paxton is an expert liar, so I need to feel his energy to confirm some findings. We're hoping that if he happens to know where Laila is, we can get that information from him as well. The Bureau is flying me there in an hour. I'd like you to call a friend to come stay with you while I'm gone."

"A friend? I don't have any friends."

"I've met several of your friends. What about that Stephanie girl? She seems nice."

I have a death grip on the corner of his sheet. "I want to come with you."

"I'm sorry. This is a private Bureau jet, and you don't have clearance."

"Can't they give me clearance? This is my best friend we're talking about here. Please, Dad."

"Addison, I'm sorry. There are policies for a reason. I can't be worrying about your safety if we want to find Laila. Do you understand?"

"Of course I do."

He zips up his bag. "Promise me you'll call a friend," he says, then studies my face as I prepare to answer.

I avert my gaze. "I don't lie to you, Dad. No need to analyze me."

"I'm sorry. I know you don't. And I'm grateful for the trust that gives me in you. I hope you can trust me again one day too." He starts to put his hands on my shoulders but stops. I can't reassure him in this moment. There are too many feelings swirling around in my chest to sort them all out. He disappears into the bathroom, and when he comes out he's dressed in a suit. He gives me a worried look.

"I'll call a friend."

"Thank you. I'll let you know as soon as I land." He kisses my forehead.

I hug him tight, and then he is gone and I stand in his room all alone, rubbing my arms. The clock on his nightstand reads 3:30 a.m. The screen of my cell phone is still black. When I run my finger across it, the light makes me squint. I go to my phone book, hesitant to call Trevor this late. I stop on my mom's number, and my thumb shakes as it hovers over the Call button. I finally let it fall and listen to it ring four times.

"Addie? What's wrong?" her sleep-deepened voice answers.

"It's Laila. She's missing. Dad's on his way home. It's bad, Mom."

I hear her bedside light click on. "What?" she says at first, and then processes the information without me having to repeat it. "Oh, Addie, I'm sorry. What can I do?"

"I don't know. I'm scared."

We share a few quiet breaths. I know she's angry with me for shutting her out. I wonder if she's going to hold it against me now.

"I'm going to make some calls, see if I can help. When they find Laila, I should be there for her, since her parents probably won't."

Hot tears fall down my cheeks. "That would be great, Mom. Thanks."

"Why don't you call Trevor? I'm sure he would come over."

"How do you know about . . ." I wipe my face with the back of my hand.

"Laila has kept me updated. I miss you. Trevor sounds great, Addie."

I smile a little. "I miss you too."

313

"Everything is going to be fine, okay?"

"Okay." I start to think that maybe it is.

I hang up. I want to call Trevor, but it's so early. I text him instead. *Call me when you wake up. It's important.*

Less than five minutes later, my phone rings. "Are you okay? What's going on?" he asks. I explain to him what's happening.

"I'm on my way."

Trevor shows up, his disheveled hair proving he rushed, and wraps his arms around me. "I'm so sorry."

"She's going to be okay," I say into his chest.

"Of course she is. She probably has no idea we're all worried about her and is just hanging out with some friends."

I want to nod my head and agree, even though my stomach is trying to tell me the opposite as it churns and bubbles with unease. He leads me to the couch, sits me down, and pries my phone out of my hands, setting it on the coffee table.

"What do you need?" he asks. "Water?"

I shake my head no.

"A milk shake?"

"Ugh."

He sits down next to me. "I wish I had that power to soothe your emotions like we gave Russell in the book."

I lean into him. "No, I'm glad you don't. I don't like to have false emotions."

"I'll be right back."

"Don't go." I know I sound like a child.

"But I brought books. Some really boring classics from my dad's library."

I smile and sit up so he can stand. He comes back holding a few books. "Do you want me to read to you?"

"Yes."

He settles into the corner of the couch and lifts his arm. I lie alongside him. He's an amazing reader, pausing at the right times, putting emphasis in just the right places. And the tone of his voice is so soothing, it makes me wish he were more talkative. "You do have the power to soothe my emotions," I say when he pauses to turn a page. "Thank you."

He squeezes my arm, and I kiss him. For the first time today I feel relaxed enough that I know I can perform a Search and hopefully help Laila. I try to formulate a choice that will most likely give me the information I need.

My phone rings, and we both turn toward it. "Will you get it?" I ask, my anxiety instantly returning.

He picks it up. I scoot back, as if putting distance between myself and the phone means any bad news won't be able to reach me.

"Hello? . . . Hi, Mr. Coleman, this is Trevor. . . . It wasn't a problem at all." After this there is a long pause. Trevor nods and grabs my hand. "Did you want to talk to her? . . . Okay, here she is."

He hands me the phone and inches toward me. His face blurs through my tears.

"Hello?"

"Hi, baby." I know pity when I hear it.

I wipe my eyes, hoping that with clear vision, a clear mind will follow. "What's going on?"

He's quiet for a while, and I can picture his face in my mind, the way it looks, serious and thoughtful, when he tries to formulate the perfect words. "It's Laila."

"Did you find her?" I say, hope filling my chest.

"We did . . . she's gone."

"Gone where?"

"Addie, she's dead. I'm so sorry."

My mind, most likely in an attempt at self-preservation, goes completely blank.

My dad continues. "It wasn't Mr. Paxton. Mr. Paxton gave us the name of a kid from your school who is responsible, but it was too late."

"A kid from my school?"

"Yes, Bobby Baker. Do you know him?"

I nod, too dumbfounded to realize he can't see me. Finally I stutter out, "M-maybe he's l-lying. Maybe he just doesn't want you to find her." Bobby may be a jerk, but I never thought him capable of something this serious.

"He's telling the truth. We've already taken Bobby into custody. I've interviewed him. Bobby is responsible."

"But maybe Bobby just thinks she's dead, and that's why you got the read that he's telling the truth. Maybe—"

"I saw her." His words effectively crush my attempt at denial. "She's gone."

I must've dropped the phone, because Trevor is holding it

and saying something to my dad. Then he hangs up and pulls me against him, smoothing my hair and telling me he's sorry over and over. I can barely feel him or hear him.

Then his mouth is next to my ear. "Addison, listen to me. Are you listening?" I nod, and he continues. "You don't pick this. This has to be a Search. There's no way you would pick this. Everything will be okay."

I wrap my arms around him. He's right, and I love him for saying it.

CHAPTER 35

PAR•A•site: *n.* a person who benefits from others
while offering no benefit in return

Bobby turns away from the heavily secured door.

"Can I use your phone?" I need to call my dad and let him know I'm okay in case Poison calls him back.

"Sure, but where is yours?"

"I left it in my car."

He peers out the long window next to the door. "I didn't see your car out there."

I point vaguely to the right. "I parked up the street."

He smiles as if he knows why. "My cell is in my room. I'll

go get it." He moves toward the stairs.

"You don't have a house phone?"

"Does anyone anymore?"

I shrug. "We do."

He disappears upstairs, and I move to the front window, parting the drapes to create a small gap. First I glance to the left at the streetlight where Poison stood earlier. He's not there, but that doesn't mean he isn't out there, waiting. Next my gaze shifts to Laila's truck across the street. I want to hurl a rock at it. Duke's window is dark, and I can't help but wonder if they are up there, in his room.

"What did my curtains ever do to you?" Bobby asks from behind me.

I quickly release the material I'm crushing in my fist and turn to face him. "Sorry."

"Bad news. My cell phone is dead. Let me plug it in and you should be able to use it in a few minutes."

"Maybe I should just go."

"It will just take a few minutes. Do you really want to go out there with that freak? I think we should call the Bureau too, when the phone is charged."

Good idea. "Yeah, okay."

"The charger is in the kitchen. I'll be right back." He walks through a swinging door separating the main room from what I assume is the kitchen.

I double-check the front door's slider. It's locked into place.

The room is dim, so I turn on a lamp that's sitting on the end table. Bobby comes back with a bottle of water that he hands to me. "Have a seat." He points to the couch. I back away from it and opt for the piano bench.

"Where are your parents?" I'm beginning to wonder if they're ever home.

"They work early, so they're already asleep." He points at a clock on the wall, and I see that it's after ten. Did I really sit in the car waiting for Duke for over an hour?

I take a sip of water and look down at my feet. "You're his best friend. . . . How long has he been . . ." I can't even finish the thought. I don't want to know how long my best friend has been betraying me with my boyfriend. "He was using me."

"He's getting desperate. He wants to know without a shadow of a doubt which college he'll do the best at."

I want to punch something or cry, but I refuse to do either in front of Bobby. "I can't tell him. Doesn't he get that?"

"You could. If you extend your ability."

My head snaps up. "What?"

"Advanced mind control. You should learn it. You could do so much with your gift."

"And risk losing all my power? No, thanks." I slide my feet forward, leaving a dark pattern on the carpet. "Is he using her too? Laila?" Is our lifelong friendship ruined over some guy's inability to pick a college? "Or does he really like her?"

"I'm not sure what he wants from Laila."

"So is that what Duke does? Teaches people how to extend their abilities?"

He blows air between his lips as if offended. "No. That's what I do. He's just one of my students."

"Why? What's the point?"

"Each person I teach teaches me a little something as well. It's like I'm able to gain a little bit of each of their powers. Did you know that before our abilities become stable, they're volatile? Our powers come out in shorter, stronger bursts than in adults. It's why they don't like us attempting to advance our abilities so young. They want them to stabilize first. But it seems the stronger a burst of power, the more I can glean from it."

An uneasiness creeps into my chest. "You can take people's powers?"

"Not take them. Just borrow a little bit of them."

"How? I thought you manipulated mass."

"Energy, Addie, has a mass. Your energy hangs around you; sometimes it's as thin as the air, but sometimes it's dense and malleable."

I stand. "Your phone is probably charged enough to use by now."

"Do you know what emotion triggers strong, dense bursts of a person's energy?"

I drop the bottle, and water splatters the bottom of my jeans. I run and dive for the door, managing to shove the slider across, and push my shoulder against the frame, waiting for it to free me. The palm pad next to the door gives a triple beep accompanied by a red flash.

"No." I bang on the pad, not knowing the security code.

"I'm surprised you didn't see this coming, Addie." He wraps an arm around my waist and pulls me away from the door, relocking it. He's stronger than I thought possible, considering his average stature. "If you can't even see your own perilous future, you could really benefit from one of my sessions," he says calmly.

I remember he said his parents were upstairs asleep, so I let out a scream so loud, he has to clamp a hand over my mouth. "Listen, I can force you to be quiet, like Poison did out there. Is that what you want?"

I shake my head no.

"Good, because I don't want that either. It limits my ability to do much more than control you."

When nobody stirs upstairs, I know he lied to me about his parents. We are alone. "So you taught Poison how to extend his ability then? Took a piece of his nervous-system control. Did you give him my phone number?"

He loosens his grip on me, and I slide to the floor. He doesn't answer my questions.

"What do you want from me?"

"I thought I made that obvious. I would like just a little piece of your Clairvoyance. I have no idea how it will enhance my ability, but I know it will."

"You're messing with things you shouldn't. What if you damage your mind?"

"How sweet of you to worry." He stands above me and runs his hand down my hair, then takes the dyed blue chunk between two fingers. "Let's get started, shall we?" He pulls on my hair until I stand.

"And then what?"

"And then I either convince you this never happened, or you become too sad to go on."

This has to be a Search. I'm in a Search. I try to test out that theory, and when only a static buzz enters my mind, I'm convinced I'm right. I'm going to be fine. Soon I will be done with this horrible vision, snap out of my Search, and everything will be okay. I would never choose this future. I let the only thoughts keeping me halfway sane loop through my mind like they are playing on an old movie reel.

"Addie, concentrate. Try to Search the future now."

I lay my hands flat on the kitchen table. "Why should I?"

He's sitting across from me. "Do you really want to play mind games with me?"

"Duke is going to be angry with you for doing this."

He laughs. "Duke is elbow deep in his own secrets, don't you think? He hardly has a right to judge."

If I can just keep him talking, I know I can figure out a way to escape. "So he doesn't know about your little project? I thought you were best friends. Have you been stealing bits of his ability too? Show me how it works. Move something."

He gives a low laugh that chills me to the bone. "Move something? Because that's what Duke does? You are so naive."

Bobby's phone chimes. It's sitting on the counter, not plugged into any sort of charger. Maybe I *am* naive. His chair lets out a moan as it scrapes along the tile. He picks up the phone and looks at the screen. With a chuckle he starts to read aloud, *Hey, Bobby, have you seen Addie? Her car is out front. I think I might be in trouble.* He looks up at me. "Is he in trouble, Addie?"

I don't answer.

"Do you know what's funny? If he had called me, he might've heard you in the background, but because he texted me, there's no chance of that." He turns his attention back to the phone. "No, Duke," he says as his fingers move over the keys. "I haven't seen her. You know she doesn't talk to me. Maybe she saw Laila's truck parked in front of your house. It was the first thing I noticed. Bad luck."

If he had called, he would have heard me. I'm hung up on those words. Duke and I have been practicing Thought Placement, but my mistrust of him lately has slowed my progress. One time, in my frustration, I told him that I would just call him if I needed him. We both thought that was pretty funny. I'm not laughing now.

I focus all my mind power on feeling Duke's energy; he's right across the street. I can do this. I picture pushing the words

I'm at Bobby's. Help toward him . . . into him. The words seem to tumble around in my brain just like they did sometimes when I practiced, when Duke would look at me and say, "Are you even trying?"

"I'm trying," I say through my teeth.

Bobby turns toward me. "Good. You're finally on board?"

"I hate you."

"Strong feelings help enhance your ability. Work with those."

I take a deep breath and try to relax. He's not going to manipulate me. *Someone help me.* As if in answer to my call, there's a pounding at the front door and then Laila's voice. "Bobby, open up. I know Addie is in there and I have to talk to her. Addie, please don't be mad at me. Just let me in."

Bobby smiles. "Poor Laila. She thinks you've barricaded yourself in my house out of anger."

I open my mouth to answer, but I can't. Bobby is constricting my voice. So I narrow my eyes at him, wishing I had the power to shoot darts out of them instead of having my useless power. There's more banging. *Help me*, I scream in my mind. From the back of the house there is a loud clatter, and Bobby's face registers shock for a moment.

"Addie!" Duke's voice is loud and coming from inside the house. "Are you in here?"

Bobby growls. "Need to change his access. I guess we're turning this into a party." He drags me out of the kitchen and shoves me onto the couch in the living room. Then he palms open the front door and pulls Laila inside. "Sit," he orders her, pointing to the spot next to me. The moment she locks eyes with me, I know she's not analyzing the situation properly. She sits down and says, "I'm so sorry, Addie. I don't know what came over me. Please forgive me."

By this time Duke is standing in the doorway between the kitchen and the living room. "What's wrong, Addie?"

"What do you mean what's wrong?" Laila says with a grunt. "She saw me at your house, Duke."

He maintains my stare. "Is that it? Because I heard you. You were asking for help. That was you, right?"

My eyes dart to Bobby, who still hasn't loosened my tongue, hoping Duke will get the hint.

"Well, say something already," Laila says.

"She told me," Bobby says, clearing his throat, "that she's too angry with the both of you to talk right now. She didn't want you to know she was here."

I remember Bobby saying it was hard to control me and do other things at the same time, so while he's talking I try my hardest to break free of his influence over me. If teenagers have stronger bursts of powers than adults do, then surely our ability to combat those powers is stronger too. *It's Bobby, it's Bobby, it's Bobby, help*, I say over and over again in my head as I try to break free.

Duke marches up to Bobby and grabs him by the collar. "What have you done to her?"

"No more than what you've been doing."

He slams Bobby against the wall with a vibrating thud, and

I break free of his control. My muscles are so tense that the second I'm released, I spring forward. My mind must've still been screaming as well, because as I hit the floor I yell out, "Help."

Duke drops Bobby and comes rushing to my side. "Are you okay?"

"Don't touch me. Get him." I point, but Bobby isn't where Duke left him. Before I have a chance to even wonder what wall he slithered through, he is standing behind Laila, who is holding a knife to her own throat, a look of panic in her eyes.

"Addie," Bobby says. His eyes are like fire. "This isn't how it was supposed to happen. Why did you have to call him here?"

"Laila, what are you doing?" Duke asks, still squatting beside me.

"First she is going to Erase the last hour of both of your memories. Then she is going to kill herself, because her father is such a loser. Right, Laila?"

She nods, and a small trickle of dark blood runs down her pale skin.

"Bobby, you don't have to do this. We're not going to tell anyone."

"Now why don't I believe you, Duke?"

Despite the situation, I feel a sense of calm come over me that helps me analyze things. "Duke," I say under my breath, "do something."

"I'm trying."

"Can't you knock the knife out of her hand or send the couch flying at Bobby's face? Do something."

Bobby lets out a low, chilling laugh. "Yeah, Duke. Do something," he says in a high-pitched impersonation of me. "Make something move." He picks up a picture frame from the bookcase next to him. "Move *anything*." He hurls the picture toward us, and Duke holds up his hand to block it. It ricochets off his palm and hits my leg. It lands on the floor between us, the glass splintered.

I look at Duke, whose face is panicked. "What's wrong with you?"

"The girl deserves an answer, Duke." Bobby gives me a look of patronizing pity. "Why don't you tell her how Ray helps you deceive everyone? Don't you find it odd, Addie, that Duke can only move things when Ray is around?"

"Stop it," Duke says.

"Oh, sorry, am I interfering with your concentration? Are you trying to give her happy feelings right now?"

I can't breathe again, but this time Bobby has nothing to do with it. The room and everyone in it seem to be underwater. Laila sways slightly back and forth with the knife pressed to her throat. I can hear her draw in a surprised breath, her shoulders rising slowly with the sound. Bobby leans one hand against the bookcase, a smile creeping onto his face. And next to me, Duke turns toward Bobby, each miniscule movement being registered and recorded by my mind. Has the world around me slowed down, or am I in another dimension?

Outside, a car's tires screech over what sounds like a mile of asphalt before car doors open and slam. And then Duke dives forward, swimming through the air. Bobby's smile contorts into rage, and Laila's hand pulls back and then moves forward, releasing the knife. It flies like an arrow through honey, straight toward me. I have plenty of time to see its exact path and move out of the way. It sticks, point first, into the wall behind me. When the front door is battered open, the spell is broken, and Duke's flying form connects with Bobby in a full-body tackle. Laila collapses in a heap on the floor, and I let out the breath I had been holding in a giant whoosh of air.

I crawl forward to Laila's side. Her neck is dripping blood, but the wound looks superficial.

"I'm so sorry," she says. "Did that knife hit you? I had no control over it."

"No, I'm fine."

"And about Duke . . ."

"Duke's a Mood Controller," I manage to say without emotion, even though I had learned it myself less than two minutes ago. "He had us both under his influence."

"Hands up where I can see them, everyone," a man in a black Bureau vest says as he enters. He's followed by three men holding guns. Soon the guns are only pointing at Bobby. Laila, Duke, and I are led outside to where my mom waits by a white, unmarked car. As I run toward her wide open arms, the tears I'd been holding in making their way down my face, the world fades to black.

CHAPTER 36

screwed: *adj.* having to choose a bad path to avoid a worse one

My eyes pop open, and I suck in a huge mouthful of air.

"What did you see?" Laila asks.

Her voice startles me and, as if on a springboard, I launch myself to a sitting position. It takes me a moment to realize everything I just saw wasn't real even though my heart feels like it's been ripped in half.

"You look horrible," she says. "Is everything okay?"

"No." I push my fingers against my temples as if that action will squeeze out a solution. There has to be a solution.

My dad.

I jump out of bed and run to the door. Just as I'm about to

open it, I stop. *Think this through first, Addie.* If I tell my dad about Bobby and Poison that will solve both problems, won't it? No. What if telling my dad about Bobby delays his leaving the Compound so he can investigate? I know the Bureau can't use my Search as evidence. First I'm underage, and second my ability is considered subjective. Too many variables. So, what if my dad can't bring Bobby in for questioning? What if that sets off a completely different series of events with Bobby still free? If I could save the murdered girls referred to in the interviews, I would march out there right now. But they're already gone. The first crime happened the second week in September and the other months ago.

I sigh.

"You're scaring me," Laila says. I had almost forgotten she was here. I turn to face her. What if I just tell her? Surely she'll stay away from Bobby. I roll my eyes. The knowledge will probably send Laila straight to his house with a knife and an attitude. And even if she does stay away, what if Bobby goes after a different girl instead? Crap. I have to live out my sucky future with Duke.

"I don't want to do this."

I throw back my head and groan. I know she has to Erase the life with my mom. If she doesn't, there is no way I could even stand to look at Duke, let alone allow him into my life so that the future plays out exactly like I saw it. Even the slightest variation can result in dire consequences. Laila got into serious trouble in both versions of the future. A completely different path, like choosing neither of my parents, or marching out and telling my dad everything, will only lead to a different variation of trouble. At least this way I know Laila will be fine.

I lean my back against the wall as the next logical thoughts come into my mind. If she only Erases Duke, the knowledge of Laila's death will paralyze me, terrify me. And there's no way I'd fall for Duke with Trevor on my mind.

She has to Erase Trevor too. I want to scream.

"Do you need to go further, or do you know which future you want?"

I feel numb. "Yes, I know."

"It was that apparent, huh?" She looks down at the bed and then back up at me. "Are you staying?"

"Yes."

A huge smile breaks out on her face, and she jumps up and flings her arms around me. "I'm so happy. I knew you couldn't live without me."

I want to hug her back. I want to tell her never to look at or talk to Bobby or Duke. But I don't. "You're right, I can't."

She pushes me out by my shoulders. "Okay, so do you want me to Erase your memories now or—"

"No. Not now," I interrupt, the suggestion making my heart pick up speed. I take several deep breaths. I don't want to forget Trevor yet.

Over Laila's right shoulder, painted on my wall, are the words ". . . we had everything before us, we had nothing before us . . ."

I remember when I first read those words from *A Tale of Two Cities*. They spoke to me. They speak to me again now.

"I just need a few minutes alone." I walk toward my closet.

"Wait, you're going to shut yourself in the closet? I can leave."

"No, I need you here. Please don't go." If she doesn't do it soon, I'm sure I'll talk myself out of it.

"Okay, I won't."

I open the door and shut it behind me. Beneath the hanging shirts and between two shoe racks, I sit down. Tears stream down my face. I feel like my life is over. I try to concentrate on my breathing, in and out. Over and over. Every once in a while it catches as an image of Trevor breaks through my concentration.

In. Out.

And then it hits me, like an alarm wailing in my ears. A car alarm, to be exact. Laila. She restored that car's "memory." That may have been in the other future, the future I wasn't going to let play out, but that doesn't mean she couldn't learn how to do it in this future . . . later. After everything happens. I wipe my tears and rush out the door. In my desk I grab a notebook and pen and run back into the closet.

On the paper, I write: *I promised someone I care about very much that I wouldn't Erase this path, but I have to. On Friday morning, the fourteenth of November, however, after certain events occur, talk to Laila about advanced ability control. Tell her she can learn how to restore memories. This is the only way I know how to keep my promise to you. . . .*

I have to keep it vague enough so that if I stumble upon this note, it doesn't give me any clues. I place the notebook and pen on the floor. My stomach aches, and I wrap my arms around it and let more tears fall for a few minutes. It makes me sick to know I'm about to let my heart get broken by one boy and Erase another boy who cares about me . . . or would care about me. Now he won't know me. Even after a memory restoration, if Laila can actually learn how to do it, I will still be a stranger to him.

I have to believe that she can learn how. It is the only thought keeping me sane. I wipe at my tears and rip the page out of my notebook. "Be strong," I tell myself. Laila can't know any of this. She will Erase my memory, but I need her to be clueless as well for everything to play out exactly the same.

Squaring my shoulders, I step back into my room. In my desk I find an envelope and seal the letter to myself inside. "I need you to give this to me on Friday, November fourteenth, okay?"

"Why are you being so cryptic? What happens?"

"Laila, promise me you will give this to me on the fourteenth and won't open it before then." I write the date on the outside of the envelope. "Promise? I'm trusting you with this."

She widens her eyes like she thinks I'm overreacting. "All right. I promise."

"Okay, put it in your purse then, so I won't see it after you Erase my memory."

"Okay." She tucks it away.

I sit cross-legged on the bed in front of her. "I'm ready. I need you to Erase both paths."

"What? Why both?"

"Please, Laila, don't ask." I'm on the verge of tears again.

She bites her bottom lip and then shakes out her hands. "Okay."

"Why do you look so nervous? Don't you Erase my memories all the time?"

"No. This will be the first."

"Are you serious?"

She nods, and I throw a pillow at her head. "You'd better be good then."

"I am."

She takes a deep breath, brings up her hands to rest on my head, and closes her eyes.

I close mine as well.

EPILOGUE

Laila scratches at the bandage on her neck as she paces the hospital room. "Are they going to let us go home already? We're both fine!" she leans out the door to yell. "I don't need a Healer for this! It was a scratch."

"Just sit down, Laila. You're making me dizzy."

"I'm sorry." She sits down only to pop right back up again. "I'm sorry for everything. I can't believe this is the future you chose. This is crazy. Duke is a jerk. We almost died. Why in a million years would you choose this future?"

"You can ask me that a million times, and I still won't know."

Laila's eyes drift to her purse on the chair in the corner. "The other future must've been really bad," she says, "for you to have chosen this one."

"Yeah, maybe you betrayed me for real in that one," I say with a laugh.

Her eyebrows lower. "I . . ."

"I'm just kidding, Laila." Sort of. Even though I try to tell myself it wasn't Laila's fault, I still get an ache in the back of my throat every time I think about it.

My mom comes whisking into the room. "Addie, Laila, I'm sorry. I promise it won't be much longer. We're filling out reports, the Healer will be in here to look you over, and then we'll be able to leave."

"How did you know where I was, Mom?"

"I didn't. Your father called. I guess Mr. Paxton's guilt got the better of him, and he called the Bureau to let them know that Bobby had you. Apparently Bobby has been teaching Poison how to extend his ability, and Mr. Paxton started to suspect he had something to do with the missing teenagers. When you went inside Bobby's house, he decided to tell the Bureau his suspicions."

"Missing teenagers?" I say.

She fills us in on the other girls Bobby had gotten to. Just like with Laila, he had forced them to hold knives to their own throats. Only unlike with Laila, he had actually used his recently acquired ability of nerve control to force them to cut their own throats.

"Why didn't he just let them go? He said if he could convince me to keep my mouth shut, he would let me go."

"This is before he had the ability to Persuade. The last girl had that ability. Thank goodness he didn't get a piece of either of your abilities. This could've been even more tragic." She kisses my forehead and then hugs Laila. "Has the Bureau taken your statements yet?"

"Yes," Laila says with a sigh. She glances out the door and then back to my mom. "You haven't seen my parents out there, have you?"

"I talked to your mom. She's at work but hopes to get off soon. I couldn't get ahold of your father."

Laila nods, her strong-face firmly in place.

My mom looks back at me and her eyes move to my hair. "I can't get used to that blue stripe. I think I'm going to take you to my hairdresser tomorrow and see if she can fix it. Maybe I should call her right now."

"Mom, it's after midnight. Don't call anyone right now."

"Oh, yeah, you're right. I need some caffeine. You guys want something?"

"I'm good."

After she's gone, Laila sits next to me and leans her head on my shoulder. "I'm sorry."

"Stop apologizing."

There's a knock on the open door, and Duke takes one step over the threshold. "Can I talk to you, Addie?"

"No!" Laila yells, jumping up. "Absolutely not. Get out of here."

"Laila," I say, "it's fine. Just give me a minute." I feel calmer

338

than I should and know it's his influence. He obviously didn't extend the feelings to Laila though, because as she goes to walk out the door, she turns back as if forgetting something, stops in front of him, and punches him in the mouth. I cringe.

A trickle of blood drips down his chin, and he wipes it with the back of his hand. "I deserved that."

She doesn't respond but resumes her walk back out the door.

"If we're going to talk, lay off your ability," I say before he can begin.

"Sorry, it's habit. It's just kind of my aura now."

"So when I always said you were naturally charming, I guess that wasn't far from the truth." I wonder who the real Duke is. What his personality would be without his ability. The blood on his lip is like a chink in his shiny armor, a flaw in his perfection. It makes me think that maybe beyond the facade, something real exists.

He smiles, and I avert my gaze.

"I didn't mean to hurt you, Addie."

"What *did* you mean to do?"

"I thought I'd just influence your emotions a little at first, make you feel happy around me. Then I thought that happiness would translate into liking me, and I wouldn't have to do it anymore. You'd see us together in the future and be able to tell me which school to pick. This one decision will affect my entire life. If I make the wrong choice, I could end up with nothing. But . . ."

"But . . ." I wait for him to continue.

"But every time I let up on the emotions, you backed away or started to question us or me. . . ."

I shift my position, and the paper on the table beneath me crinkles loudly. "In other words, when you took away my feelings of like for you, I didn't like you?"

"Exactly."

"It's because I don't like you, Duke. You're not my type. I didn't like you before, and I especially don't like you now." I don't want him to know how heartbroken I am. He had accomplished his goal of making me fall for him, but then he had ripped away my ability to ever trust him again. Even now I wonder why he's in my room. What he wants from me.

And something else is bothering me as well. "Why Laila? Was she just for fun?"

"No. I thought what Bobby was doing was harmless. He was going to teach Laila to extend her ability. He told me if I could talk her into it that it would help you learn how to master the future. I never wanted to hurt you."

"I don't believe you were willing to play this game for years just because I have a convenient ability. Don't you want to be with someone who likes you? Don't you want to like someone?" I look up and realize through the course of our conversation he has gotten closer. If I wanted to, I could reach out and touch him. I don't want to.

"I do like you. A lot."

"No . . . you've manipulated emotions so much in your life

340

that you can't possibly know what real feelings are. . . ."

"I do, Addie."

"You need to man up and come clean about your ability. Why did you feel the need to lie about it to everyone in the first place?"

"Do you honestly think the coach would've put anyone short of a mover in the quarterback position? On the team for that matter?"

"I have no idea."

"Well, he wouldn't have, no matter how amazing my aim is without Telekinesis. My dad thought it was the only way to make sure I got on the football team."

"Which is very important to you."

"Yes."

"So important you're willing to soothe people's emotions so your teammates can deliver career-ruining injuries?"

He doesn't say anything.

"How does Ray do it? How does he injure people?"

"He can move a lot more than just footballs. Muscle, bone."

I hold up my hand, needing him to stop.

"If Coach finds out my true ability, he won't let me play on the team."

I'm ready for him to leave now, so I stand. "That sucks. I'll make you a deal. You get your team to stop using their abilities when you play Norm schools, and I won't tell Coach about your real ability." I walk toward the door. He brushes his hand along my arm as I pass by, and I immediately jerk it away. "Oh, and

341

you wanted my help picking a college?"

"Yeah." It kills me to hear the hope in that single word.

"I think that school in California might be your best choice after all. Unless there is something even farther away." I walk out the door.

Laila is nowhere around. Did the Healer come by to discharge us?

Halfway down the hall I see my dad walking toward me. I run the distance between us and throw my arms around his waist. "What are you doing here?"

"They flew me out to interview the suspects. I would've come either way, to see you. Are you okay?"

"I will be."

"I was thinking . . ."

I look up.

"Maybe you'd want to stay with me in Dallas for the holidays to get away from the Compound, away from everything, for a while."

I see Laila coming down the hall behind him. "Did they discharge us?"

"Yeah." She nods to my dad and gives him a side hug. "The Healer said it looked fine." She touched her neck.

"You okay?" he asks her.

She shakes out her hand. "My knuckles are a little sore, but I'm all right."

"I was just telling Addie that she needs to come stay with me for the holidays. You should come too." My dad reaches into his back pocket and pulls out two tickets. "The high school football team is playing in a holiday bowl."

I raise my eyebrows at Laila. "You can see your Norm boyfriend. What was his name? Rowan?"

She laughs. "Whatever. If I remember right, there was a certain cowboy that you set your sights on."

"Cowboy?"

"Yeah. He had the boots, the relaxed pose . . ."

An image of his brown eyes and dark hair come into my mind. "Trevor."

A warmth spreads through my chest, and suddenly Trevor's there, his image so clear that I almost reach out and touch him. The hallway, the hospital, is gone. He's kneeling in front of me as I sit on a wooden staircase, an intense expression on his face. His chest brushes against my knees, and my heart picks up speed. "Are you okay?"

I open my mouth to answer, but the question comes again, in Laila's voice. "Are you okay?" She has a hold of my arm and shakes me a little.

The wide hallway of the hospital is back. I take a deep breath, confused. That felt like a Search, but . . . no. I look between Laila and my dad. They both stare at me expectantly. "I'm fine. I'll be fine. Yes, I want to go home with you, Dad."

ACKNOWLEDGMENTS

As with most babies, this one would not have come into the world without a team of specialists. First, I'd like to thank my agent, Michelle Wolfson, because this book would just be another manuscript in my documents folder if she hadn't believed in it. She is my anchor in this industry; I don't know where I'd be without her to hold on to. Thank you, Michelle. Also, a special thanks to Sarah Landis, possibly the best editor in the universe, whose love for my book helped me believe in myself. And my copy editor (who would probably tell me I shouldn't have started that sentence with *and*. Or maybe she'd tell me that's an old rule. See? I need her.). Thanks to all the other people at HarperTeen who helped make *Pivot Point* a reality.

I'd like to thank my entire family, especially my kids—Hannah, Autumn, Abby, and Donavan—who allow me to share their time pursuing my dream; my husband, Jared, who supports me in all I do; and my parents, who instilled a love of books in me that only grew as I did—thank you for being amazing parents. I miss you, Dad. And Mom, your strength is an example to me every day.

This book wouldn't have even made it to the query stage without my amazing readers, who've stuck with me since the beginning. Your advice and friendship are invaluable to me: Stephanie Ryan, Heather Garza, Chris DeWoody, Rachel DeWoody, Candice Kennington, Jenn Johansson, Natalie Whipple, Renee Collins, Julie Nelson, Linda Cassidy-Lewis, Tricia Sutton, Ed DeFranco, Kevin Ryan, Melissa Braithwaite, Rachel Braithwaite, Nicki Broby, Jenny Weech, Heather Hague, Misti Hamel, Brianne Seamons, and Elizabeth Minnick. And to all my other readers, who are too many to name, who read parts or all of early manuscripts (you brave souls).

It's not often you get a best friend who is also a writer, and a sister who reads as much as you do. So, an extra thanks to Candice for being the best friend a girl could ask for in and out of the writing world. And my sister, Stephanie, who reads every word I am willing to write and always makes me feel like a rock star. Your support means the world to me. To Jenn for talking me down from ledges and Natalie for picking me up when I'm down. To Renee, who wouldn't let me give up, and to Julie, who finds all my unfindable errors.

Finally, I'd like to thank my friends who remind me that there is life outside of writing (I still struggle to remember this, but I try): Elizabeth, Stephanie, and Rachel, who share my love of chick flicks. And Brittney, Courtney, Emily, and Mandy, who motivate me to work out.

PIVOT POINT

Kasie's Playlist

I love music. It inspires me. As I listen to music, stories often swirl in my mind. A good song can conjure up a whole plot. I'm lucky to have very musical people in my life—mostly my teenage daughter—who introduce me to new songs constantly. This is a list of songs that I listened to while writing *Pivot Point* or that remind me of *Pivot Point* in some way. I hope you enjoy these songs as much as I do.

1. "Little Wonders" by Rob Thomas: When I heard this song for the first time, I immediately thought of *Pivot Point*. It talks about how life is made up of small moments and how fate can be defined and changed in an instant. It made me think of Addie and how she needs to move past memories and let things go. I adore this song.

2. "The One That Got Away" by Katy Perry: Obviously, every song can't be a perfect match for a novel. But the general feel of this song made me think of the fact that in the end Addie has to let go of one of her lives and with it one person she cares about.

3. "Timing Is Everything" by Garrett Hedlund: First of all, have you ever seen the movie that this song is from—*Country Strong*? The movie is amazing and inspires me as a writer. And this song talks about how many things in life are based on timing. Plus, Garrett Hedlund is hot. Just sayin'.

4. "Waiting for the End" by Linkin Park: I love Linkin Park in general. Their songs make me want to write. But this song reminded me of *Pivot Point*. Just some of the lines— "holding on to something that's invisible"; "waiting for the

end to come"; "it's out of my control"—drew me right in to memories of the story.

5. "Over My Head (Cable Car)" by the Fray: This is another band that I adore. This song was on the playlist on repeat while writing *Pivot Point*.

6. "Kiss Me Slowly" by Parachute: This is another song I listened to a lot while writing. This song conjures up so many feelings and images in my mind. I love it.

7. "Stay" by Mayday Parade: I feel like a broken record, but again, this song makes me think of *Pivot Point*. The opening line, "I need some time just deliver the things that I need for now," takes me right to a certain place in the story. I love this song.

8. "Trouble" by Never Shout Never: My fourteen-year-old daughter, who plays guitar and has a wide taste in music (from the popular to the obscure), introduced me to this band. This song was one she played a lot in the car while *Pivot Point* was circling in my brain. So when I hear this song, I automatically think of *Pivot Point*.

9. "Already Gone" by Kelly Clarkson: "It doesn't matter where we take this road, but someone's gotta go." That is basically the bottom line of *Pivot Point*.

10. "Give in to Me" by Leighton Meester (featuring Garrett Hedlund): This is another song from *Country Strong*. And this song reminds me of one of the boys in *Pivot Point*.

11. "Why Don't You Love Me" by Hot Chelle Rae: And this song reminds me of the other boy.

12. "Half-Life" by Duncan Sheik: This is another song that can describe some of the elements of *Pivot Point*. Addie is definitely living a sort of half-life throughout the novel.

13. "Chasing Cars" by Snow Patrol: Yes. Love this song.

14. "She's So Mean" by Matchbox Twenty: This song reminds me of Laila, Addie's best friend in *Pivot Point*. It's not that Laila is mean . . . well, she can be. She's superloyal to her friends but sometimes treats boys as expendable.

The Scene You Never Got to Read

In *Pivot Point*, Addie mentions a Search she did where she picked the safer path. The Search involves Laila and an incident with a stolen golf cart. Enjoy!

• • •

I pulled out my lunch and sat under a tree, waiting for Laila. My mind scrolled through the study program I had just watched on Tech Innovations for the test later today.

Laila walked toward me across the grass and even if she wasn't holding a skateboard and wearing a mischievous smile, I would know she was up to no good. It was kind of her permanent state of being. I started thinking of my excuses for whatever she was going to suggest. When she reached me, she pointed to the outdoor stage off to our right, where most of the upperclassmen sat. "By the time we're juniors, we will own that spot." Of course she'd want that spot, the focal point of the entire outdoor area. People would be forced to notice us.

I just laughed and let my shoulders relax. If that's all the trouble she was looking for today, I could handle that. "You have two years to plot our rise to the stage, then."

"Yes, I do."

"What's with the skateboard?" I asked. "You couldn't get a ride to school?"

She pressed a slip of paper into my hand.

"What's this?" I read four digits off the paper—5837. It didn't clarify anything.

"A code."

"A code to what?"

Her smile became even more playful. "The janitor's golf cart." She grabbed hold of a rope attached to the end of the

4

skateboard and lifted it up, causing the board to dangle in front of me as if it were a hypnotist's brainwashing device.

"No."

"You don't even know what I'm going to say."

"It's pretty obvious, Laila."

She laughed. "Okay, you're right. It is. But come on, it will be fun."

"No." I started looking around now to see if she'd drawn the attention of other students. Laila drew attention without even having to try. And a girl holding up a skateboard on a rope was even more likely to catch someone's eye.

"Stop worrying about everyone else and think about how fun this will be."

"Don't you think the janitor will know his golf cart is missing?"

"That's the beauty of it. He's sick today. It's been parked by the supply building all day. Not a soul in sight. Come on, we'll stick to the outskirts. Just a few minutes of skateboard practice."

"You act like you ride a skateboard on a regular basis. Have you even been on one before?"

"Oh! Search it!"

"Shhh," I hissed, looking around again. I didn't need the whole school to know my ability.

"Sorry," she whispered. "Search it. You'll see. It will be fun."

"I'm not Searching it. I don't Search stupid choices."

"Please."

It would only take a few seconds to Search. She wouldn't even know I'd done it if I didn't want her to.

"You'll see this . . ." She continued to talk, but I took a deep breath. If I Searched it, I could decide if I wanted to keep fighting her about this. I relaxed my shoulders and looked into the future. Into two futures.

"Okay. Let's do it," I say, stashing my untouched lunch in my backpack and walking toward the supply building.

It takes her a second to follow after me. "Wait, what? We're doing it? I knew you'd see the light."

By the time we reach the golf cart and she's tying the rope to a hitch on the back, my stomach is turning. I really don't want to do this. Why does Laila talk me into doing stupid things?

"Do you want to drive or ride first?" she asks, straightening up.

"I've never ridden a skateboard. Where did you get it anyway?"

She shrugs and toes the board. "Start slow, okay? I don't want to fall and mess up my face. It's my currency, baby."

"Did you steal the skateboard?"

"Steal is such a strong word. And if someone didn't want me to borrow it, it shouldn't have been left all by itself outside meditation." She steps on top, arms out to the sides. "Drive, woman. We don't have all day."

I climb carefully into the golf cart and stare at the buttons next to the steering wheel. It isn't too late to change my mind.

"It's too late to change your mind!" Laila says, and drums on the hood a few times. "Start her up."

I enter the code she gave me earlier and the engine hums to life. I had hoped for a second that the cart hadn't been charged, but the green bar on the dash indicates full battery power. Great.

"Head toward the track," Laila says before I've even started.

"And use the horn liberally. I'm not going to have a whole lot of control back here."

I take a deep breath and press on the gas. Maybe she'll fall off right away so she won't get hurt too bad and we can be done with this. But the excited *whoop* confirms that she doesn't. Probably because I'm going as slow as possible. She steers the board back and forth like she's on a wakeboard being pulled by a ski boat. In order to get to the track we have to pass some very busy hallways.

"Horn!" she reminds me as we approach the first one.

I just have to cut to the left and then right and we'll be out of this section. I lay on the horn, my face flaming as people make way, staring at me with annoyed expressions. I'm going to kill Laila when this is done. A baseball cap sits on the seat next to me, obviously the janitor's. I pull it on and shade my eyes.

We pass the first hallway and enter a more deserted area of the school again. My anxiety eases.

"Stop!" Laila yells, and I apply the break. She jumps off, the smile of adrenaline now on her face. "Your turn."

"I'll fall."

"You won't. I'll go slow. I promise."

I'm not sure I believe that, but the longer I argue the longer it will take to get to the track and be done with this. I pat my backpack sitting on the floor of the cart. "Don't let this fall out. My favorite book is in there."

"You have a favorite? Isn't that like picking a favorite child? Aren't the other books jealous? You're an awful book mother."

I smile at her. "It's my favorite for the day."

I step carefully on the skateboard and test out my balance. I wobble a little and we're not even moving. This isn't going to end well, I can sense it. I squat and grab onto the sides of the board, knowing that's the only way I'll be able to stay on.

"That's not going to work. You have to steer it. You'll have no control that way."

"I won't have control either way so I'm good."

She shrugs, and the golf cart slowly moves forward. She's right. I have no control. The board dictates where we go and it doesn't make good choices. I get a face full of leaves at one point and Laila laughs. After a few minutes it seems as though she's learned how to steer the golf cart to control me. This could be good or bad—I haven't decided yet. But there's something freeing about the ride. Joy bubbles up in my chest and I find myself laughing right along with her.

"Uh-oh," Laila says as we turn the last corner, heading toward the track.

"What?" I want to jump off but we're going a little fast.

"Nothing." She says it like it's something, though. I can't see around the golf cart, so I slowly start to stand.

"Watch out!" Laila yells out. "Coming through." Then she turns the wheel sharply to the side and the skateboard continues forward. That's when I see the entire football team in front of me, heading toward the practice field.

"It's like bowling for boys," Laila says right before I fly off and straight into a padded chest. Strong arms catch me, and I look up to see a wide smile and bright blue eyes.

"Well, hello there," he says.

My heart thumps a few times and my cheeks catch fire. "Hi."

"Are you okay?"

"Fine."

"Good," he says, still smiling down at me.

8

I twist out of his hold and shoot Laila narrow eyes.

"Be careful," the guy says as I nearly trip on the skateboard behind me.

I scoop it up, give him a small wave, then head for the golf cart. I plop the skateboard into the back and slide in the passenger seat next to Laila. As soon as I'm seated, Laila takes off, laughing.

"Tell me you at least got his name," she says.

"Of course I didn't." My face is still hot from the collision.

"Opportunity wasted." She skids to a stop around the back side of the bleachers. "What now?"

"Now we go return the golf cart?" I ask.

"Too bad we don't have a second golf cart or we could race around the track."

"It's a tragedy."

She powers off the engine, grabs hold of the bar supporting the roof of the cart, and leans back. "Want some doughnuts? I'm hungry."

"And you have doughnuts?"

"The teachers' lounge does. And they leave the back window open a lot."

"How have you not been kicked out of school multiple times by now?"

"Teachers love me too much. But I can tell you find this idea as awful as cleaning up under the bleachers. So come on, I have a different idea." She takes over the driving and heads toward the football field. There's an equipment shed between the track and the field, and she pulls up behind it then gets out of the cart and uses it like a ladder, climbing first on the back, then on top, and finally to the roof of the shed.

"They'll see us."

"They're not even looking. They're playing."

I join her, and she's right—nobody is paying attention. She starts back into her game of choice. "Would you rather fall off this shed or be tackled by the entire football team?"

I glance down at the ground then over to the football team. "The shed."

"Not me."

"Of course not." We were only freshmen, but I saw the way guys already looked at Laila. She loved it too. Sometimes I wondered if it was because she didn't get a lot of attention at home. I worried about her, though—that she'd thrive too much on the attention here and get into trouble. I tried to keep her grounded when all she seemed to want to do was keep her head in the clouds. "Would you rather have a best friend or a boyfriend?"

Her head whipped over to me and her normally playful smirk softened to her genuine smile. "Best friend. Every time."

"Ladies." The voice butting into our conversation was low and angry. I jumped and turned, nearly making my choice of falling off the shed a reality. The principal stood behind us, arms crossed, disapproving look directed right at me. I tried to think of an excuse that would explain why we were here.

Laila just stood up and stretched. "Is lunch over already? We lost track of time."

"My office. Now."

"Can we take the golf cart?"

He wasn't amused.

The other possible future blended seamlessly into my mind.

"No, Laila. I don't want to steal the golf cart."

"It's not stealing when we're going to return it."

10

Sometimes diversion is the only way to get out of something Laila has her mind set on. "Guess who asked about you today?"

"Who?"

It doesn't hurt that what I am about to tell her is true. "Cooper Lathrop."

"What did he say?" She puts the skateboard on the ground and sits on top of it.

I draw out every detail of the exchange until the bell rings. Then I look up. "Oops. Looks like we missed our chance."

"I know you did that on purpose, Addie. One day, you're going to take a risk and I'm going to be there to see it."

I smile. Maybe she's right. But it will be a risk worth taking.

I snapped out of my Search and Laila was still midsentence. "So?" she finally asked, the skateboard still dangling.

"Guess who asked about you today?"

An Interview with Kasie West

How did you come up with the idea for *Pivot Point*?
Pivot Point was inspired by the movie *Sliding Doors*. I love the idea that one little choice, one little moment in time, one little pause can produce such different futures depending on which path you choose. And I've always loved the thought of exploring alternate realities, seeing how they overlap versus how they don't, deciding which path would be better versus which one would be better for you.

Have you created a character you feel closest to?
The characters I feel closest to are usually the ones I'm writing at the moment. When I have to immerse myself in their lives, get in their heads, I almost feel like they're immediate-family members. But, of course, then I have to move on to another project and they become more like distant cousins. Oh wait, I just reread this question, and maybe it's asking if I feel like I've created a character that closely resembles me? Hm. Well, I can answer that, too, just in case. The answer is . . . I'll never tell. Muahaha. Oh, I mean, I'm supposed to be professional here. The answer is, all my characters get a little piece of me—I can't help it; I'm their brain—but none of them handle things in the exact same way I would.

What is your writing process?
I'm supposed to have a process? Maybe that's what I'm doing wrong. My process is different every day. I have four kids, so they dictate a lot of my life. If I get a phone call from school or have to take an unexpected trip to the doctor, I have to drop everything. So I've learned to write when I can. I mostly write

at night when everyone is asleep. There's something about the stillness of the night that allows my brain to fill with plot elements. I'm not an outliner. My first draft, which I usually put out fairly quickly, becomes my outline and I work from that to flesh out the story and make it better. I also read my books a bajillion (that's totally a number) times as I'm editing/writing. Because in order to get back into the story I have to sit down and read everything I've written. It's a bit obsessive, I'll admit, but it works for me. I remember someone once told me that it might benefit me to write an outline. And at the time I thought, *you're right, that's what real writers do—they plan.* So I wrote an outline. It was one of the only books I couldn't finish and what I did finish ended up a huge mess. So I now say, *Do what works for you. Don't try to write like someone else.*

Do you have a book that you know—one day—you'll write but haven't written yet?
That's a great question. With a very uninteresting answer. I do have a lot of half-finished books in my documents folder on my computer. But am I dying to write a book that I haven't yet? No, not really. I'd love to rewrite the very first novel I attempted because I love the idea, but I didn't have the skills to write it well enough at the time. So maybe I will. Writing a book is hard, so if I have an idea and the proper amount of desire to do it, I have to sit down and write it because you can't write a book you don't want to write. It's too hard of a process to have anything but desire pushing it forward.

Are there any novels that inspired you to write?
I love to read. Always have. My parents were both readers. They always had at least a few books stacked up on their

respective nightstands. And some of my fondest memories from childhood are of my siblings and I piling onto my parents' bed and listening to my dad read to us from *The Hobbit.* I have four siblings, so it was quite a party. Then as I grew I had amazing teachers who required me to read equally amazing books for class. Books like *To Kill a Mockingbird, Their Eyes Were Watching God,* and *The Joy Luck Club.* Books that made me think and broadened my outlook on life. I honestly had no idea I wanted to write, though, until I was much older. I think I would've been happy reading my piles and piles of books for the rest of my life. But one day I had an idea for a book, told it to my husband, and he said, "Yes, you should totally write that." He's been my constant support ever since.

If you could have a superpower, what would you like it to be?
As you might imagine, considering the book I wrote, I get this question a lot. And every time the answer is different, depending on my needs at the time. This week, I'm very pressed for time. I have a million things to do and not enough time in each day to do them. So I'd love to be able to manipulate time. . . . I would explain what a Time Manipulator can do, but that's something you'll have to find out in *Split Second.*

CHAPTER 1

Addie: Meet me at my house later. If I'm not already dead.

My car sat on the far side of the parking lot, and I couldn't get to it fast enough. The day had been horrible, matching perfectly with the rest of my first week back to school since the whole Duke's-a-huge-jerk-who-had-been-using-me revelation. I could almost handle conversations stopping dead when I entered a room. But the looks of pity had me seething. I did not need pity. If luck were on my side, the winter holiday that began as soon as I exited the parking lot would make people forget. If it didn't, maybe Laila could zap the whole school with amnesia. Ah, schoolwide amnesia, the first happy thought of my day.

I stepped off the curb and realized too late that I hadn't looked

15

first. Tires screeched across asphalt and my hands instinctively flew up, bracing for the impact. The impact that didn't come. At least not yet. The motorcycle skidded my way in slow motion. So slow that I easily stepped out of its way as it moved past. Connor, the driver, let the bike drop to the pavement as he crawled his way off it. Pieces of glass from the shattered side mirror floated by my head. I reached out and touched one with my index finger. It dropped like a brick to the asphalt, where it rocked back and forth—the fastest-moving piece of the world around me—until it stopped.

Back at the bike, Connor slowly ripped his helmet from his head and turned a full circle, searching the ground. His movements gradually picked up speed until he no longer appeared as though underwater. When our eyes finally met, relief washed over his face.

"Addie, I thought I hit you. I was going to hit you."

"I'm fine." At least physically. I had no idea what was happening to me mentally. My ability had always been the same—I could see both outcomes of a choice. In essence, I could see the future. Two futures, really. There had never been any variation to that. It was predictable.

Until now.

Now my ability was acting up. At certain moments, time slowed down around me. The same thing had happened at Bobby's house last week, and I wrote it off as an isolated incident—a fluke that had come out of the extreme stress of the situation. He'd said something about extreme emotions. And it wasn't every day that someone tried to kill you. Everything that day had been weird—the time slowing down, the Search-like vision of Trevor at the hospital. But now I could no longer blame it on that day. I hadn't been almost killed today. I glanced at the motorcycle lying on its side. Well, maybe I had.

A pain shot up the back of my neck and then radiated through my head. I tried not to wince and pressed my palms against my temples, scanning through a pain-relief mind pattern. It didn't help.

"Are you sure you're okay?" Connor asked. "Because you look like you're going to puke."

"I'm fine. Sorry about your . . ." I was about to say *bike*, but then saw Duke, coming toward the scene at a jog.

I spun on my heel and walked as fast as my throbbing head would allow in the direction of my car.

"What happened?" I heard him ask Connor behind me.

"I almost hit her. I should've hit her. One second she was there, the next she was gone."

Just thirty more steps and I'd be at my car. I positioned my thumb, ready to unlock the door, so there would be no delays when I reached it. My head had finally calmed, so I walked even faster. But then his voice was right behind me.

"Addie."

"No." It was a lame response, but the only one my lips would allow passage to.

"Did you get hurt?"

The many answers I could've given to that question flooded my brain: *Not nearly as much as you hurt me. Not nearly as much as I will hurt you if you come any closer. Why do you care? Were*

17

you hoping to be the sole provider of painful experiences in my life?

Of course I didn't say any of those things. I led him to believe he hadn't hurt me. That I had never liked him at all. That when he stopped manipulating my emotions with his ability, everything I ever felt for him vanished. And that was the story I would stick to no matter what. That story let me hold on to a shred of dignity.

"No." I reached my car and pressed the pad, unlocking it. I opened the door and let it act as a barrier between us when I turned to face him. "I'm good." I threw in a smile as proof of the statement.

"The rumors were brutal today. Sorry. They'll die down soon." His ever-present smile made his words seem like the setup to a joke. Unfortunately, I was probably the punch line he'd tell his buddies later: *And then she fell for me again. Ba-dum-bum.*

He ran a hand through his tousled blond hair, pushing it off his forehead and making his blue eyes stand out more. "You still haven't told anyone, right?"

And there it was, the reason he was still coming around. I knew something that could ruin him—he was a Mood Controller. Everyone still thought Duke Rivers, football star, was Telekinetic, which was what he wanted everyone to think so he could play. More specifically, so he could play quarterback, a position the coach would only fill with a Telekinetic. It made all the pity looks even worse this week, because they probably just assumed I was the poor girl with no willpower to resist Duke's charm. If only they knew I had no choice. "I made you a deal. Get your buddies to stop injuring the Norm players and I'll keep

18

your secret. Is that still the arrangement?"

He nodded. "But you think I should tell either way."

Yes! "I could not care any less." I climbed in and pulled the door shut behind me. *Don't look at him, Addie, just start the car and drive away.* I turned my whole body away so I could look over my right shoulder to back up. If I backed over his toes, that was all on him. When I straightened out the steering wheel, I managed not to check and see if he still stood there. I just drove away. Maybe now that Duke Rivers knew I wouldn't spill his secret, he'd leave me alone.

I lay perfectly still as the music flooded my bedroom, attempting to drown out all thoughts. I stared at the words on my ceiling, pretending the answer to what I should do with my life was written somewhere among the quotes painted there over the years. After an hour of staring, my eyes tricked me into thinking some stood out bolder than others, so I read the darker words. Life. Other. Sometimes. Eat.

Not helpful at all.

My door flew open and Laila walked in. "Is this Journey? Are you grieving to Journey?" The lights illuminated. I hadn't realized they had turned off with my lack of motion, but my now stinging eyes proved otherwise. "There are bands of this era that are perfectly acceptable to cry to."

I rubbed my eyes. Was it that obvious I had been bawling all afternoon? "Nobody can sing a love song like Journey." My down comforter puffed up around me, as if slowly trying to swallow me whole. I hadn't put up much of a fight.

There were things I should've been doing: laundry, a half hour of meditation, packing for my dad's house, and then there was the hair appointment my mom had scheduled for me. That was in five minutes. And just like the first three items on the list, I was ready to forgo that one as well. I found the blue strip of hair and twirled it over and over again around my finger. It had faded a lot, but I wasn't ready to give up all the blue quite yet.

Laila stood at my wall monitor, probably searching for the right background music for my suffering. I waited to hear her pick when the room went completely silent. She sat down at my desk and riffled through my drawers.

With every noise, I sensed my desk becoming more and more disorganized. "What do you need?"

"Paper."

"Top right."

She pulled out a clean sheet, and before she could ask, I said, "Pens are in the center drawer."

"Perfect. Time to start a list." She leaned back in the chair, propped her feet, clad in red heels, on the desk, and put the paper on her knees. "It's entitled 'Revenge.' Subtitled 'How to pay Duke back for using not only his ability but his exceptionally good looks against two unsuspecting, perfectly innocent girls.'"

Before I had a chance to object to this pointless exercise, she said, "Number one, figure out a way to make the whole school think he's turned ugly. You know that would kill him. Ooh, I bet we can get a Perceptive to help us. They can just alter everyone's perception of him. It will be awesome. Okay, your turn. Number two."

I smiled. Maybe this would be a good healing ritual after all—just imagining Duke ugly made me a little happier. "How about we get a Persuasive to talk him into doing something really stupid in front of everyone?"

"Kalan would totally do that." She wrote it down and then tapped the pen on her teeth. "What else . . . ?" She stood and walked to my bookcase, tilted her head sideways, and started reading the titles. "Don't you have any books in here about somebody plotting revenge?"

"I'm sure there are revenge subplots in one of them."

She turned to face me and leaned back against my bookcase. "How about we sneak into his room at night and put lipstick on him?"

"How would we get in?"

"A Mass Manipulator can walk through the wall and unlock the front door for us."

"You don't think their security system covers that possibility?"

"We'll find a way."

"Why? I'm sure he showers in the morning. What would putting lipstick on him do?"

"It would let him know we were there, always watching, able to get in whenever we want. Plus I've always kind of wanted to put lipstick on him. He has amazing lips." After she said it, she realized she shouldn't have and dropped her gaze.

I finally sat up and scooted back against the headboard.

21

"What did you two do anyway?" I asked quietly, not sure I wanted to know the answer. "I guess you kissed?"

"Do we really have to talk about this? He tricked us both, right?"

"He betrayed me and then made you betray me."

"He made you do things too."

I started to nod but then wondered what he had ever made me do, aside from like him. He gave me the feelings, but I was pretty sure I was the one who acted on them. *Stop,* I told myself. I had lost Duke; I wasn't going to let him take away my best friend with his betrayal too. I had to let it go.

"We're not going to do these, are we?" she asked, holding up the revenge list.

"No. But it was fun imagining them. Thanks."

She gave a long sigh, then slid the paper into the slot on the recycle bin. She glanced at her purse on the desk and then started playing with the zipper. "If I had something important to tell you, something that might stress you out, would you want me to tell you now or when you got back from your dad's?"

She probably wanted to go into detail about her and Duke. Get it off her conscience and put it onto mine. I sighed, the slight pressure behind my eyes reminding me that things weren't quite right. My life was a huge mess. "I just need a break right now, from everything. Can we talk about it when I get back?"

She dropped the zipper on her purse, seeming relieved, and turned to face me. "Yes. So what are you packing for your dad's house? Six weeks is a long time."

DON'T MISS THE SEQUEL TO *PIVOT POINT*!

Reeling from her ex-boyfriend's betrayal, Addie decides to spend winter break in the Norm world. There she meets the achingly familiar Trevor. Meanwhile, Laila has discovered she can restore Addie's lost memories. Now Addie must piece together a world she thought she knew before she loses the love she nearly forgot . . . and a future that could change everything.

MORE FROM KASIE WEST

Seventeen-year-old Caymen Meyers learned early that the rich are not to be trusted. Enter Xander Spence—he's tall, handsome, and oozing rich. But just when Xander's attention and loyalty are about to convince Caymen that being rich isn't a character flaw, she finds out that money is a much bigger part of their relationship than she'd ever realized.

With so many obstacles standing in their way, can she close the distance between them?